The Shoreless Sea

J.B. Toner

For information, or to order additional copies, please contact:

Beacon Publishing Group
P.O. Box 41573 Charleston, S.C. 29423
800.817.8480| beaconpublishinggroup.com

Publisher's catalog available by request.

ISBN-13: 978-1-949472-04-2

ISBN-10: 1-949472-04-2

Published in 2020. New York, NY 10001.

First Edition. Printed in the USA.

For Ellie—
My Reason, My Rose.

1

Monday was named for the moon. I guess we worshiped her once, or at least looked up to her—like a big sister maybe. Patroness of poets and madmen. But then we went trampling around up there, way back when my parents were younger than I am now and came back from what used to be the luminous, untouchable face of a goddess bearing ordinary rocks and dust: the shrapnel of another shattered dream. I think that's why Mondays are always a little sad. Well—okay, that and the fact that the weekend's over.

When this whole mess got started, it was midway through my first semester of junior year at Zevon High and gold and crimson leaves were swirling in a bright, sharp blue November sky. My house was only a couple of miles from the school, and I liked to get up early and walk most days. It gave me time to wake up, collect myself, and also to grab my first coffee of the morning.

It's a tiny little town, our Zevon, Massachusetts (that's ZEE-von, by the way, pronounced to rhyme with absolutely nothing in the English language). It lies about forty miles south of

Boston—but we've still got a Dunkin Donuts. Steam was rising from my Styrofoam elixir, and the crows were cawing overhead as I came pacing up to the long grey house of learning at six minutes till eight.

"Faith!" A familiar voice. "Hey, Faith! Wait up."

I turned and gave a bleary, not-quite-awake-yet smile. "Hi, Tommy."

He came trotting across the parking lot, beaming like a little kid. "Hi! How's it going?"

"It's Monday morning, Connor. You're way too happy for a normal person."

"Normal's boring," he said cheerfully. "Rage against the dying of the light, Avalon."

"Oooh, someone did their English homework."

Tommy Connor was new to Zevon, a denizen of bustling Beantown who transferred to our dozing hamlet back in September. I tended to pick on him a lot—he made it way too easy not to—but I'd liked him instantly.

He had an open, honest-looking face, with blue-grey eyes and a mop of light brown, almost sandy blondish hair. Though he was seventeen like me, he had a tousled, unguarded look that made him seem far younger somehow. On this particular occasion he was wearing a green polo shirt and the same plain blue jeans he wore every single day. I hadn't been to his house yet, but I suspected it must contain a vast subterranean chamber full of identical pairs of blue jeans, forever hidden from the light of the world above.

As we headed inside, we passed Old Luke the janitor: a grizzled, gangly fellow in a dingy brown jumpsuit with a peculiar knack for being there whenever you turned around. Sarah and I had decided he was the dark spirit of the school itself in human form.

"Morning, Luke," I said politely.

"Is it now," he muttered. "Is it now."

On we went, down the long narrow hallway, past the classroom doors, the water fountains, and the endless dull red lockers, shouldering our way through the scurrying hordes of our peers, to our homeroom at the far end of the school. There were only about sixty of us in the junior class, but it was enough that they'd split us into two homerooms; some rampaging tyrant of an educator had decreed that the A-L section would be quartered in Mrs. Mara's room at the very back of the building. It may not have added more than a minute or so to my commute, but that can be everything when you're racing the late bell.

Today, however, we made it with a couple of minutes to spare. Sarah Featherstone, my best friend, was slumped at a desk near the front, so I headed over and claimed the empty seat to her left.

"Hey, you," I said loudly, over the babble of our classmates. "Want some wake-up juice?"

She blinked sleepily at me and mumbled, "Gimme." She clutched at my half-empty cup and started guzzling. Finally, she wiped her mouth and cracked a smile. "Hey, you."

I shook my head and smiled back. Unbelievable—barely five percent conscious and she still looked like she'd just stepped out of a modeling shoot. She was a blue-eyed redhead, gorgeous, and a sorceress with all things fashionable. The only times I was really happy with my hair were the times she did it for me. My hair's sort of a plain pine-bark brown, incidentally. I had it yanked back in a ponytail this morning.

"Anything left in there?"

"Um. . . yes?" She swished the cup apologetically. "Maybe like a sip or two, if you tilt it way back and exhibit great patience."

"Well, it's only two periods till break."

"You are an actual registered saint."

"It's true. So, did you do the reading this time?"

She winced. "Not exactly. Mr. J's gonna go berserk, isn't he?"

"Oh, you'll be fine, just read it during math class. Say, did you know that *berserk* literally means 'bear-shirt'? It comes from the belief that a warrior could don the strength of a raging bear."

"No, sweetie. Why would anyone know that?"

At that moment the bell rang and the general chatter in the room faded away. One of the seniors came on the PA to read the announcements and lead the Pledge, and then Mrs. Mara started taking attendance. "Faith Avalon?" she commenced, and I waved at her.

"I'm here! Hi, Mrs. Mara!"

She smiled and nodded at me. "Hello dear. Roy Belmont?"

I loved Mrs. Mara. She was a short, plump lady in her sixties, with deep smiles lines and white hair in a bun, and she looked like everybody's favorite grandma. The only downside to her (apart from having a homeroom lost in the shadows of the back hallway) was that she taught Chemistry, which was not one of my stronger subjects. Despite this, I knew the sciences were important. Without them, the poets would all starve to death.

After homeroom came Mr. Spenser's Algebra class: a black fifty-minute fog of gobbledygook and fatigue. Then Spanish with Mr. Valenzuela, which I enjoyed a lot but was still not entirely awake for. And then at last came morning break and the mad beeline to the cafeteria for coffee, and there was joy in the universe once more.

Roy Belmont came striding over as I was basking in my first few sips. "Heya, Faith."

"Heya, Roy." I threw him a little mock punch, which he answered with a friendly mock parry and a mock knee-stomp that would've crippled me forever.

Roy was another old friend, and also my father's top student. His parents were refugees from the Congo, so he stood out a bit in a mostly white Irish town, but he and his siblings had been born in the States and spoke with no trace of an accent. He was a good-looking guy, and knew it, and he wasn't shy about dressing up a bit. Today, for example, he was wearing a white silk button-up and pleated silver slacks that set off his dark features and close-cropped midnight hair. It *definitely* worked on him.

"So, how's your dad liking San Francisco?" he asked.

"Pretty well so far, I guess. The first conference started this morning, so we'll see how it goes. I'm sure they'll call tonight to make sure we haven't set ourselves on fire yet."

Dad owns and operates the dojo here in town. He teaches Karate, Jiu-jutsu, Aikido, Kung-Fu, and that wacky MMA that all the cool kids are doing these days. He and Mom flew out to Frisco on Saturday for a week-long series of martial arts conferences. Well—he went for the conferences; she went for the shopping. Mom's a Lit teacher at the local college, and she happened to have some vacation time saved up, so it was just me and my kid sister Hope this week.

"Cool. Take it they got there safe and everything."

"Yep. They checked in with us on Saturday night. I asked Dad if he remembered to wear flowers in his hair, and I think he tried to put me in an arm-bar through the phone."

Roy grinned. "Sounds like Sensei, all right."

The bell rang again. "Catch ya in gym," he said, and moseyed on down the hall. He had Physics next; he was a big math and science guy, so third period was his favorite. As for me—I had English. So, it was my favorite period too.

As I came into Room 14, Mr. Jameson was bouncing up and down on his heels and nodding with his usual slightly alarming ferocity. We were all busy taking our seats and no one had spoken to him. He was just nodding to himself, or to the air, or to the gods themselves. I guess that sounds kind of odd, but it was very normal for Mr. J. He was a loomingly tall man in his mid-to-late thirties, with a magnificent mustache and a yellow-striped azure bowtie that no student at Zevon High, nor any of our parents, had ever seen him without. He kept nodding and bouncing like the world's most exaggerated marionette until we were all at our desks and the bell rang to start class.

"Now, now, now," he said instantly in his booming voice, "yes, good, let's begin. We've all done our reading, hrm? Have we?" We all nodded dutifully. "Good, good, good! Dylan Thomas, yes, indeed. Then we're all caught up through Chapter Twelve of our textbook, are we not? Yes?" More nods. "Ah, good, excellent. Then today, before we go on to study the development of the villanelle throughout recent literature, we shall pause to perform—" he lowered his voice for a moment "—an exercise. Now, quickly! If you're in an odd-numbered row of seats, look to your right. If even, look left. Quickly, my friends, time is like an eagle on the winds. Have we all looked?" We had. "Then behold your partner. Now, turn your desks. Come, come, be swift!"

My partner turned out to be Tommy Connor. It also turned out that Sarah was right behind me, so when we all made our quarter-pivot, she and I wound upside by side.

"Did you get your coffee?" she whispered.

"Yep. I'll be functional till lunch."

"When the next cup will be waiting."

"Don't you ever worry about exploding or something?" Tommy asked, sounding genuinely concerned.

"Now, now, don't let's yammer," Mr. J proclaimed. "We have work, much work, to do. Today, after steeping ourselves in Western poetry for the past two months, we shall attempt an original piece of our own composition. But! In order to help train our minds to adapt to new perspectives, we shall not write it alone. You and your partner will alternate, each writing one line in turn. Your poem must be at least ten lines in length. The question of rhyme and meter I leave to you, but don't let yourselves lapse into mere prose, hrm? No, indeed." Melody Firiel raised her hand, and he nodded violently. "Yes, yes, Ms. Firiel."

"Can we write about anything we want?" she asked.

"*Mrmm!*" He came up, not merely on the balls of his feet, but actually onto the points of his toes. "Poetry, Ms. Firiel, is the stuff of life, and vice versa. There is no topic which cannot yield worthy verse. Other questions? No, yes? No? Then let us begin!"

"All right then," I said to Tommy. "What do you want to write about?"

"How about the meaning of life?"

I raised my eyebrows. "That's a bit vague my friend."

"Hmmmm. . ." His brow furrowed, and he cocked his head from one side to the other with a sort of kittenish solemnity. It was funny to watch, but at the same time almost—kind of beautiful. Then, suddenly, his face lit up and I had to drop the "almost." He leaned way forward and just glowed at me. "I got it! How about coffee!"

I burst out laughing. "You're a genius, Connor. Let's do it. Why don't you take the first line?"

"Kay." He chewed on his pen for a few moments, and then shot me a glance, scratching his head. "I'm not really much of a poet."

"Sure you are. Everyone is. Just write whatever comes to you."

"Okay. . ." He paused for another long moment, then abruptly lunged forward and scrawled something in his notebook. Our desks were touching, so when he turned the notebook sideways, we could both read it easily. At the top of a fresh page he'd written, *COFFEE by Faith Avalon and Tommy Connor*. And under that, *Coffee, coffee, comes inside a can.*

"Perfect." I thought about it for a minute. I'm a leftie—a southpaw, as Dad puts it—hardly surprising, considering how right-brained I am. My pen hand tapped rhythmically on the edge of the notebook as I contemplated possible rhymes, and my right-hand lay palm-down on my desktop, pressing hard against the grainy wood as if to help push me upwards. Finally, I reached over and scribbled, *Transforming water like a wizard's hand.*

"Nice!" Tommy exclaimed. I was surprised at how happy that made me. I gave a dismissive sort of "no big deal" wave with my left.

Then I jumped in my seat. There was water running into my lap from somewhere. I lifted my right hand and realized there was a puddle underneath it. *What in the world?* Can your palms even sweat that much? What, was I going through menopause or something? I didn't feel hot.

"You okay?" he asked.

"What? Oh—yeah, fine. Go ahead."

He drummed his fingers for a second and then wrote, *We like the beans, the yummy crunchy beans.*

Well. Whatever that leaky hand incident was about, it seemed to have stopped. I returned my attention to our growing poem, deliberated, and wrote, *We love the fruitful earth that grants such gleams.*

And there was a tiny, but noticeable, tremor under our feet.

"Whoa," said Sarah. "Did you feel that?"

I heard myself say, "Um," and realized my mouth was hanging open. Tommy wore a puzzled look, and his head was cocked to the side again.

Weird—but nothing else, just weird. Weird things happen every day. Maybe a really big truck just went by.

Slowly, my poetical partner lowered his eyes back to the notebook.

"Lessee," he murmured. A few beats went by, and then he penned the next line: *They grow it in a field in Mexico.* Another few beats, and I added: *Where sunlight glows and all the four winds blow.*

The pages of the notebook began to rustle, and Tommy's messy hair fluttered in a sudden breeze. Inside a classroom with the windows shut. Sarah frowned at him, blinking, as if her brain was struggling to edit out what it was seeing. Tommy gazed at me with an alert, interested expression. I just stared.

"You made it wind," he said matter-of-factly.

"*Wind* is not a verb," I snapped. "And don't be ridiculous. It's—it's probably just the air conditioning."

"In November?"

"Then you're doing something. Stop it."

He spread his hands. "It's not me."

The breeze died away. We sat there looking at each other; he with curiosity and total calm, and I with completely irrational hostility.

"Let's keep going," he said.

"I don't—maybe we shouldn't."

"Don't you want to see what'll happen?"

"Nothing's gonna happen. *There's nothing happening.*"

He gave me that strange, childlike smile of his again. "Then what's the problem?" He turned back to the poem, raised his pen, and wrote, *It makes your heart go thumpy-thumpy-thump.*

"Tommy. . ." I almost pleaded.

"Hey—it's okay. You can stop if you want. My uncle always says I'm too nosy for my own good."

I thought about it. I hadn't consciously decided to weave in the four elements when I started this piece—but re-reading it now, I realized I'd already mentioned three of them. If this craziness continued with the fourth—

But that was silly. There was nothing happening here, nothing. Just a funny coincidence. And, besides—I *never* give up on a poem. So I set my teeth, gripped my little wand, and wrote, *A secret fire within that bloody pump.*

Tommy's notebook burst into flames.

2

Name's Roy Belmont. Six foot one, a hundred and seventy pounds, seventeen years of age; Congolese by blood, American by birth and loyalty, Zevonian by the whim of chance. Or the will of fate, if you prefer. Of course, technically, that's the oldest question in the cosmos, as well as the most important—which doesn't necessarily mean a ruggedly handsome young man from Massachusetts couldn't answer it once and for all. If I figure it out, I'll let you know. But right now we've got other concerns.

When Faith and I parted ways in the cafeteria, I headed straight for Mr. Valenzuela's class, Room 9. In the hotbed of cultural diversity that is our Celtic pinprick of a town, Mr. V was the only native Spanish-speaker on the school faculty, which put him in charge of Spanish class despite the fact he was a physicist by education, and thus also in charge of *my* subject. Today we were starting the chapter on superstring theory, so pass around the energy drinks and crank up the "Ode to Joy." I'd been waiting months for this.

I automatically surveyed the room as I walked in, like Sensei taught us. Two exits, not counting windows. Nearest potential weapon—fire extinguisher. Six tables, each with six stools and a

Bunsen burner. Usual number of occupants: twenty-two kids, not counting myself, and the teacher.

Valenzuela had a stocky build, good balance and the bearing of a man who knew how to handle himself. While he was off teaching other tongues, Mrs. Mara used this room for Chem class, which I also enjoyed—but Physics was the high point of the day. Once we'd all gotten settled, he clapped his hands together briskly and started right in. Didn't even wait for the bell.

"Dimensions! How many dimensions? Dave—what's the first dimension?"

Dave Albion was one of my better friends. Kind of a twitchy guy, with no muscle mass to speak of, he had a seemingly boundless supply of nervous energy. His hair had a tendency to spike out as if he'd just stuck a fork in an outlet, and he was constantly playing with things—in this case, the Bunsen. He looked up with a slightly guilty expression and said, "Um er um uhhhhh—length? *Length!*"

Mr. V nodded and went over to the whiteboard. "Very good." He picked up the marker and drew a single line. "Ms. Darrell, what's the second?"

Leah Darrell: pretty blond girl, great legs (for kicking). She was a cheerleader. Outta the gutter. "Width?" she said.

"Good." The line became a square. "Third dimension, let's see. . . Jason?"

Jason Locke, linebacker for the Zevon Hawks. Tough kid. Smart, too. "Depth."

"Outstanding." Mr. V walked back to his desk, picked up a Rubik's cube, and held it high for all to see. "And now the hundred megaton question. Mr. Belmont, the fourth dimension is what?"

"Time," I said.

"Time indeed." He paced slowly through the room, passing each table, still holding the cube way up in the air. "If we could see fourth-dimensionally, we would perceive this cube as a long stream spooling itself out into the future and the past. It would stretch all the way back to the factory where it first took shape, and all the way forward to that unknown moment when it will break down and cease to be a cube. And it would stretch not only from the factory to the store to my car to my desk, but millions of miles out into space, because we're also flying around the sun at a rate of 67,000 miles per hour. And the sun itself is hurtling through the universe as the Milky Way and every other galaxy continues to expand—or contract, or fluctuate, or whatever the experts are saying this week."

We chuckled. The extreme lack of consensus on almost any given theory in physics was an old joke for Mr. V.

"So, in short—four dimensions. We all agree?" Nods from us. "Then what if I told you that a prevailing theory in physics now states there may be as many as *twenty-six* dimensions?"

Hullaballoo in Room 9. Dave waved his hand frantically in the air, restraining himself with obvious effort from jumping up and down. Mr. V nodded to him, and he practically shouted, "Does that mean there could be a Dimension of the Slime People?"

Mr. V gave him the look that so many of our teachers reserve for Dave, sort of three parts amusement and one-part exasperation. "Spatial dimensions, Mr. Albion, not 'alternate' dimensions. Is there a Length or a Width of the Slime People?"

"Ummmmm. . . no?"

"Good guess. Now, just to muddy the waters—this is only one of several variants of the theory in question. Other versions suggest there could be eleven dimensions, or ten."

"We sure they're not just throwing darts at a calculator?" I asked.

"Oh, we'll get to the math, Roy, don't you worry about that. But let's start with an overview. Super-symmetric string theory was developed in response to an old difficulty in physics. There are four fundamental forces in nature: gravitation, electromagnetism, and the strong and weak nuclear forces. General relativity mainly studies gravity and operates on an extremely large scale—solar systems and interstellar space—and quantum mechanics mainly studies the other three forces and operates on the subatomic scale. However! —no one has yet succeeded in creating a single theory which can adequately study all four of those forces."

Interesting, I thought. Four dimensions, four forces. But if it turned out there were actually more than four dimensions. . . Suddenly I could hear Sensei in my head, chiding me for the fiftieth time: *Learn the rules first. Then worry about bending them.* Right. Focus Belmont.

"As you recall," Mr. V was saying, "Einstein demonstrated that matter and energy are ultimately one and the same: a very small piece of matter is in fact a very large amount of energy bound together. In other words, energy provides the building blocks of the physical universe. Therefore, a better understanding of energy could help us to unify our understanding of the four forces. And that, my young friends, brings us to superstring theory. In the simplest possible terms, the theory states that energy itself is a series of vibrations created by inconceivably tiny 'strings' or 'loops' vibrating at different frequencies."

"Like music?" I said, involuntarily.

Mr. V waffled a bit. "Yes—well, yes, that's a common analogy. But, obviously, it's just an analogy. Now, let's look at the mathematics. These strings, if they exist, are measurable only by what's known as the Planck length, which is 10^{-33} centimeters. . ." He went back to the board and started drawing equations.

I spent the rest of the period taking notes and being a good student, but only half my head was listening. The other half was busy spinning wild, unscientific speculations—which I might be embarrassed to admit, if they hadn't mostly turned out to be true.

After class I wandered down the hall, still half-lost in hidden forces and impossible dimensions, and took that second left toward the gym. I had Phys. Ed. for fourth period, which worked out nicely since lunch came right after. I cruised through the locker room, stripped my threads, and threw on some sweat clothes. The gym itself was pretty standard fare: wide open space, bleachers, B-ball hoops, mats along one wall. Nearest weapon—broomstick in the corner.

We lined up at half-court, exactly thirty of us by my count, awaiting the onset of our teacher, Coach Strothman. She swept in through the double doors at the very second the bell rang and came stalking toward us like a brunette velociraptor. Tall lady, early thirties, broad shoulders, great legs—and I won't even try to pretend I don't mean that in a completely inappropriate way. Whenever she walked into a room, I started hearing the "Ride of the Valkyries" in my head.

"It's dodgeball day," she announced. "Belmont—Connor—let's do this."

Not a verbose individual, our coach. What she meant was that Tommy Connor and I were team captains and should get started on picking our teams. Tommy was new this year; I hadn't gotten to know him much, but he certainly seemed like a nice guy. Always smiling. Had a lean build and a way of standing that somehow made it seem as if his body was weightless. Like myself, he was a perennial frustration to Coach Strothman as an athletic student with no interest in student athletics. I think she kept making us captains in the hope of sparking some dormant sports-related ambition within us.

We picked our teams and I casually led my flock over to the side of the gym with the big windows in the wall. Those would be at our backs, and it never hurts to put a little sun in your adversary's eyes. "Dave!" I barked.

Dave snapped to attention and threw a surprisingly sharp salute. "Sir, yes sir!"

"Take those two—" I pointed randomly "—and go grab some balls out of the supply closet, stat."

"Am I authorized to keelhaul mutineers?"

"Wouldn't have it any other way."

"Come on, you sea-dogs," he said to his helpers, and they went scuttling off.

I glanced around. "Hey, where's Faith?" I asked.

Sarah Featherstone leaned over to me and whispered, "Something really weird happened in English. She and Tommy were doing a poem, and his notebook caught on fire."

"Say *what?*"

"Yeah, it was bizarre. We couldn't figure out what started it. There weren't any matches or lighters around or anything. It was like spontaneous combustion."

". . .Huh. She okay?"

"Oh yeah, I think so. Tommy put it out with his jacket, and Mr. J said, you know, 'Hrm, well, these things happen from time to time,' or something like that, and that was it. She stuck around for a while and then she said she had a headache and took off. I dunno if she went home or what."

"Well, that sucks."

Just then, a volleyball came flying at my head. I raised a hand, negligently, and palmed it in midair.

"Victory is ours!" Dave shrieked.

"Game hasn't started yet, doofus-knave."

"We've brought a selection of spheroids. Basketballs, volleyballs, medicine balls."

"Dude, we're not throwing medicine balls at each other. Those things weigh like thirty pounds. Don't we have any of those big red plastic ones?"

"Just use the volleyballs," Strothman commanded.

"All right, you heard the lady. Prepare for combat."

"Who leads off?" Tommy called. "Wanna toss a coin?"

I grinned and spun the dodgeball on my finger. "Possession's nine-tenths of the law, buddy."

"What's the other tenth?"

"Speed!" I yelled and flung the ball at Matt Rooker. He was crazy fast when his head was in the game—a wise pick on Tommy's part—but he was also flighty, and I was confident I could catch him daydreaming. Know your enemy. Sure enough, I nailed him right in the chest.

Strothman jabbed a thumb at the sidelines. "You're out, Rooker."

"But I—but he—but—awww." He shuffled away.

Tommy picked up the ball and bounced it a couple of times. There was a long, tense standoff. An imaginary tumbleweed went drifting by. Then he pointed at the half-dozen unclaimed balls lying in the no-man's-land between sides and shouted, "Go get 'em!"

And there was dodgeball.

As usual when two armies collide, the casualties were heavy at the outset. My front line scrambled to get to the balls first, and Tommy picked off one of my best people immediately, beaning him right in the skull. A second later, the air was full of speeding volleyballs—plus a soccer ball that almost ripped off one of my eyebrows. I narrowly side-stepped and snatched it out of the air, spun, and hurled it back into the faceless ranks of our foes. To my right, I saw Dave go down, fatally clipped on the shoulder. To my left, Sarah took one in the leg. Their sacrifice would never be forgotten. After a few minutes, both sides were down to five or six people, and the action slowed as we began to play more strategically. Both Tommy and I were still in the mix.

I got a hold of a ball and prowled the half-court line, scanning potential targets, watching how they breathed and how they shifted their weight, following their eyes and their hands and their feet. I'd sparred and grappled a thousand times, and been in some street-fights besides, and I had a talent for reading my opponent. But now, as the game continued, I gradually became aware of something different in my reading, something new.

This'll sound strange, I know, but it felt as if my sense of sight was developing a tactile aspect. All of a sudden, I could *see* the inner strength of another person pushing back at me. At first I tried to shake it off—just battle-stress playing tricks—but then I happened to glance at Melody Firiel as she was raising her dodgeball to throw.

A pulse of energy shot up from her feet as she planted them, gathered power in her core, and fired a ray of light from her hands a split-second before she released the ball. The light was some bright color, a lovely color, but one we have no name for. And it traced the exact speed and trajectory of the ball as determined by Melody's output of force. It was aimed right at me—the light passed right through me—but I sprang out of that ray and the ball missed me by a fraction of an inch.

What is this? What's wrong with me? No one reacted to the light; obviously no one else had seen it. But as I looked around, I could now that same light spearing across the room every time someone launched a ball. I could see the ebb and flow of their balance and their strength, like vibrations in water or running my fingers through sunlight. And after a few moments of shock and bewilderment, I felt a huge exhilaration rising up inside. I realized I was laughing out loud.

Tommy came running toward me with a big grin on his face. "You ain't won yet, Belmont!"

Whoa, wait a second. This can't be right. The power coming off that kid was way too strong. Way, way, *way* too strong. *Nobody* could be that—

WHAM!

3

HI, I'M TOMMY! I'm a pretty normal guy. But sometimes weird things happen around me. I don't mind that—it keeps life interesting (I kind of get bored easily). What I do mind is not knowing *why* stuff happens. I like getting to the bottom of things. Uncle Syme once told me if I try too hard to fit everything into my head, I'll end up squeezing all the wonder out. I get what he meant. But I still think something can make sense without having to lose its—I don't know—its wonderfulness. Is that a word? Faith would know.

Oh yeah, speaking of weirdness. She set my notebook on fire with her brain. It was awesome. I was dying to figure out how she did it. I mean, not because I wanted to go around starting fires with my brain or anything. I was just curious. But she seemed pretty shaken by the whole thing—she left class a few minutes later. I borrowed a piece of paper off Sarah and re-wrote the lines we'd already written. I've got a good memory. It might not have been exactly right, but it was definitely close. Mr. Jameson said we could do the last two lines later.

Maybe I shouldn't have pushed her to keep going. Tonight's top story: under severe peer pressure, more and more teens are falling victim to iambic pentameter abuse! But seriously, I hoped she wasn't mad at me. Faith was a special girl. You could see in her eyes that she was smart and tough and kind—but even beyond that, there was something in there I'd never seen before. They were bright, bright green, like staring at the sun through a leaf, almost *ancient* somehow. Or something like that. I don't know, I'm not making sense.

Anyway. I had PE next period. That was usually fun. Today Coach Strothman put me and Roy in charge of picking teams for dodgeball. Now Roy—he was a super-cool guy. But man, he was kind of intense. He had these keen, coal-black eyes, and you could just see him sizing you up when he looked at you. We'd been on opposite sides before, and he was always a good sport whether he won or lost—but he sure played to win.

Except today, something weird happened. Another weird thing, I mean, apart from Faith setting my notebook on fire with her brain. Both teams were down to their last few people and things were getting desperate, and when I finally landed a shot on Roy, it knocked him like ten feet backwards. Literally.

Everything stopped. You know how when there's a room full of people and something bad happens, you can hear that giant gasp from everybody inhaling at once? That happened. Then Coach ran over and yelled for everyone to step back, and they did. A few people sort of glanced at me and then quickly looked away.

Then Roy sat up. He was coughing, and he looked slightly pale, but he seemed to be in one piece. I ran over to him, and he gave me a little smile.

"Dude, you've been working out," he said. He sounded hoarse.

"Roy. . . Roy, I'm really sorry. I don't know what happened."

"Eh." He waved the apology away. "Don't sweat it. Just glad you didn't mess up my dashing profile."

I realized he'd been holding his own ball against his chest, and my ball had bounced off of that, so it cushioned a lot of the impact. Lucky. "Are you sure you're all right?" I asked.

"Let's find out." He got his legs under him and rose slowly, wobbling a bit.

Coach put a handout to steady him. "Easy, Belmont."

"'Sokay, Coach. Not ecstatic about losing the match, but otherwise I'm fine."

Dave Albion raised his hand. "Ah— technically, we still have three players left standing?"

Melody smacked her forehead and muttered, "For Pete's sake, Dave."

"Yeah, no, it's okay," I said hastily. "We concede. Unforeseen circumstances or whatever."

"Nonsense," said Roy. "You've got more players left than us."

"Well—how about we call it a draw?"

"Done." He offered his hand. "Good game, Captain."

I shook it and found myself smiling back. "Same to you, Captain." Like I said—cool guy.

Since Dave had already brought out a bunch of basketballs, Coach had us spend the rest of the period working on free throws. Roy got his wind back pretty fast. I guess he did judo or something with Faith's dad, so he must've been used to getting tossed around a lot. Nobody said much for the first few minutes after the game ended. But once Roy was better, he started goofing around and got everyone laughing again.

Toward the end of class, Melody came over and punched me on the shoulder. "Hey, chief. You okay?"

"Me? Yeah, I mean—I think so. What do you mean?"

"I mean, you looked like you just ran over someone's puppy for a while there. Whatever happened, it's not like you did it on purpose. It must have been some kinda crazy adrenaline thing. Not your fault, you know?"

"Yeah, I suppose."

"Good." Then her cheeks dimpled. "All the same, you're not safe with this." And she stole the ball out of my hands and went dribbling away down the court.

I scratched my head. I can never tell if girls are flirting with me or just being friendly. Melody was really nice. She had wide hazel eyes, and she looked right at you when you spoke, like whatever you were saying was the most interesting thing ever. I wondered if I was supposed to go chase after her and try to the steal the ball back? I'm not so great at this stuff.

But as it turned out, Coach ended class right then anyhow.

"All right, hit the showers," she bellowed. "Have a good lunch and don't do anything stupid."

So, I showered and changed and headed for the cafeteria. I didn't feel hungry though. About halfway there I changed my mind and went outside. There was a small courtyard-type area between the rear exit and the tall wooden fence that cut off the rest of the world, with an elm tree and a bench, and there was usually no one out there. I went and sat and thought about life.

We moved around a lot. Uncle Syme was a consultant for Surtex Industries and every few years they sent him to a new plant to help them do efficiency stuff. Right now he was working over in

New Bedford. I liked Boston; it was an exciting place. I liked Zevon too, since it was nice and quiet. I guess I liked most of the places we'd been. I had a couple of good friends here and there in New England and sometimes I'd take the bus to go visit them—or even borrow Uncle Syme's car for the weekend, once in a while. But I've always spent a lot of time by myself.

More weird things had been happening lately. A few weeks ago there was a thunderstorm, and lightning hit the lightning rod outside our house six times, but it didn't strike anywhere else in town. Animals had been coming up to me—even big ones, like deer—and sort of nuzzling me. I didn't mind that, I love animals, but it was still odd. And the last time I was in Boston, I went to give a hot dog to a homeless guy, and he gave me this awful stare like I was some kind of monster, and then he screamed and ran away. I told Uncle Syme about it, and he said lots of homeless people have mental problems, which I'm sure is true. But again: weird. Plus, I was having dreams almost every night now where I was flying.

A squirrel came over and climbed up next to me on the bench and sat there blinking at me and twitching his nose.

"Hi, squirrel," I said. He (or she? —I don't know if there's a way to tell without checking) sniffed my leg for a few seconds, like a dog saying hello, and then sat back and blinked at me some more. Then he scampered off. "Crazy day," I said out loud. "At least it can't get much crazier."

You know how there are some things you should just never, ever say?

Well anyways, I had European History for fifth period and then Chemistry with Mrs. Mara, and that was it. Nothing else out of the ordinary happened at school. I didn't see Faith again, so she must've gone home. I didn't have her number. I thought about stopping by her house to check on her, but I figured she might want to be alone or something. I went home and did my homework and made some mac and cheese and put in a movie. Uncle Syme was supposed to be back late tonight.

I think I dozed a bit on the couch. It was already evening—the days were getting shorter. I got up and discovered I felt restless. I paced through the house for a while, then grabbed my jacket and went out for a walk.

There was deep, deep violet in the west. No stars yet in the east, but Mars and Venus were out, alone in the sky. Cold gusts of wind kept stirring up and dying down. It was a perfect night for walking. I went fast, but not in any particular direction, up one street and down another, wherever the wind was going. A few cars and a pedestrian or two went by, but the streets were mostly empty. It got darker, and a crescent moon came out.

Then I started to feel something peculiar. A very faint prickling in my scalp, like I was standing too close to a power line. I slowed my pace and glanced around, and I couldn't see anything unusual—but the feeling got stronger. Somebody was watching me. And now they knew I knew. I came to a stop. I'm not sure why, but I didn't feel either scared or excited, just kind of irritated. I wasn't much in the mood for this.

"What do you want?" I called. I was on a back road, lined on both sides with birch trees, with only a couple of houses in sight. It was full dark now.

No one answered, so I decided to see if they could keep up with me. Whoever they were, I was betting they couldn't. I'm pretty fast. I took off sprinting down the road, and another strange thing happened: I realized I'd gotten faster. Like, a *lot* faster. I hadn't been doing any special training or anything, but all of a sudden I felt lighter, like the gravity around me had gotten dialed way down. I went tearing along like a panther, like a jet fighter, and I noticed a floating trail of fallen leaves getting sucked through the air behind me as I passed. I forgot all about whoever was watching me. I forgot about everything and just ran for the sheer joy of it.

I zipped through town, all the way to the outskirts, three or four miles from where I'd started, and then I saw the old clock tower. It was five stories tall, made of old marble and dingy white wood, and it had been out of commission since before we came to Zevon. They were trying to restore it, but I heard they were having budget problems. A ramshackle chain-link fence went around the whole site, and there were scaffolds crisscrossing the building all the way to the top floor where the bells must be. I had one of those instantaneous "wouldn't it be fun?" ideas that usually end up getting me in trouble, but I was feeling lucky right then. And I like climbing.

I was breathing hard by that time, but I was still full of energy. I wondered where it was all coming from. I would definitely have to sit down and try to figure out what was going on here, and why—soonish, like maybe tomorrow sometime. For now, I had a clock tower to climb for no reason.

Hopping the fence would've been easy even on a normal day. Once I was over, I headed straight for the scaffolding. At first I planned on going up the outside of the building. But then about midway up, I came to a window they'd taken all the glass out of. I guess I mentioned already that I might have a slight problem with my curiosity. Anyway, I'd never seen the inside of a clock tower before, so I thought I'd just stick my head in and peek around.

It was a wide-open space, but full of clutter. Boards and sawhorses were sort of strewn about, plus an old desk, and then there were all the wheels and gears, and in the middle was a big gap in the floor with ropes running through it. In the starlight coming in through the windows, you could see all the way to the bottom of the tower and all the way up to the top. Everything was covered in cobwebs.

Gazing at the dust and the shadows, I had a funny little flashback to a few weeks earlier when we were covering Greece in history class. Mrs. Draper told us a bit about the Greek philosophers and some of the stuff they said, and it really stuck with me for some reason. Plato said life was like being chained up in a cave and only ever seeing shadows on the walls from the firelight. But once in a while, someone got loose and made it outside, and then they had to try and figure out what the daylight was and where it came from and what it meant. Maybe that's what was happening to me, I thought—maybe one of my chains was coming loose.

There was a tiny sound like the sigh of moving dust, and I turned back toward the window. A figure was crouching on the sill, black in the moonlight behind it. I'd completely forgotten I was being tracked. Might have to turn in my panther-man card.

"Who are you?" I asked.

"My name is Alyra." It was a girl—well, no, a lady—and she had the prettiest voice I'd ever heard. She was only talking, but it sounded like singing. In fact, it sounded like the *moon* was singing and it was somehow coming out through her lips. I couldn't see her eyes—she was still just a silhouette—but now that I looked closer, I could see the long hair and the long graceful limbs. I must have lost her for a while when I started running, but she'd caught up pretty fast. "And you are Thomas Gabriel Connor."

"Um, yeah. I mostly go by Tommy, though."

"Very well," she said, and I could hear a smile in her voice. "It is an honor to meet you, Tommy." She stepped in through the window and stood facing me, a few steps away. It might sound silly, but I was starting to wonder if she was some kind of ninja, here to assassinate me. But then why would it be an honor to meet me? And for that matter, why would a ninja want to assassinate some random kid?

"So, uh, you're not here to assassinate me, then?"

She laughed and shook her head. I noticed something protruding from her hair—a couple of long thin pointy things like horns or antennae. "I rather doubt that I could, even if I wished to.

You've been growing stronger these last few days, have you not?"

I stared at her. "How do you know about that? And—and what's going on with me, anyhow?"

"Your true nature is awakening, Tommy Connor. I know of it because the rising force of that nature has sent ripples through many pools in many lands. And I've been sent to help you take the first step—if you believe you're ready."

Looking back now, the whole conversation sounds—I don't know, surreal. But at the time, it not only felt totally normal, it felt like everything else was just a dream, like everything I could remember had been waiting for this one moment to give it all meaning. Like I was about to step out of the shadows and into the sun. There were about a hundred and fifty million questions I could have asked her in that moment. But all I said was: "I'm ready."

Alyra raised her face and began to sing.

4

Did you know that the word "glamour," as in charm or enchantment, comes from the word "grammar", as in—well—grammar? Same with "grimoire" and "gramarye", as in a magic tome or book of spells. All my life I had thought that I believed in the power of words to accomplish miracles. I never thought I'd actually see one myself. Much less cause one.

When I left Mr. J's class, I didn't have any clear destination in mind. I just needed to get out of there. Down the hall I went, through the doors, and out into the cold, sweet autumn air. A breeze ran softly through my hair and brought back Tommy's words: "You made it wind." But that was impossible. That was insane.

Impulsively, I raised my hands and said aloud, "Where sunlight glows and all the four winds blow!"—which, in retrospect, might not have been the wisest move. Nobody wants to start a hurricane. I didn't have any rational motive, but perhaps a part of me wanted to see if I truly had magic in my veins—and besides, if I could summon up the wind, then surely I could banish it again. But in any case, nothing happened. Part of me was relieved; part of me was so, so bitterly disappointed. *Maybe it only works once*, I thought. *Maybe the same image, but in different words. . .*

I stopped myself. This was absurd. I would have loved to believe it—I could admit that—but it wasn't real, it couldn't be. I had no idea what might have caused the—the phenomenon. Despite my little outburst back there, Tommy would never do something like this as a prank. He was one of the nicest boys I'd ever met. Also, there was obviously no way he could have known in advance what I was going to write. So if it wasn't magic, then what on earth was it?

My head hurt. What I really needed was a bath, a blanket and some hot chocolate, and possibly one of the old battered Winnie-the-Pooh books hidden away in my closet. I'd get in mild trouble for skipping the rest of the school day, but—whatever. I typically had perfect attendance, but I was prepared to rebel for Pooh's sake. "Rage against the dying of the light, Avalon." Hmm— Tommy in my head again. He sure kept his cool when the fire broke out: ripped off his jacket and slapped the flames out like a pro. I was not unimpressed, if the truth be told. *And now I'm picturing him ripping off articles of clothing. It's definitely time to go home.*

We had a cozy greenhouse atop a steep hill at the end of a long gravel driveway flanked by firs.

As I came through the front door, I was instantly accosted by our six-month-old calico Pendleton, a supersonic blur of adorable fuzziness who could still fit comfortably into my cupped hands.

"Hey, Pen," I said fondly, petting him for as long as he was physically capable of sitting still, which was just about three seconds—then he darted away again. His matriarchal mama cat, Queensbury, was hulking on Dad's recliner like a vast quivering amoeba, taking up the whole jumbo-sized seat.

"Hey, Q." I scratched her giant head, and she acknowledged me with a rumbling purr and a twitch of the ears. Then I was off to the inner chambers where a steaming bathtub full of bubbles had my name on it.

After that, I put on my fluffy yellow robe and made myself some grilled cheese and tomato soup. And after *that*, I made a huge mug of hot chocolate and whipped cream, dug out a couple of my favorite books, and bundled myself up in the comfiest blankets I had. This was turning out to be a pretty good Monday after all.

Hope got home around 3:30. She came into my room without knocking, which was a mid-range evil—somewhere between kidnapping the prince and blowing up the planet—but I let it slide because she looked worried about me.

"*There* you are!" she said. "Ever hear of answering your phone?"

"Hey, sis. I take it you talked to Sarah?"

"Yuh-huh. Glad to see you haven't burned the house down."

"Funny."

She looked very professional today, in her navy blouse and light grey skirt. The skirt was maybe a tiny bit shorter than necessary, but what the heck, our parents were out of town. She was a wiry little thing, a year younger than me, with curly shoulder-length brown hair and light brown eyes flecked with green. We looked quite a bit alike, considering—well—anyway.

"So, you're definitely okay?" She came over and sat next to me on the bed.

"I'm fine, monster-baby. It was just some zany fluke of nature."

"Could've been qi!"

"I suppose. That's more your department than mine."

Naturally, our father brought his girls up to protect themselves. We both carried around some fairly advanced combat techniques in our personal arsenals, just in case; Hope was a lot more enthusiastic about the martial arts than me (I'd stopped tickle-torturing her years ago, when she started putting me in triangle chokes). Most of what Sensei Dad taught us was purely practical—go for the eyes and so forth—but he didn't neglect the mystical aspect of the arts. He was a firm believer in the reality of qi, the life-force.

She nodded gravely. "Prob'ly better we don't tell the old man about this, at least for now."

I smiled. She was so cute when she picked up Roy's speech patterns. She used to have quite the crush on young master Belmont, till she started dating Jason Locke.

"That works for me. Speaking of not telling Dad—what're you up to tonight? Going out?"

She heaved a great world-weary sigh, barely restraining herself from pressing the back of her hand to her forehead and flopped down with her head in my lap.

"*No*," she mourned. "Jason's got football practice all afternoon. Like *always*. And he'll be too tired to go out afterwards."

"Sorry, Hopi Mesa." I smoothed her hair, shifting from co-conspirator back into big sister mode. "How about we make some popcorn and have movie night? —*after* you finish your homework?"

"That sounds nice." Then she sat up and poked me in the ribs. "And you can pop the corn with your qi. Think of all the electricity we'll save!"

"Oh, get outta here."

Once she scuttled off to make some pretense of doing her homework, I sat there in silence for a while, pondering what she'd said. It's a tricky word, *qi*—there's no exact analogue for it in English. I've seen it translated as "breath" or "essence" or "spiritual energy", but it seems to mean something our culture lacks a concept for, something that's all of those things at once. The essence of a thing, I thought, the quintessential spirit of a thing. And that got me thinking about elements. The word *quintessential* grows out of *quint-*, as in quintet, as in five. It almost literally means, "the fifth element". And here I was, stuck at the end of a poem with two lines left to go and four elements already accounted for.

Don't be stupid, Faith. We're playing with fire here. Or—okay, not fire, but some mystery element that could be even more *dangerous.*

Yes—true—of course. Better safe than sorry. At any rate, my partner wasn't here to write the next line, so it was kind of a moot point. What would Tommy write? Something direct, something simple—something that summed up everything we'd written so far. Like, say, *Coffee is the best thing in the world*. Bam: line number nine.

Don't do it, Faith.

Okay, okay. I got up and went out to the kitchen to make some more hot chocolate. What rhymed with "world"? Hurled, furled, twirled. . .

Stop it!

Fine. Jeez. I could be awfully bossy sometimes. I peered into the fridge to see if we had any cherries. It was past four—too late for coffee—but I could build a mighty edifice of cocoa, with sprinkles and marshmallows and whatever else I could think of. It still wasn't quite the same, though. "Coffee is the best thing in the world," I murmured.

Oops.

But hey, I hadn't written it down. It didn't count if you didn't write it down. According to the rules I just made up. I went back to my bedroom and stuck my nose in my book and tried not to think about qi or poetry or Tommy. Especially Tommy.

Sometime after six, there was a knock on my door and Hope poked her head in. "Faith? Homework's all done. Time to fix some junk food and curl up on the couch."

Curled. That was a good one. "Be right there."

I marked my page, threw on some grubby clothes and rendezvoused in the kitchen. We made chicken quesadillas and a big overflowing bowl of popcorn for dinner/dessert and raided our Dr. Pepper supply for beverages. Everyone knows that if you want to have a proper movie night, you've got to commit to eating food that will take a few years off your life. Then we settled into our soft blue couch and cued up a few of our favorite zombie movies. Queensbury came padding over and sprawled herself across both of our laps, and Pendleton zoomed by occasionally to have his fur stroked for a few tenths of a second before zooming away again. We got a call from Mom and Dad late in the second movie, and we chatted for long enough to convince them we weren't starving to death or throwing any wild parties or forgetting to brush our teeth before bed. We didn't tell "the old man" about the qi incident.

Before diving into the next movie, we took a quick break to go run pee (that's a little gem of a phrase from my Hope-cabulary, since she's such a bad influence on me). I'm not sure why—maybe she's just girlier than me—but my sister can take up to four times as long in the bathroom as I do.

So there I was, sitting on the couch with the beasties, munching on the dregs of the popcorn, and abruptly the final line burst into my brain. That's how it is with poetry. Sometimes you toil and agonize for hours looking for the right word, the right balance of syllables, the right flow of syntax, and come away bone-tired and nothing to show for it; other times, the perfect phrase will just appear in your head like, like. . . well, we're not saying the "m-word" right now, but like that.

I sat there rolling it around on my tongue. I knew two things for certain. First, I probably shouldn't say it out loud. And second, I was definitely going to. A few parts of me—skepticism, wariness, apathy—tried to talk the rest of me out of it, but I wasn't really listening. Most likely, nothing would happen anyway. And what was the worst that *could* happen? And, like I said before, I don't give up on my poems.

"It makes my spirit glitter like a pearl," I murmured, and instantly everything became luminous. The chairs, the tables, the carpet, the couch, the cats, the walls, the whole room—it all began to shine, gently, with some inner radiance. It was like the moment when the very first ray of dawn peeps over the Atlantic: one second, grey and black; the next moment, pink and orange and scarlet fire and sea-blue sea and sky-blue sky. Nothing *changes*, but the beauty that was hiding right in front of you suddenly lifts its head and winks. I didn't move—I didn't even breathe. Somehow I didn't feel any surprise; just a deep, quiet joy. I wished I could show this to Hope. I wished I could show it to Tommy.

And then, inevitably, the strangeness started in. Stranger than the glowing couch, I mean. The room began to tilt forward. I clutched at the cushions and realized after a second of panic that nothing was actually moving—it was just my sense of balance, or perspective, or something. It felt as if the gravity in the house was re-orienting to pull me forward instead of downward. I held up a piece of popcorn and let go, and it went straight down like it was supposed to. I let go of the cushions and leaned slightly forward, and to my relief, I didn't start plummeting toward the wall. This was strictly inside my head.

So, I got a bit braver. I got to my feet and drifted along with the pull, and I found myself heading for the front door. "Okay, hang on," I muttered to—whatever. "Lemme at least get a jacket on."

Hope came out of the bathroom at that moment. "Ready for round three?" she asked, impossibly perky for nine in the evening.

"Hey, sooooo. . . I actually need to go out for a while. I'm sorry to break up the rhythm, but you can start the next one without me."

"What? Where? Why?"

"It's—it's sort of a—thing. I just need to go for a walk."

She rolled her eyes. "Poet stuff again?"

I smiled. "Actually, yeah. I guess it is."

"You people are all nuts."

"No argument here." I went over and hugged her. "Love you, lady. I'll probably see you in an hour or two—if not, don't forget to brush your teeth."

"Sure thing, *Mom*."

I slipped on some shoes, grabbed my tough red and white windbreaker, and headed for the door. "Love you too!" she called after me.

Down the hill. Up the street. Across the town, through the square, past a score of darkened shops and lighted homes. All the way to the outskirts of Zevon I followed the steady tugging in my qi. Funny—until a couple of hours ago, I was a firm skeptic regarding this qi business, to say nothing of magic. I wondered if they were the same thing, or separate forces, or maybe different facets of some larger force, or what. While I was absorbed in random speculation, I stumbled my way into the edge of a construction site and stopped at a chain-link fence.

The clock tower? They'd been trying to repair this thing for years. All the money kept going to snow removal—the past few winters had been pretty blustery. The gravitation, or whatever it was, very clearly wanted me to go inside. I hesitated. My parental units would not be pleased if they heard of me committing arson, truancy, and breaking-and-entering all in the same day.

Then the bells began to ring. But not with the precision of clockwork, not with the harmony of bells. Discordant knells and jangles, like a madman's funeral dirge. I squeezed through a gap in the fence and ran toward the tower—the front door must be locked, but there was a network of scaffolding I could climb up—and then I skidded to a halt and stood staring upwards, too horrified to scream. It was a long way down, and he seemed to fall forever, and I had plenty of time to see his face.

5

Must be qi. Everybody I looked at was giving off that eerie force like tangible light waves—but nothing else gave it off, only people. The trees, the birds, the fish in Mrs. Draper's tank, all looked the same as before. Inanimate objects didn't give it off either, but they still followed that arc of nameless color whenever somebody tossed something. I could pre-track the flight of every basketball and see whether or not it would go through the hoop.

Now, I know what you're thinking—and you're right. It may have been somewhat of a leap, especially for a scientist, to assume a quasi-mystical explanation for a phenomenon he'd barely begun to observe. And trust me, I considered the most obvious explanation: that something in my brain was acting wonky. I knew about disorders like synesthesia that cross sensory wires and cause people to see sounds and smell colors and suchlike; it was a reasonable hypothesis that I was just subconsciously calculating vectors and velocities and then translating them into a visual matrix. Except for one thing: Tommy. There was no way my subconscious could have known in advance how strong he was. For that matter, there was no way he could be that strong. And Faith's notebook spontaneously combusting, what was *that* about? Whatever was going on here, it was way too big to be all in my head.

I bumped into Locke during lunch.

"Yo, I heard Connor dominated you in gym," he said, with deep sympathy. "You gettin' old or what?"

"Nope. Might be getting wiser, though. I've discovered a new fundamental force. $Qi=mc^2$." I caught myself on the verge of giggling.

He peered at me. "Dude, seriously—are you okay?"

"Yeah, yeah, fine. Ribs're a little sore, that's all. Now go! Go forth and feast, my esteemed colleague. To a mayfly, lunch comes but once in a lifetime."

"Uh—sure. Catch ya later."

He had a good solid aura; no surprise there. But Tommy could've flicked the melon right off the top of his spine. I began to fell giddy again. Settle down, Belmont. The whole thing was just so freakishly fascinating.

Mrs. D's history class for period five. Tommy sat two rows up from me and I kept scanning him with my new "five-and-a-half" sense; oddly, his qi had subsided back down to normal parameters. To look at him now, you wouldn't think he was any stronger than the next guy. Maybe it really was just some senseless fluke, like Melody said. But then why had I suddenly manifested this qi-sight of mine?

I noticed that I couldn't get a reading on myself. Squinting at my own arm, I just saw an ordinary limb like a picture in a textbook, with no glimmer of otherworldly energies. And it didn't work in reflections either—but it did work through windows. I wondered if it would work in the dark.

French for period six (kind of a free ride for me, what with my parents being native French-speakers and all), and then we were out the door. Hadn't seen Faith since morning break; she must've gone home after English class. Figured I'd leave her be—I knew she loved her solitude, and I wanted some alone time as well. I walked quickly through the parking lot, hopped into my car, and took off at highly illegal speeds.

Do you mind if I talk about my car for a second? She was a sleek, black and yellow '98 Pontiac Firebird with pop-up headlights and a VS1 eight-cylinder engine—got up to 160 if I red-lined it. Plus, my buddy Hodge from Plymouth had outfitted her with a nitrous-injection system which, needless to say, I would never, ever use. I called her Betty Lou. Why? —don't know, just did. When Betty Lou and I tore out of the lot that day, we took a left up Overlook Drive and headed out of town. Needed to cruise and process things.

I went east for a while, out past Wareham and Bourne, stopped in Hyannis for gas and kept going up the coast till I saw the rolling breakers in the distant bay. I parked among the dunes and sat there in silence, watching the cattails waving in the salted breeze and the last few determined beach-goers straggling along in the cold November surf. Even at a distance, I could sense the energy levels in their bodies, the way you can feel the coiled potential in your hand when you make a fist. I couldn't *not* sense it. I couldn't switch it off.

"Something's wrong with me, Betty," I said in a low voice. "Something's wrong with my head."

Or heck, maybe something was right. Maybe it was some benign mutation. Maybe it was my "third eye," as the Zen folk say. Sensei always said that qi was how the soul communicated with the body, and that made sense to me as a theory—assuming one believed in the soul, which I was still debating over. My folks were Catholic, and I was baptized and confirmed and all that jazz, but I considered myself sort of undecided on the matter. The thing about it was that belief affected *everything*. I knew that the precise speed and trajectory of every single particle in the universe had been explosively established at the moment of creation, and absolutely everything that occurred, including the very thoughts in our brains, was therefore pre-determined by the inevitable interactions of those particles. Unless!...unless you believe in free will, in which case every time a human being thinks, he or she is forcing the atoms of the brain to deviate from their pre-determined course, *merely by wishing it*, and is thus ground zero for nothing less than a literally supernatural event. We don't notice it because it happens continuously all around us, but if the soul exists then our every thought represents an invasion from some higher mode of existence into the material plane. So, as an aspiring physicist, it wasn't a question I could afford to take lightly. But hey, perhaps my newfound power of perception could help me find a solid answer.

"Ugh." Enough of this. I needed to hit something.

I fired up the engine and gunned it back toward Zevon. Still didn't feel like seeing anyone right now, so I dug out my cell phone and called home. Mom answered on the third ring. "Yes, hello?"

"Hey Ma, it's me. I've gotta head over to the dojo for a couple hours, okay? Don't wait for me for dinner."

"Roy." She said with slight reproach. "I have made mashed potatoes, just as you like them best."

"Can you stick some in the fridge for me? I've got some special training I need to work on."

"Yes, I can, but your brother, he wants your help with his math homework. When will you be home?"

"Oh, eight or nine-ish. Tell Joe he can go into my desk and get my notes if he needs to, but don't let him touch anything else."

"Roy, slow down your car. You are speeding again, I can hear it."

Busted. "Yes, Mother."

"I thought Mr. Avalon is out of town for the week?"

"He is, but I've got a key. He doesn't want me getting rusty while he's away." That was true. Soon as he got back, I knew I'd be his top *uke* to help him practice and teach whatever new moves he learned out there. That's pronounced "oo-kay"—which basically means "rag doll". The person on whom a technique is executed during training is the uke.

She sighed dramatically. "Very well, we will miss you. Work hard. And Roy, you eat something. Do not forget."

"I will, Mom. See ya tonight."

"Goodbye, dear one. Drive safely."

I can't say I obeyed that order, but I did heed the command to eat. Around 7:30 I stopped at a diner outside of town and wolfed down a giant meatloaf sandwich, some spicy home fries, and a big glass of iced tea. Then I made my way to the dojo.

Sensei had bought an old defunct art studio near the edge of town, about fifteen years back and converted it for his own violent purposes. It was a squat, ramshackle building on a lonely windswept back street, one story tall and made of faded brick and aluminum siding. On the outside, it was unimpressive at best, on the outside. When I pulled into the dirt parking circle, dusk was creeping in and shadows loomed all around me. By long habit, I surveyed the area for any hidden menace as I neared the door; as usual, no desperate ruffians leapt out to rob me of my virtue. Their loss.

I unlocked the door and went inside, re-locking it behind me. In the dim anteroom I kicked off my shoes and took a lighter out of one of the drawers. I bowed over the threshold of the training ground and went to light some candles. The windows were shuttered, and I had no desire to stand beneath fluorescents.

The dojo's interior told a very different story from its outer appearance. The whole structure was a single wide-open space, floored with immaculate wall-to-wall tatami matting and punctuated by six polished oaken columns. From the twelve-foot-tall ceiling there hung four banners: Old Glory, the

Massachusetts state flag, a white coat of arms depicting a black wolf and raven, and a red flag inscribed with Japanese characters and a picture of a sheathed katana. The coat of arms belonged to the legendary Grandmaster Hiko, my teacher's teacher, whom I hoped to meet someday. The red flag contained a samurai motto: "Swift as the wind, silent as a forest, fierce as fire, immovable as the mountain". One wall was lined with gleaming mirrors, the other with well-maintained punching bags, wing-chun dummies, pommel-horses, and weight benches. And at the back—weapons. No need to search this room for makeshift implements; three broad ebony racks bristled with sais, nunchucks, escrima sticks, bo staffs, an assortment of swords and spears, and Sensei's razor-edged Filipino machetes, Biter and Beater. Absolutely no one was permitted to touch them, and even I had yet to hear the tale behind the old black stains on Biter's blade that had been never washed away.

Candleholders lined the wall that faced the mirrors. I lit three of them, and then went to the back of the dojo where extra uniforms were hanging on pegs. Once again, I stripped my threads and dressed myself in a blue gi top and baggy grey pants. The last of the sunshine was gone by now, and I stood in the center of the floor in nothing but flickering candlelight. I closed my eyes and breathed slowly, in through the nose, out through the mouth, letting the air fill my stomach. Hands loose at my sides, knees relaxed, my heartbeat whispered in my ears. Feeling the flow of my qi.

Qi.

Twenty feet to the closest heavy bag. From a full stop I broke into a dead sprint, closing the distance in the breath between heartbeats and sailed into the air to cross the last few yards with a flying jump kick. The bag pitched back and boomed against the wall, and I landed already swinging— knees and elbows, fists and feet, I unloaded on that thing.

The impact knocked a burning candle out of its wall-sconce. I spun, caught it in the air, and used the momentum to nail the nearest speedbag with a spinning heel kick. Holding the candle in my right, I unleashed a blur of hand-strikes on a wing-chun dummy, completing a two-handed strike pattern with my left alone—then I vaulted off a pommel-horse, popped the candle back in its holder in mid-dive, and rolled to my feet, panting. The equipment rocked and swayed in my wake. It felt good. I jogged over to the weapon-racks and grabbed a pair of nunchucks. Meditation is for nursing homes.

See, much as I admired Sensei Avalon, I had doubts about the martial path he'd chosen to tread. It seemed ultimately more contemplative than active; in fact, his teaching style was almost backwards from what you might expect. He taught us the most brutally efficient techniques early on (basically as soon as he felt he could trust us), and once he was satisfied that we could protect ourselves adequately, he began introducing more and more metaphysical aspects of the arts. It was all about conflict avoidance and inner peace and so forth. Whenever I tried to get at the kernel of true violence within some esoteric maneuver, he would utter his old refrain about learning the rules before trying to bend them. I knew if he were here right now, I'd be stuck doing forms and breathing exercises all night to help me "visualize". Screw that noise. I could see qi with my naked eyes now—who needed to visualize anymore?

I trained for over an hour, briskly but not exhaustively, sacrificing speed and force in favor of precision and focus. I was trying to feel the flow of energy in my own body the way I could feel it in everyone else's—but for some reason, it didn't seem to work that way. Eventually it occurred to me that it might be sort of the same reason you can't see your own eyeballs: maybe my qi was the very thing powering my qi-sight, and that's why it didn't register. Whatever the case, I finally quit worrying about it and blew out the candles. Time for some homework, a few video game s, and the slumber of a hard-workin' stiff.

But. When I stepped outside, I saw something gleaming over the tree line. It was just a glimpse, a fitful radiance—but it wasn't ordinary light. It pushed back against my vision, from at least half a mile away. There was some serious qi happening over there.

Well hey, I was already warmed up and dressed for the occasion. Couldn't turn my back on a mystery.

"Tally-ho," I muttered, and took off down the road at a trot.

A few minutes later, I found myself at the old clock tower. The gleam was coming from the third floor; as I got closer, I could hear what sounded like a woman singing. Without a second thought, I hopped the fence and started climbing the scaffolding. The singing stopped, but the light was getting stronger. And as I slipped through the empty window-frame, I saw—

"Tommy? What are you doing here?"

It was too dark to see his face, I realized belatedly. I had actually recognized him by his qi-signature. Over to his right was someone else—a lithe female form with a powerful life-force, no doubt the singer I'd heard. But I couldn't spare much attention for her. Tommy's energy was skyrocketing. He stood in the center of the room, his eyes squeezed shut, his whole body clenched, trembling, with waves of power pulsing out of him.

I could hear his teeth grinding, and I could hear
something else: the floorboards starting to rattle.
Dust came sifting down from the rafters. The walls
were shaking.

"Uh. . . Tommy?"

His eyes popped open. They were glowing
white.

"Ohhh, crap."

6

I WISH I could describe Alyra's singing. It was strong and sweet and kind of sad, and so, so beautiful. It wasn't English and it didn't sound like any language I'd ever heard, but somehow the sound of the words brought an image into my head all the same—or rather, not an image but a light, a bright white light that kept getting brighter and brighter and brighter. She only sang for a minute or two, I think, but then something funny started happening to the time in the room. It felt like it was slowing down somehow. But the singing didn't change, just everything around it. And yes, I know that doesn't make sense.

The light kept getting brighter, and she kept singing, and everything kept going into more and more extreme slow motion around me. I shut my eyes, but then I realized that actually made the light even stronger, but then I couldn't open them again. I couldn't move at all. My whole body seized up, and I started to shake. Then everything exploded.

You know that feeling when you've had way, way too much sugar and you're trying to sit still but you can't help drumming your fingers and tapping your feet and shifting around and you just want to jump up and run around the room and scream? Imagine that feeling times, like, a thousand. I can't exactly remember how the next part happened, but I think I snapped out of the paralysis and started throwing stuff around—like the gigantic desk, and a couple of the big metal gears that were riveted to the floor, and maybe one of the pillars holding up the ceiling. And then someone was shouting at me to stop, but half of me couldn't hear it and half of me didn't care, and then whoever it was tried to grab me by the arm but I shook him off and ran to the open part of the floor and *jumped up through it.* I wouldn't have tried that if I was thinking straight, and I'm pretty sure it wasn't even physically possible, but I went soaring up through the air and landed on the fourth floor.

That insane rage was still frothing away in my limbs and I found myself tearing up more of the tower. There were footsteps running up the stairs behind me, and then the same guy from before came running up and shouted at me again, but it was all fuzzy, like a radio station that was three-quarters static, so I didn't listen. And then the guy kicked my feet out from under me, and I fell hard, and all of a sudden I was really, really mad. I bounced back up like someone had switched off the gravity, and I grabbed him and hurled him all the way across the room and he smashed through a whole giant stack of old boards piled up on the far side of the floor.

But whoever he was, he was tough as nails. He got back up, grabbed a two-by-four, and came running all the way back to where I was standing and shattered it on my face. I swung at him like a bear slapping salmon and he ducked under it and then hit me like a machine gun, maybe twenty times all over the torso. It knocked me back a step or two. Then I slammed him in the chest with my palms, and he went flying backwards again and crushed a sawhorse in the corner. I came stalking towards him, and my vision was a thudding white haze, and I don't really know what I would've done, but this guy just wouldn't stay down.

He jumped back to his feet and picked up a huge slate tile that must have been a roof shingle and bashed it to pieces over my head, and it almost hurt. Getting angrier, I heard myself roaring, and the floor was trembling for some reason, and then the guy turned and ran and I chased him, still howling at the top of my lungs.

We went pounding up the stairs to the top floor and he kicked me in the face and I caught his leg and swung him in a circle and launched him into the air and his plummeting body destroyed a huge wooden crate and a million tiny metal cogs came spilling out and rolled across the floor like skittering spiders. Five metal bells, each ten feet tall, were hanging from the ceiling, and I straight-armed the nearest one as I passed, and it set them all off in ear-splitting clangs and rattles and bongs. I was panting, not because I was tired, but because some part of my head was finally waking up and trying to stop me from killing a man. I paused a few feet away and stood there shuddering, fighting for control of myself. Then I heard this awful rending groan, and he dragged himself back to his feet and made a spear out of his fingers and jabbed me right in the eye. I screamed and stumbled back a few steps, and then I screamed again and charged at him. He fell straight backwards and grabbed my shirt and stomped a foot into my chest and flipped me over his head, and I crashed right through the face of the clock. And there was wind and floating debris all around me, and I couldn't get a hold of anything. There was dark wet grass hurtling up at me like a wall.

After the impact, the blazing light and the craziness went away. The ground felt cool and soft, and I lay there for a while just enjoying how comfortable it was. It couldn't have been more than a second or two, I guess, but time was still misbehaving and it felt like a long restful snooze. Gradually, I started to realize that someone else was yelling at me now—a girl, this time. And even more gradually, I realized I knew her voice.

"Oh my God, Tommy! *Tommy!*" But she wasn't yelling. She was crying.

It took a lot of effort, but I slowly raised my head. It felt like my mouth was full of cotton. There was an actual indent in the grass where my face had planted, and I basically had to peel myself out of it. "F—Faith," I mumbled.

She went quiet, and there was a pause. "Tommy?"

"Hi."

". . .Hi." Another pause. "Are you okay?"

"Yeah—I think so." I got my arms under me and started pushing myself up, but she put her hands on my shoulders.

"Wait! Wait, don't try to move. You could be hurt, you could be in shock."

But my wind was coming back now, and my head was clearing at least. "Nah, I'm okay." I sat up. "Whew."

She was kneeling next to me, and the whites of her eyes were showing. "Are you—are you sure you're not hurt?"

"Yeah. Sorry if I scared you." I could see the tears on her cheeks in the dim light. Without thinking about it, I reached up and wiped her face, and she took my hand in both of hers.

"Tommy, please, what is going on?"

"Ummmmm. . ."

There were footsteps behind me, and I craned my neck around to see. It looked like Roy Belmont from school. He was limping and clutching his left shoulder like he'd just been hit by a car. Blood was running down his face.

"Tommy?" he said.

"Hi, Roy. What happened to you?"

"You, uh—you don't remember the last few minutes?"

I frowned. "No, I mean—I think I do." Then it dawned on me, and I got to my feet. "Oh God, was that you in there? Roy, I—I—"

"Eh." He waved the whole thing aside, again, just like in gym class. "How you feelin'?"

"Me? I'm fine. What about you?"

"Still breathing, more or less."

Faith got up as well. "Roy? What are *you* doing here?"

"Why wouldn't I be here? It's a public place."

"Ah, no, actually, it's fenced off and clearly marked 'no trespassing.' And don't be disingenuous with me."

"Disingenuous, for crying out loud, can't you just say 'coy'?"

"I'll use as many syllables as I please, Roy Belmont. Now somebody tell me why Tommy just fell five stories out of a disused clock tower!"

"I myself would love to know the answer to that question," he said, and turned back towards me. "Why don't you start?"

"Huh? Oh—okay. Well, see, I was going for a walk and I felt like someone was watching me, so I started running and I ended up here. And then I just felt like climbing, so I went up the side, but there was this lady who followed me up there, and she started singing, and then—I dunno, everything kind of went white, and I felt really weird. And then, you know, you and I had our—our fight, and then I guess that's it. I think I'm back to normal now."

He pinched the bridge of his nose. "Faith, did you get any usable information out of that?"

"Not really. Let's take it from the top."

We sat down on the grass, and they asked me a whole bunch of questions, and we went over it and over it until they were satisfied. "So you have no idea who this Alyra was?" Faith asked.

"Nope."

"Don't suppose she stuck around," Roy said.

"Probably not, once you two started busting up the place. My God, Roy, you could've killed him."

"Listen sis, he was throwing hundred-pound clock-wheels around like beach balls in there. Of the two of us, he was not the one in mortal danger."

"Okay, okay, fine. But seriously, what were you doing here in the first place?"

He sighed. "I was at the dojo. And I could see his qi from the parking lot."

"What, exactly, do you mean by that?"

He told us about how he started being able to sense people's energy that same day during gym. Then Faith talked about what happened in English class and told us about the spell (or whatever it was) that brought her here. And then there was a long silence.

"There is no way this is all a coincidence," Faith said eventually. "There's something happening to all of us, and it's tied together somehow. And this Alyra person has to be at the center of it."

"Unless she was telling the truth," Roy said. "Unless Tommy's the center of it and she only showed up when she did because of him. You and I were both interacting with him when our own weirdness manifested."

"So now we're getting our information from a shadowy psychopath with antennae?"

"Even granting that she's a psychopath, which we have no way of knowing, it doesn't mean her intel's faulty."

"Whatever she did to Tommy, it almost got the both of you killed."

"Maybe she didn't know what was gonna happen."

"Maybe you're so into girls with antennae that you're not thinking straight."

"You're really fixated on the antennae, aren't you? We don't even know they were antennae, it was dark in there."

"Oh, well, *horns* are much better. If you can't trust someone with horns, then you can't trust anyone in this world."

I raised my hand. "Guys?" They stopped bickering and looked at me. "I'm kinda tired. Do you think we could talk about this tomorrow?"

Faith hesitated, but Roy blew some air through his cheeks and nodded. "Actually, I'm pretty run down myself. Might be better if we all slept on it."

"But, Tommy—are you *sure* you shouldn't go to the hospital? Just to double-check?"

I shook my head. "I'm okay. I promise if I don't feel good tomorrow, I'll go see the nurse."

"All right. Roy—I know better than to ask you to see a doctor. Although you really should, you know."

"Eh. Come on, my car's back at the dojo. I'll give you guys a lift."

We didn't talk any more as we walked over to his car. I got in the back and Faith took shotgun. We didn't talk as we drove, either. He dropped Faith off at her place, and she reached back and squeezed my hand, kissed Roy on the cheek, and got out without a word. I gave him a few directions and he took me to my house.

"Listen," he said as we pulled into the driveway. "I want you to know I didn't mean for you to go through the face of the clock like that. I mean—I didn't mean for you to fall. I just miscalculated your momentum. And—you know—I'm glad you're okay."

"You too. I, um. . ." I never know what to say to people. "Yeah. Thanks for the ride."

"You bet." As I was getting out of the car, he said, "Hey—good fight."

I smiled. "You too. See you tomorrow."

Uncle Syme was in his study. I went in kind of fast because I didn't feel like explaining stuff, and I called through the door and told him I was home and tired and going to bed. He said okay. He seemed distracted.

I washed my face and went up to my room. I was exhausted. My head hurt. Plus I'd just gotten tossed out of a five-story building. That was weird. I'd have to sit down and think about that. But not right now. I hit the lights and flopped down on my bed with all my clothes still on.

But after I lay there for a minute or two, I started to wonder about something. When I hit Roy with the volleyball in gym class, I was totally caught up in the game and sort of, you know, firing on all cylinders. And back at the tower, I was caught up in some kind of berserk fury. I wondered if that crazy strength was still around now that I was all relaxed and calm.

I got up and went over to my dresser. It was a big wooden thing, full of clothes, probably somewhere in the neighborhood of a hundred and fifty pounds. I squatted down and got my fingers under it and lifted, and I almost fell over backwards. It came into the air so easily that I had to catch it before it broke the ceiling.

Slowly, I eased the dresser back down to the carpet. Then I stood back up and frowned and ran a hand through my hair. Whatever Alyra did to me, it looked like it might be permanent.

7

I didn't even try to sleep that night. Hope was dozing on the sofa when I came in, so I pulled a blanket over her and went on up to change into my pajamas. Then I turned out the lights, climbed into bed, and lay there with my hands laced behind my head, gazing at the little glow-in-the-dark stars on my ceiling. I kept seeing him falling.

Roy could be cocky—and belligerent—and I couldn't help wondering if he'd jumped into that fight when there might have been other options. But for all that, he was one of the smartest people I knew, and he had a point: both he and I had been engaged in some fairly intense give-and-take with Tommy when things started getting odd. I didn't believe for a second that Tommy would deliberately cause—whatever had happened. And yet, I had watched him fall a hundred feet onto his face and then get back up with barely a wince. I kept circling around that fact in my head. Obviously, it wasn't possible. But there it was. Whatever else it might mean, it meant the world was a different sort of place than I had thought.

Outside the window, an owl was hooting somewhere in the darkness. It was funny people always ask "why?" but the owls skip right to "who?" when posing the endless question. I wondered if they knew something we didn't. Far away in the deep starry silence, at the very edge of hearing, a coyote sent up a dolorous call. It reminded me that midnight had gone by and Tuesday had arrived; Tyr's day, named for the Norse god who sacrificed his hand to bind Fenris the demon-wolf. Were there really monsters in the world? I didn't seem to feel afraid, just puzzled. Did that mean something was wrong with me too? Oh, wait—I was the girl who set fires with rhyming couplets. Of course something was wrong with me.

"Sleep on it," Roy said. Sure. It was past three now. I wondered if the boys were sleeping. Roy could probably fall asleep at will. He could probably decide when to wake up without even setting an alarm. And Tommy, he was—he was like a little kid, he probably jumped up and down on his bed until ten and then slept all night with a smile on his face. On the other hand, they probably both had concussions. They could both be slipping into comas right now. Drifting away.

Then Hope banged on my door. "Hey! Sleep through your classes when you get to college, ya slacker."

I groaned and sat up. I must've finally dropped off around five—it was past seven now, so at least I'd gotten a couple of hours. Slowly, feeling half-suspended in amber, I raised my hands and rubbed the sand out of my eyes before dragging myself out of bed. Yaaay, school.

Hope had fixed us some cereal and bagels. "You look dreadful," she chirped.

"Uff."

"Jason's picking me up in a few minutes. Maybe you'd better skip your morning schlep and ride with us today."

"Kay." I chewed my bagel.

"Are you all right? How was your—late-night walk, or whatever?"

I stopped in mid-munch. "Mmff—'sokay."

She looked dubious. "If you say so. Come on, get your shoes on. I promised I wouldn't make him late again."

One thing I hadn't thought about during my interminable ponderings was what to tell my sister, if anything. It went without saying that Mom and Dad were not to know—or anyway, not over the phone, which meant not till Sunday at the very earliest. It might have been a relief to share it with Hope, but I discovered I wasn't ready for that. Either to deal with her reaction or to accept the guilt of burdening her with all this. No rush, I supposed. The weirdness would most likely still be here tomorrow.

Locke showed up right on time—or to be specific, right after I finished making coffee. I poured it into a couple of travel mugs while he and Hope were being mushy, mixed in cream and sugar while they were arguing about something, and led the way out the door as they were blissfully reconciling. It all took about thirty-five seconds. Ah, young love.

Everything came crowding back into my head as I brooded in the back seat, and with it a swirl of perplexity and fear that cleared my sinuses and woke me up fast. All the same, I'd had a stressful day and a long night and I didn't want Sarah pillaging my caffeine supply again. Hence the second mug.

"Hey, you!" she said as I came into Mrs. Mara's room. She looked bright and merry this morning. At least one of us remembered to sleep last night.

"'Eya." I handed her the auxiliary coffee and slurped noisily at my own as I sank into an empty seat.

"Aw, thanks." Then she peered at me. "Honey, you look awful. Are you okay?"

"Dunno yet." I sat nursing my cup and watching the door.

"Faith, seriously, I was worried about you. I didn't call you because I know how you are about your alone time, but some crazy stuff went down yesterday. Did you hear about Roy?"

"I heard. Have you seen him yet?"

"Nuh-uh." She glanced at the clock on the wall. "He's got a few more minutes."

I started drumming my fingers on the desk.

"Faith? Maybe. . . you should slow down with the coffee?"

"Maybe." People were still trickling into the room, including Locke. Mrs. Mara came in and went up to the front to start organizing her desk. My fingers drummed faster.

Then at long last, Tommy walked in and I jumped up and flew over and threw my arms around him before I realized what I was doing. He looked a bit startled, but he hugged me back—kind of gingerly, like he was afraid of breaking me. "Hi, Faith," he murmured.

I pulled away, a little, and looked at him intently. "Hi. How are you? You're not hurt?"

"Nope, feel fine." He didn't have a scratch on him that I could see. "How about you?"

"I—I'm not sure. Pretty flummoxed, I guess."

His forehead wrinkled. "Is that like confused?"

And suddenly I was smiling again. "Exactly like confused."

"Gotcha. Me too, then."

"So..." At that moment, Roy walked in too. "Roy!" I hugged him too, and he flinched slightly.

"Heya, Faith," he said in a pained voice.

"Oh! —sorry. How are you feeling?"

"Bit stiff. Be okay in a day or two. Heya, T. You look—pretty good."

Tommy nodded, looking unhappy. "Not too bad. I'm sorry you're—"

Roy held up a hand. "We've been over this, buddy. I already said, 'eh.' Remember?"

"That means everything's cool," I translated. "Gotcha."

The bell rang, and Mrs. Mara gestured placidly. "Take your seats, please, everyone." We were the only ones still standing, so we slunk back to our desks before we roused her benevolent ire. Sarah was glancing at Tommy and waggling her eyebrows at me. I gave her the death-glare and focused on the fascinating world of my empty desk.

As usual, my first two periods were uneventful, and the lack of sleep was starting to catch up with me. When I went to the cafeteria to re-caffeinate during morning break, I opened one of those little creamers, poured it into the trash, and caught myself half a second from throwing the empty container into my coffee. I sighed and reached for another creamer.

"Long night?"

I sighed again. That was the bright Arctic voice of Kira Quinn, my doe-eyed nemesis from the senior class. I'm not sure what I did to attract her venom. It could have been the fact that our fathers didn't get along (her dad was a developer who kept trying to buy and bulldoze the Avalon dojo), or it might possibly have been that she overheard me saying uncomplimentary things about the art of ballet during lunch awhile back—not knowing that she was an aspiring ballerina—and that I went on to defend my position rather loudly when she called me on it. Personally, I liked to think she was simply jealous of my looks. Whatever the case, she rarely missed a chance to pick on me about something or other and I was in no shape for a battle of wits right now.

"You know, most of us wait till Friday to run out and misbehave," she said in a "friendly advice from your elders" sort of tone. "But then again, most of us don't set our boyfriends' books on fire in the middle of class either."

Ugh. "He's not my—how did you even hear about that?"

"It's a small school, Faithie. Word gets around."

The only comeback I could think of was, "Well—you're dumb." So, I kept my mouth shut and concentrated on fumbling with the sugar.

"I've gotta hand it to you, though, Tommy's not hard on the eyes. It'd be a shame if he ran off with someone who was less of a firebug. You know, someone more mature. Like a senior."

I lifted my chin and gazed at her. She was about as subtle as a brick to the face, but she certainly had style. Her blouse was precisely low enough, and her skirt precisely high enough, to maximize her appeal while still being classy. She had a way of cocking her hips and shoulders that looked totally relaxed but unconsciously reminded you of every cover girl you'd ever seen. I couldn't even remember what I was wearing—a hoodie and sweatpants, maybe? But at that moment, she seemed a lot less intimidating and lot more annoying, like a mosquito whining in your ear when you're about to drop off to sleep—or a terrible dream that hovers around you and keeps you awake after two of your friends have practically butchered each other in a ruined tower on the edge of town.

"Kira," I heard myself saying in a level voice, "I'm about five seconds from setting your *head* on fire, so why don't you go pester someone else?"

Her eyes widened, and she missed a beat, but she came right back with, "That's about what I'd expect from a psycho. He'll get tired of you soon enough." Then she turned and sashayed away at a nice slow pace to show that she wasn't scared of me.

Whatever.

When I got to English class, Mr. Jameson let me, and Tommy go off in the corner for a couple of minutes to complete our assignment. Tommy had re-written our little poem, not exactly as it had been (my memory's generally spotty, but I've got great recall when it comes to poetry), but close enough.

"Hey, so—I'm sorry if I bugged you to keep going yesterday," he said. "We can just take a B on this if you want. It's still better than I normally get in this class."

"No, I want to test something. I tried repeating the line about wind yesterday, and it didn't do anything. Let's see about the line that brought me to the clock tower." I started to write, and then paused. "And you don't have to apologize, Tommy. You haven't done anything wrong."

He nodded, looking unconvinced.

"Anyway—here goes." I gave him a quick look, hesitated a second, and then wrote it down: *It makes my spirit glimmer like a pearl.*

We exchanged another look, then looked back down at the paper. Nothing happened. I let out my breath.

"Well, that's good to know," he said.

"Ha, yeah. I can only torch your stuff once per poem."

"Just move everything flammable out of the room before you start writing, I guess."

"You're a riot, Connor. Better save some of that wit for the last line."

"Oh yeah." He scrunched his eyes shut and thought about it for a couple of minutes. I didn't rush him. They were talking about Sylvia Plath over there, so I wasn't in a hurry to rejoin the class. Plus, I kind of liked watching him think.

"Got it!" he said finally, and scribbled out, *It bringeth joy to every boy and girl.*

"Oooh, 'bringeth'! Very Shakespearean, I like it."

He beamed. "Thanks."

"Well. . . I suppose we'd better get back to learning about the villanelle."

"Right. Nice working with you."

"Likewise." I went up and put our poem on Mr. J's desk, then settled back into my regular seat next to Sarah.

With characteristic subtlety, she gave me a broad wink and then leaned over and elbowed me. "Didja get his number?" she whispered loudly.

"Oh, just shut it."

The next half hour went on for hours. I couldn't summon up the interest to take any part in the class, so I sat there staring blankly at my notebook and listening to the babble in my head. Several of me were occupied in wild speculations about what was causing these apparently supernatural events and how it was all tied together, while a few more of me were busy pointing out the holes in my theories and reminding me that there was no actual evidence to support anything yet. A couple of me were bickering about whether this was anyone's fault and, if so, whose. One or two of me were wondering about Alyra, and at least one of me was wondering what Roy found so compelling about the idea of a woman with antennae. I myself—the Faith who makes the actual decisions—floated above the fray and watched the glacial dripping of the minutes. I was tired. And hungry. And tired. And the fruitless, free-wheeling debate in my head was starting to sound almost hypnotic, like white noise. I nearly jumped out of my sneakers when the bell went off.

Gym class was excessively uneventful. Coach Strothman must have been nervous about Tommy smashing things again, because she announced that this would be an extra yoga day (we typically did yoga on Fridays). So, the mats came out and she led us all through a nice calm session, barely strenuous enough to keep me awake, and I had lots of time to think about being hungry. I tried whispering something to Roy at one point and our illustrious coach snapped at me to stay focused. By the time she let us go, I was seriously considering shouting a poem about roast beef sandwiches. I took an ultra-quick shower and slipped out of the locker room a minute early to beat the crowd to the caf.

As soon as they started serving, I constructed a mammoth grinder out of sesame buns and roast beef and sliced cheddar and mustard and mayo and lettuce and tomatoes and pickles. Then I made myself yet another big cup of coffee, and then I tracked down a couple of fudge brownies from the dessert tray. And *then* I went looking for my boys.

They were already waiting for me by the door. Roy had an insulated bag that no doubt contained all sorts of high-protein athlete-approved foodstuffs and Tommy was fiddling around with a sandwich made of white bread and that telltale purple stain that bespeaks the presence of PB&J— but he didn't look very hungry.

"You guys wanna go outside?" he asked. "I've got a place I like to go sometimes."

"Sure," I said, and Roy shrugged. We followed him down the hall, and he brought us out to that tiny courtyard beyond the back door that no one ever went to, for some reason. I looked around and found myself thinking it was a really nice spot and wondering why I never ate lunch out here. Leave it to Tommy to find the one enormous glowing diamond sitting right out in the open in the middle of a barren field.

Have I mentioned that I was hungry? Once we got seated on the bench—they put me in the middle, Roy on the right and Tommy on the left, like I needed protecting—I started devouring my grinder and let them do the talking. Roy opened with the inevitable, "So."

"Yup," said Tommy.

There was a silence. I said, "Mrmpf." A true meeting of the minds, this.

Roy rolled his eyes, very slightly, and said, "All right, look. Obviously there's a whole lot going on that we don't understand. So in the absence of any other data, we've basically got two options. One, we can be very patient and just hope that everything somehow works itself out if we wait long enough. Or, two—"

At that moment the back door opened, and a man walked through. He had a grey suit and tie that hung a trifle loose on his slight frame and thinning hair shot through with grey. He looked to be in his late forties and couldn't have weighed more than a hundred and fifteen pounds. He wore bifocals and was in every possible way unimpressive. But somehow the second I looked at him, I could feel my hackles rising—and until that very second, although one hears that phrase all the time, I'd never been exactly sure what a hackle was or what it would feel like if they rose. I could feel my lips pulling back from my teeth, and a scalding trickle informed me I'd crushed the paper cup of coffee in my hand.

What—what's going on here? Who is this guy?

"Good morning," he said, in a fantastically ordinary voice. "My name is James Wingrove."

8

So James Wingrove walked into the courtyard. I'd never heard of the guy, but I felt something strange as soon as I

maggots

My eye twitched. There was something lice about him, but I couldn't put my finger on it. He was extremely average-looking, with thinning grey beetles and dismal brown eyes. Conservatively dressed, in oozing leprosy and a grey tie, with brown loafers and flies breeding in sores. I shook my head sharply. What the bloody hell was corpses, rotting corpses, grinning skulls and writhing flesh worms burrowing in filth? I couldn't

needles

Faith clutched at my hand, and it gave me an anchor. I shook my head again, even harder, and got a hold of myself. I squeezed her hand, got to my feet, and stepped between her and him.

"Name's Belmont," I said—growled, in fact. "What can I do for you, Mr. Wingrove?"

It was already a lousy day. Woke up so sore I could hardly move. Spent over an hour in the shower—luckily my siblings were used to me coming back from the dojo in rough shape, and we had more than one bathroom in the house—then scarfed down a small fistful of ibuprofen and slathered myself with zheng-gu-shui, an Oriental muscle ointment. 'Far as I could see, my erstwhile opponent was completely unscathed—his five-story fall notwithstanding. For which, of course, thank God; I certainly didn't want Tommy hurt. But, still—that was a lot of power for an untrained random to be carrying around.

"I represent an organization called, ha, called The Eye," Wingrove said dully. "We're interested in speaking with Mr. Connor if that's, hee, if that's all right."

"This is a school, Mr. Wingrove," I replied. "I don't see a visitor's pass on your lapel. Have you cleared this visit with the principal's office?" I was trying to feel him out with my qi-sight, but I kept getting waves of rot and corruption whenever I looked at him. It made me want to squash the life out of him, but at the same time it made me afraid of whatever was giving off that ugly ghoulish vibe. And I ain't afraid of much.

"I may have bypassed a few of the, hee hee, the customary niceties," he said. "But I hope we can, ha ha, we can overlook that little detail for the time being." Despite the giggling, his tone remained absolutely flat, and nothing about his posture seemed even remotely threatening. I had no idea how to respond to this guy.

"Say what you want," Tommy said. I realized he and Faith had gotten up and were flanking me, and it made me feel surprisingly reinforced. "Then go."

"Mr. Connor," said Wingrove. "We of The Eye are very interested in some of your abilities. We would be most appreciative if you would, hee, care to, ha ha, care to meet with us this evening, Mr. Connor. I am authorized to assure you it will be most profoundly to your benefit, Mr. Connor."

"Where?" he asked.

"Tommy," I said in a low voice, but he made a shushing motion and I followed his lead.

"Perhaps outside the school, after sundown?"

"Yeah, maybe. We'll see."

"Very well, hee hee, very well, Mr. Connor, very well. We hope to see you very soon indeed." Without another word or glance at any of us, like a jerky little grey-clad puppet, he turned and walked away.

The jagged edge in my vision faded, and I found myself relaxing. I hadn't even realized how tense I'd gotten. "Did you guys—?"

"Yeah," Faith said, in a faintly quavering voice. "Way, way, way beyond creepy."

"Yeah, that was definitely the creepiest guy I've ever met," Tommy confirmed. He sounded almost cheerful about it. I suddenly realized why I couldn't decide if I liked this kid or not: the exact same things about him were both endearing and infuriating.

"You're not actually planning to meet him and his—whatever, his organization tonight, are you?" I demanded.

"Nah, prob'ly not. I just wanted to get rid of him."

I nodded slowly. "Well. . . good. But all the same, this is even more craziness we have to worry about now. I don't suppose he and his group will go away if we ignore them."

"Do you think they're connected with Alyra?" Faith asked.

I glanced at Tommy, and he shrugged. "Dunno," I said. "We need a lot more data before we can formulate a meaningful hypothesis."

"I do love it when you talk dirty, Belmont."

"Just warmin' up, Avalon." I laced my fingers together and pushed them outwards, knuckles popping and snapping like a string of firecrackers. "I think we should get together after school, someplace we won't be interrupted by lunatics, and at least get a handle on what little we *do* know. How about Dunkin Donuts?"

Tommy scratched his head. "Well. . . what if we meet at my house? You guys've never been there, and—you know—we could have dinner and stuff. And nobody would bug us to keep buying crullers or whatever, and we could listen to something other than elevator music."

Faith lit right up at this suggestion. "That sounds really nice! Right, Roy?"

"Ah—sure. Yeah. I can give you a lift, if you like."

"You remember how to get there?" Tommy asked.

"'Course I remember," I said, trying to keep the acerbity out of my tone. I was trained— *highly* trained—to observe and retain minor details. Part of the warrior's way. Not all of us got handed superhuman strength for no perceptible reason.

"What time?" Faith asked. "I'm gonna need a nap after we get out of here, so later might be better."

Tommy made a kind of "meh?"-like gesture, so I said, "How about seven-ish?" They both agreed. "Now, about these misbegotten 'Eye' people. . ."

"I told you, I'm not going to meet them," Tommy said.

"You said you probably weren't going to meet them."

"Okay, I definitely won't meet them."

"You sure? Because if you do talk with these people, I want to be there too."

"How about neither of you talks with them," Faith said in a severe (and slightly maternal) voice.

"We'll have to deal with them sooner or later," I said. "I just don't want our boy here running off to do it on his own."

"I know this is gonna sound crazy, but we *could* try, you know, calling the cops."

Tommy and I glanced at each other. "I think this is something we should handle in-house," I said, and he nodded confidently. Nice to know we were on the same page here.

Faith shook her head disgustedly.

"Anyway—gotta get ready for next period. Catch you guys inside." I headed in and went to my locker to collect my history stuff. As I was turning away with an armload of books, I bumped into Old Luke, the janitor. "Oh hey, Luke. How's it going?"

"On and on and on," he muttered.

"Uh—right. Good, then." I swung back through the caf, grabbed a table, and scarfed down my meal. Didn't feel much like eating after the encounter with Wingrove, but growing boys need their carbs. By then it was nearly time for Mrs. Draper's class.

"Hey babe, you got a sec?" That was Sarah, gliding in from nowhere and slipping sinuously into the chair across me.

"For you? I've got like three or four. What's up?" In spite of everything, I felt my mood lifting. Sarah and I went back a long ways. My folks made me learn ballroom dancing when I was eight and she was my partner every Thursday. I actually looked forward to that silly class, knowing I'd get to see her there. We'd even dated a couple of times, although it never quite worked out—too much of a brother-and-sister vibe, I think. Our most recent attempt was this past summer, and there was more friction during the break-up than either of us wanted. Recently we'd been starting to get close again.

"Have you talked to Faith today?"

"Yeah, I—um—I was just talking with her a few minutes ago."

"Really?" She leaned forward, looking concerned. "Roy, is she okay? She's been acting awfully strange."

"Yeah, it's been a strange week."

"Sweetie, it's Tuesday."

"I know! Let's hope it normals down some from here."

She made my very favorite expression: that grimace you make when you're trying not to smile. "Optimum helpfulness not achieved."

"She's fine, Red, honest. I'm not exactly sure what's up yet, but it's nothing she can't handle. Especially with you and me watching her back."

"Got that right." She offered a pretty little fist and I bumped it with my own. "So! —next item. What's going on with her and Tommy?"

"Oh, for Pete's sake. . ."

The bell rang.

"Whoop. So much for gossip hour."

"This ain't over, stud."

"Yeah, yeah. See you in French class."

"*Mais oui!*"

Faith and Tommy both had European History with me. It was a quiet period today—no explosions or fistfights or magical singing women with antennae—but I was only partially relieved. Unlike yesterday, when I spent this class scanning Tommy with my qi-sight and having him read totally average, I was unsettled to see that today his aura was holding steady at about ten times stronger than everyone around him. No dips, no flares, just a solid force at rest like an idling tank. Glancing around at our classmates and then back at him was like brushing my way through a bunch of hanging laundry sheets only to walk into a brick wall.

French class was—French class. I let it wash over me. I know, I know, taking a class in a language I already knew was ethically shady at best. All I can say is I had a moment of laziness when I was picking electives that year. I think at least some of the blame goes to the grown-ups who let me get away with it.

After school I went to the dojo and did some very slow, easy stretching for about an hour, then went for a long slow walk around town. I was still sore—about as sore as I'd ever been, in fact—but as long as I kept my muscles loose and my blood flow brisk, I figured I'd be back to about 90% by tomorrow. I heal fast. When I finished that, I retrieved Betty Lou and then headed on back to the school as the sun was setting. I had no intention of confronting Wingrove and his band of freaks, but I wanted to make sure Tommy kept his promise. Plus, it wouldn't hurt to get a look at these people.

I cruised by Zevon High at a leisurely, but not suspiciously leisurely, speed—didn't see anything stirring in the parking lot. I turned around in the law office down the road, came back, and pulled into the school. Sat there for about ten minutes, slumped way down in my seat, peering around: still nothing out of the ordinary. A few teachers and parents came and went. A couple of football players late for practice went straggling by.

The van for the coffee vendor pulled up to a side door, and some schmoe in a cap started carrying supplies into the building. Qi signature looked normal—if he was an evil spy of some kind, at least he was a human evil spy. And he couldn't be all bad if he stocked our larders with the coffee that kept Faith from lapsing into a permanent vegetative state.

Eventually I got out and did some brief reconnaissance on foot, but there was no one crouching in any of the trees or bushes, no one lurking around the back corners of the school. Either they'd blown off the meeting, or—more likely—they were watching the place from a distance to see if Tommy showed. In any case, it was time for me to get out of here.

Tommy had said something about having dinner at his place, but Ma Belmont wouldn't much care for me passing on her mashed potatoes two nights in a row. I went on home, walked through the door, and got tackled by my kid brother Joe. We sprawled halfway out onto the front step, giggling like idiots and knocking over a potted plant, and then I trapped the little punk's torso with my legs and threw him in a guillotine choke. If *I* didn't teach him not to expose his throat to a grappler, then who would?

"Boys!" That was Mom, swatting at Joe's defenseless hind quarters with a broom. "You stop that fighting—" horrified gasp "—*and you fix my ficus!*"

"Yes, Mother," we said, grinning. She left the broom by the door and bustled back off to the kitchen, praying loudly to St. Monica for her unrepentant urchins.

I winced involuntarily as I was getting up, and Joe stooped to give me a hand. "Feelin' any better?" he asked.

"'Course. Why wouldn't I be?"

"I thought you had some kinda super-intense training session last night or something."

"Psssh, that was like twenty hours ago. You start sweeping, I'll grab a dustpan."

"How come I gotta sweep?"

"Your butt was the last thing to touch that broom, young Joseph. You. . . are the chosen one."

We were just finishing up when Dad pulled into the driveway. He was an electrical engineer, working over in Plymouth while Mom raised the kids and kept the house. Old-fashioned, I suppose, but I think they did a halfway decent job with us. He gave us the somber stare that was his patriarchal version of the grimace I mentioned earlier. "Boys, I hope you are not fighting again."

We pointed at each other and said in chorus, "He started it, sir." It was practically an evening ritual.

He shooed us. "Inside, inside."

Amarantha came skipping up to me as I went to help set the table. "Heya, Roy. Feeling better?"

"I'm fine, why does everyone keep asking me that?"

"One other person asked you that, Einstein. Aren't you supposed to be the math whiz in the family?"

"Keep it up, princess. I'll go Schrodinger on your cats."

She stuck her tongue out at me.

Amarantha was a month shy of fourteen. She got her looks from Mom, which meant she was tiny and beautiful (and also much smarter than me). Joe took after Dad, which meant he was already bigger than me despite being two years my junior.

Watching our parents dance was like witnessing a titan's courtship of a pixie queen. Me, I basically split the difference between my genetic contributors. For my purposes, I was exactly the size I wanted to be. I was big enough to throw a heavyweight punch and small enough to duck the counterblow. We had another sister, Isabel, who was the eldest and had gone off to Notre Dame this past September.

All of us were born Stateside, which is why we spoke American and considered French a second language; our parents had gotten asylum here after a

particularly brutal round of atrocities by one of the
Congolese militias. I had an aunt once, my mother's
sister, whom I would never meet in this world.
Some days I dreamed of visiting my ancestral home
and snapping some vertebrae, but I know life isn't
an action movie. Usually.

Squabbling with my siblings always made
me feel better, but tonight it was only temporary.
Dinner was great—grilled salmon, asparagus,
French bread fresh-made that morning—and it was
cool enough these evenings to start lighting a fire in
the hearth. We had a nice home, a good family, and
life was kind to us. But somehow, something got
me thinking about Aunt Jeanne, and that got me
thinking about my own sisters, and that brought me
back to James Wingrove. By the end of the meal, I
was putting on a conscious act of levity so I
wouldn't bring down the mood, and I excused
myself as early as I could. "Gotta go pick up Faith,"
I said, glancing at the clock. "We're going to this
guy Tommy's house to do some studying tonight."

"Tommy Connor?" Amarantha said brightly.
"He's cuuuuute."

"Wretched girl, go back to your books."

I was in my room digging a jacket out of the
closet when Mom knocked lightly and came in.
"Roy?"

"Yeah, Ma."

"Will you tell me what is troubling you?"

"Nothing's—" I stopped and gave her a rueful smile. "Mommy radar, huh?"

She reached up and put a hand on my cheek. "And X-ray vision, dear one."

I heaved a sigh and stood there fiddling with my jacket for a long time. "Mom. . . do you think there's such a thing as Evil? Like, not bad people doing bad things, but an actual separate entity all by itself?"

Her face was grave, and unafraid. "If you mean the Devil, then yes. I have seen his face, behind the eyes of men with guns. Most were as you say, only bad men—but some of them were *things*, evil things, that had taken men's bodies and their hearts. They are older, and stronger, and wiser than men. But, Roy—even the Devil and his creatures are still only people, things, doing what is bad. There is no such thing as pure Evil, not the way that God is pure Good."

"How do you know that?"

"Because being is good. Existing is good. If a thing had no good at all, it would no longer be."

I thought about that. "Huh," I said eventually.

She stepped closer and put her arms around me, and I hugged her back, tightly. "I love you, Roy."

"Love you too."

"Go on now. Do not keep a lady waiting."
I burst out laughing. "Yes, ma'am."

9

I WENT HOME right after school. I was curious about that guy James Wingrove and his secret club, but I did promise Roy I wouldn't talk to them alone. Plus, it might not be safe. I woke up this morning still pumped up on magic-strength or whatever, but for all I knew, these guys could have a way to switch it back off again. Of course, it might be better for everyone else if I didn't have magic-strength. But then again, it might be better if I did. Maybe I had it for a good reason, even if I didn't know what it was yet. All I knew for sure was, Alyra felt trustworthy to me and Wingrove didn't.

The bus stop was only a couple of blocks from our house and I kind of felt like stretching my legs. I thought about going for another run around town, but that didn't seem like a very good idea, so I figured I'd go inside and do some jumping-jacks or something. Also, I hadn't really eaten lunch and I was getting hungry. Come to think of it, I hadn't really eaten breakfast either.

Uncle Syme came home late fairly often, but he always made sure there was plenty of food around. I went straight to the kitchen and started poking through the fridge and the cabinets, trying to decide what I felt like eating. I settled on a tuna fish sandwich and some Coke, and I sat and watched cartoons for about fifteen minutes while I was munching away. Then I got restless.

I remembered jumping up a whole floor in the tower last night, and I didn't want to risk breaking the house with my head, so I stood in the stairwell to give myself lots of room. Then I flexed my knees and tried a short, easy hop. It sent me up several feet higher than it should have, but at least I didn't go through the roof or anything. I hopped up and down for awhile, until I got the hang of going no higher than I meant to. Then I picked a spot on the ceiling and tried jumping exactly that high, and it worked perfectly: I bounced all the way up to the second floor, touched the spot with my finger, and dropped back to the bottom of the stairs without smashing anything. I did that a bunch of times, and then I started trying it with only one leg at a time. I was laughing out loud by now, and I didn't feel tired or worried about anything at all.

That went on for a pretty long time (it turns out that super-hopping is really, really fun). But eventually I thought I'd better get my homework done and tidy up a little for when Roy and Faith showed up. I had a hard time focusing on my assignments for the evening, but luckily, I didn't have much to do for most of my classes, and some of it could be put off till later in the week. I did a little work and then puttered around neatening up the living room and stuff. When the sun went down, I found myself glaring out the window and thinking about Wingrove and The Eye, but I shook it off and tried to think about something else.

At a few minutes after seven, there was a knock on the door. I trotted over and glanced through the spyhole to make sure it wasn't anyone sinister, but sure enough, it was my friends. I opened up and waved, and they both smiled. Faith looked sleepy.

"You guys hungry?" I asked. "I was thinking about throwing a pizza or two in the oven."

"That sounds great," Faith said.

Roy shrugged. "Not starving, but I can always eat."

"Cool. Come on in."

They came on in. Faith followed me into the kitchen and started preheating the oven while I dug a couple of supreme pizzas out of the freezer. Roy wandered off into the living room—prob'ly looking for alternate exits in case we got attacked by a rival warrior clan or something.

"So how was your afternoon?" Faith said.

"Oh, uh—pretty good, thanks. Nothin' special. Did some homework. Jumping jacks. That sorta thing. You?"

"Same here. Mostly napped the whole time."

"Dude!" Roy shouted from the other room. "You've got actual vinyl out here. Can I put a record on?"

Faith smiled fondly. "He thinks better with music."

"Yeah, go nuts," I called. It was funny—Uncle Syme spent a lot of his time updating the technology at Surtex, but he mostly used old-fashioned stuff in his own house. We still had a toaster oven instead of a microwave, and none of our clocks were digital.

"Sweeeeet." A classical piece came on a second later. I think it was called "Spring"—you know, the happy song with all the violins?

I set the timer on the oven and we went out to the living room. Roy was peering at the old scimitar over the fireplace. Uncle Syme brought it back from Spain before I was even born. I was pretty sure he'd never taken it out of the sheath. Faith looked around and smiled again. "You've got a nice house, Tommy."

"Thanks! I like it too. So, um, yeah, have a seat." I gestured vaguely at the furniture. Faith plunked herself into the comfy old rocking chair, and Roy sat down right on the edge of the couch. I took Uncle Syme's chair by the hearth, so we were sitting in a circle—or a triangle, I suppose. That way we could all look at each other. "Okay."

Faith nodded. "All right."

Roy ran a hand through his hair. "Yeah. Now that there's nothing interrupting us and we can finally talk about what's going on, I'm realizing we don't actually know anything. I wonder if we should've gone to that meeting with Wingrove after all."

"No!" Faith said, almost angrily. "I don't want anything to do with that guy. And I don't want you two having anything to do with him, either."

"It's not an option now anyway. We've got no way of finding him. On the other hand, I strongly doubt we've seen the last of him."

"I don't like the idea of sitting around waiting for him to turn up again."

"Me neither. Maybe we could ask around town, see if anyone's heard of him and his group."

"Or gee, I don't know, maybe we could try the police?"

"And tell them what, Faith? That someone's running loose in our town giving off a sketchy vibe? It's not like we can tell them we're all suddenly manifesting super-powers." He glanced at me. "I see you've still got 'em, incidentally."

"Yep," I said. "Which—I assume that means you've still got yours too."

"Sure do. Definitely not complaining, but it would be nice to know where they come from and why. I don't suppose you've got any ideas on tracking down your friend Alyra?"

I thought about it. "Well. . . we could try going back to the clock tower, I guess."

"That sounds dicey. The only reason she was there—" He frowned. "Wait a sec. She was following you. And I was following a qi-signature, which was also you. But Faith was there because of—because of what, for lack of a better term, we may as well call magic for the time being."

"Why Mr. Belmont, how very gracious of you," she said. "But whatever you want to call it, I was still following the same thing you were. It drew me toward the brightest spiritual energy in the area, which was Tommy. You said yourself that antenna-girl's aura wasn't as strong as his."

"Granted, but we haven't tested the limits of your gift yet. Maybe it could lead us to a specific person."

She opened her mouth and then closed it. "Hmm," she said softly.

"It sounds like a good idea to me," I put in.

"I'm just not sure it's safe."

"Aw, what's the worst that could happen?" Roy said cheerfully. "Lessee, what rhymes with Alyra?"

I scratched my head. "Nearer?"

"Hey, nice! That's perfect: 'Lead us nearer to Alyra.'"

Faith shuddered. "Forget it. I *hate* half-rhymes. Even Shakespeare does it—pretending the 'Y' in 'eternity' rhymes with 'die.' It's so lazy! As long as you're phoning it in, why not just draw a smiley face and write, '*lol omg 2 hard 2 rhyme*'?"

"Okay, okay, jeez!" He held up his hands. "No more suggestions from the peanut gallery. But seriously, don't you think this is at least worth a try?"

She looked worried. "I don't know. I mean—it probably is, but what if something bursts into flame again?"

"From what you've said, it sounds like the—you know, the magic—has a fairly specific response to your word choice. Besides, Tommy's already an expert at stamping out your little infernos." He grinned and she suddenly looked embarrassed.

"I didn't mean to pick on your rhyme," she told me.

"Oh, *that's* okay. I was just spitballing."

"All right then." She set her jaw. "I'll give it a shot. Let me think for a minute."

Roy got up and took the needle off the record player. The three of us sat in silence as the old grandfather clock in the corner ticked away. Faith was glaring at the carpet so hard I half-expected it to start smoldering before she even said anything. Then she raised her head and spoke:

"Guide my spirit, guide my mind, to find the one we wish to find!"

Roy and I tensed up, and we all glanced at each other. A few more seconds went by. Then Faith let her breath out and shrugged.

"Sorry, guys. I'm not getting anything."

"Are you sure?" Roy demanded.

She nodded. "I thought I felt a slight tingle for a second there, but it went away. It was probably just stress."

He exhaled through his nose. "Yeah—maybe."

"It *might* help if you used her name," I said. "Things aren't really themselves until they've got names, you know?"

Before she could say anything, the front door opened. Roy jumped to his feet, and I half-rose as well, but then I heard Uncle Syme calling hello. I said hi back and Roy relaxed. Faith reached up and straightened her hair.

Then he came into the room, and everyone started smiling. People almost always smiled when they met my uncle.

"Guests!" he bellowed and flung his arms wide. "And *new* guests, who haven't heard all my jokes yet! Welcome, welcome. Wayne Basil Syme, at your service."

Uncle Syme was very, very big. Normally I would say "heavy-set" to be polite, but he insisted on calling himself fat—possibly because it goes so well with "jolly." He was six foot six and nearly three hundred and fifty pounds; somehow that seemed to be the proper size for him, like he was designed that way from the outset. Like God sat down about fifty years ago and went, "So I'm working on this new thing called a Syme. It's gonna be a gigantic fat guy." He had short salt-and-peppery hair and a big bushy moustache, and some people said he looked like Teddy Roosevelt. He also had a fedora. It looked awesome.

Roy introduced himself and offered his hand, and Uncle Syme caught it with both of his own and shook it like they were old friends who hadn't seen each other in twenty years. Faith got up and introduced herself too, and he grabbed her and kissed her on the cheek. She giggled, and I'm not totally sure, but I think she actually blushed. Then he turned around and tousled my hair, like he does.

"Thomas! How was school?"

"Pretty good. We're learning about World War II."

"Ah, cheery stuff. Have you fed our visitors? Wait! —never mind, I smell the impending answer to that question. You'll no doubt be wanting Scotch with your pizza?"

"I wouldn't say no to a glass," Roy said hopefully.

"Kidding, Roy. Come back when it's not a school night and perhaps we'll see."

"Yes sir."

"Now!" He clapped his hands together. "I'm sure you have important things to do, but might I intrude for just a few moments? I'd love to get acquainted with Tommy's friends."

We all said of course, so he took off his hat and set down his briefcase and sat with us for a bit. It was fun watching Uncle Syme talk to people, because he had this amazing way of knowing stuff about whatever you were interested in. He chatted with Faith about Shakespeare and poetry and with Roy about math and science. When I mentioned that Roy did martial arts, Uncle Syme turned out to know all kinds of stuff about feudal Japan too. Finally, the buzzer on the oven went off, and while I got up to fetch dinner, Uncle Syme excused himself and went to his study.

Roy came into the kitchen to help me cut the pizzas, and Faith came in to get Cokes out of the fridge for everyone. "You have the coolest uncle ever," she said.

"It's true," I admitted.

"So, is he your mom's brother, or your dad's?"

"Um, neither. He's not technically my uncle, but he and my mom were really good friends before she passed away, so he took me in. They don't know what happened to my dad."

"Oh." She got a look on her face that I couldn't identify. "I'm sorry, Tommy."

"'Sokay. I was just a baby."

She hesitated, and glanced at Roy, and he gave her a little smile like he was encouraging her about something. "Actually—I'm adopted too," she said.

"Really? I didn't know that."

"Hardly anyone does, apart from Roy and Sarah. I don't remember anything about it—I was a baby too—so Mom and Dad have always been my mom and dad." Then her face lightened. "It's this old joke in our family. They were told they couldn't have kids of their own, so they adopted me—and then a year later, they got pregnant with my sister."

"That's pretty cool."

". . .Well," Roy said. "Shall we go and eat our pizza?"

"Absolutely."

For some reason, none of us brought up Alyra or Wingrove again that night. We ended up eating and talking about random stuff for a while, and then we watched some reality show and made fun of it. Roy and I got laughing so hard that Faith started shushing us in case we disturbed Uncle Syme. Eventually we all got tired, and Roy said he'd better take Faith home.

"Thank you for dinner," she said, and gave me a hug.

"Anytime. It was nice having you guys over."

Roy put his fist out. "See ya tomorrow, big guy."

"Yep." I bumped his fist, and they headed for the door.

"Good night, Uncle Syme!" Faith called. "Thank you!"

He came bustling out of his study. "Wait, wait! Please, a proper farewell." He was in such a hurry to catch them that he was still holding whatever device he'd been working on. It looked kind of like an eggbeater, except it was made of some shiny reflective metal like mercury. He switched it to his left and went to shake hands with Roy.

"A pleasure, Mr. Belmont. Come back as often as you like."

But Roy didn't answer. He was staring at the thing in Uncle Syme's other hand. Slowly, he raised a finger and pointed at it. "What—what is that?"

Uncle Syme frowned. "This? It's just a stabilizer. For one of our machines. Forgive me, I'm not at liberty to say more."

"Ah—sure. No, of course." Roy glanced back up, like he was snapping out of whatever had distracted him. "Sorry. I'm up past my bedtime. But yes, anyway, thank you very much. Nice talking with you." He shook Uncle Syme's hand.

Faith stepped forward and hugged him. "It was lovely to meet you."

"Likewise, my dear. I hope to see you both again soon."

They said good night and went out the door. I waved and closed it behind them, and then turned around. Uncle Syme was still standing in the hallway, and the frown was back on his face.

"Hey," I said. "Are you okay?"

"I'm fine, my boy."

"So, what *is* that thing, anyhow?"

"It's not really anything. As I said, it's merely a stabilizer. But it's extremely curious that your friend would be so affected by it."

"How come? Roy's big into physics and stuff like that."

"Yes, but he didn't look interested. He looked stunned."

"Yeah, well. . . he's had a rough couple of days."

"Oh? Is something wrong?"

I raised my shoulders. Part of me wanted to talk about everything that was happening, but it didn't feel like the right time somehow. "Just school stuff."

He nodded. "My days of school stuff are long behind me, but I remember well enough how complicated they could be. I'm here, if you ever need to talk."

"I know."

"Good night, Thomas."

"G'night, Uncle Syme."

10

Whatever Roy saw, he clearly wasn't ready to share. All he said in the car was that his eyes were playing tricks on him and it wasn't anything to worry about. Maybe I should've pressed the matter, but I was used to him being needlessly cryptic about things—partly to get on my nerves and partly because he was Roy and he tended to be a little dramatic. I figured if it was important, he'd get around to telling me soon enough.

It looked as if Hope had gone to bed, or at least retired to her chambers for the evening, so I sank into Dad's recliner to ruminate. Pendleton whizzed by a couple of times, practically outstripping his own meow, and finally stopped to let me pet him for a moment or two before he whizzed away again. I didn't see Queensbury; she slept with Hope sometimes, in between sleeping in the recliner and brooding over her food bowl and cuddling with her hyperactive little spawn. Tough life these creatures had; I'll tell you what.

I leaned back and gazed at the ceiling. It was funny—I'd never noticed it was covered in stars, like the ceiling in my room. At first I wondered why they were rippling like that, but then I realized they were only the reflections of stars in the water below. I lowered my head and gazed down at the floor and saw the shining heavens far above me, and a hundred million quiet worlds glimmering in the darkness far away. I heard the rigging of the mast creaking all around me, and the waves splashing gently on the keel, but somehow my feet couldn't seem to find the deck. I worried they would sail away and leave me here, trapped between the starlight and the sea. It was beautiful—so beautiful—but it wasn't enough, and there was someplace I had to go.

When I raised my head again, I was still in the living room, but now there was someone else. It was a man in blue—a royal blue, a strong solid blue that could have held a summer sun. I saw the color first, and then the clothes: a simple well-fitting smock-like top and pants. It was almost exactly like a Kung-Fu uniform, in fact, except without a sash or cuffs. And then I saw the man himself. He was tall and lean, with high cheeks and a dark complexion; at a guess, I thought he might be Hawaiian. His face was calm and kind-looking, but the furrows in his brow were far deeper than the smile lines at his mouth. Somehow it was impossible to guess at his age. His eyes might have been those of a centenarian, but he carried himself like a man in his prime. He was standing in the center of the floor with his hands folded, watching me with an air of patience. I felt neither fear nor surprise, but I was a bit puzzled. "Hello?" I said.

He inclined his head. "Ms. Avalon," he said, very quietly. "Nice to have seen you again."

"Again? Do I know you?"

"I wouldn't always know the answer to that question at a given moment. Certain laws would forbid it."

"Certain laws forbid breaking and entering, boyo. You don't seem to have troubled yourself much about those."

The furrow in his brow lightened, almost imperceptibly. "There have been different types of laws. If you're to kill a man, you might escape the law that will make you go to prison—but not the law that will make you carry his blood on your soul."

"Oh, dear. More enigmas. Do you at least have a name?"

"A moment will have come soon. You will have crossed a bridge and found three gifts. Keep them close."

"Okay. . . Could you be a little more vague, please?"

"I could not have known any more, in this moment, than what I would have told you already. I'd wish that I could have."

"Your grammar is giving me a headache."

I said it as a joke, but I realized it was starting to be true. Or rather, there was no pain; my head was going light, and sort of distant, like the time Roy accidentally caught me in the jaw with a crescent kick. There was a very faint sound like the gleam of sunshine on steel, and a spatter of spots in my vision. I shook my head sharply, and got to my feet, and the man in blue was gone.

"Crap."

It didn't feel like waking up. It hadn't felt like a dream. And with all the odd things happening this week, it seemed silly to rule out the possibility of visions. Of course, it hadn't been a particularly helpful one. But maybe that very fact vouched for its authenticity. Maybe messengers from higher levels of reality have such a hard time operating on our level that they occasionally lose some of their faculties. On the other hand, even if that were true, it still didn't make an unhelpful vision any more helpful. Whatever. It was time for bed.

If other dreams came visiting that night, I don't remember them. I slept straight through till my alarm went off and woke up actually feeling rested.

It was Odin's Day—king of the gods, possessor of ancient runes and second sight, who sold his eye and hanged himself on a tree to gather hidden knowledge. To the French, today was *mercredi*, named for the herald of Olympus, Mercury the messenger. Another bearer of words and secrets.

My sister was still asnooze—probably waiting for Locke to swoop in and take her away from all this—so I slipped into the bathroom and took a nice long shower. There was another shower off the master bedroom, mind you, but it was full of Mom's stuff and it didn't have the right water pressure and it sometimes went cold for a second or two and, anyway, ours was better. She was barely stirring by the time I was done, so I stuck my head into her room and yelled at her to get up. She threw a pillow at me and I called her a brat—which was true—and went back to my room to get dressed. Happily, I didn't feel like quite such a ragamuffin this morning, so I opted out of the rumpled sweat clothes and settled on a rather professional-looking pantsuit, with a teal top and black legs, that I'd somehow never gotten around to wearing before.

Queensbury came padding heavily into the kitchen as I was throwing my lunch together, and I heard the shower running upstairs. Obviously, Hope was now functional, so I'd done my sisterly duty. "Bye, Q," I said, and she nuzzled my leg just enough to shed on me. I brushed myself off, grabbed my bag, and headed out the door. Plenty of time for a coffee run this morning.

When I walked into Dunkin Donuts, Sarah was waiting for me. It was a frosty morning, so she was clad in a long brown duster and her trademark purple scarf, and she looked like—Sarah. You couldn't envy that girl for her looks; it was too much of a blessing just to share a planet with her.

"Heya, love," she said. She was already holding two big Styrofoam cups, both trailing wisps of steam.

I felt myself smiling before I even finished registering her presence. "Heya, lady. One of those for me?"

"I figured it was my turn. Better take it before my willpower gives out though."

"Done and done." I took one of the cups and we went back out into the parking lot. Her sporty little blue and silver Jetta was parked on the leeward side of the building, and I climbed into the shotgun seat. "Good thing you turned up. It's colder than I thought out here."

"Hey, I got your back." She fired up the engine and pulled out into traffic. "So! We *are* best friends and stuff, right?"

"What? Yeah, of course."

"So, if you had a crush on a guy, you'd tell me about it, right?"

I sighed. "Sarah. . ."

"Oh come on Faith. You know I hear everything at that school. You were at his house last night! Were you even gonna throw a bone to my endless hunger for gossip?"

"Okay, okay, I'm sorry. I swear I wasn't trying to keep it from you, I just—you know—hadn't quite gotten around to telling you yet."

"Well, get around to it, for crying out loud."

"Yes, ma'am." I started talking about Tommy and Roy and Syme and dinner and that asinine reality show, and somehow, I could feel the world falling back into place, as if simply telling Sarah my story was enough to make that story a part of the everyday world we'd always shared. We ended up sitting in the lot outside the school, twenty minutes early, laughing hysterically about practically nothing, as we'd been doing together since we were in pigtails. I couldn't tell her everything—not yet—because it involved the others too, and they deserved a say in what should be revealed. But it felt really good to tell her even a little of it.

"Uncle Syme sounds like a trip," she said, and polished off her coffee.

"Definitely. Wow, you beat me." My cup was still almost half-full.

"That's cause I tricked you into doing all the talking. But hey now, seriously. Are you honestly telling me there's absolutely nothing going on with you and Tommy? And don't get all, 'Why yes, we have a stimulating intellectual relationship, my dear Sarah.' You know what I mean."

"I know what you mean." I paused and sipped my coffee. "I don't really know. I do like him a lot. But—it seems like things are happening awfully fast all of a sudden."

"Yep, that's how it goes. Nothing, nothing, nothing, then *bam!* True love."

"Is that how it was with you and Roy?"

"Oh, don't change the subject. You heard every teensy detail of that whole soap opera unfolding in real time. And for the record, yes, that's how it was. Not *true* true love, obviously, but still. Like Milton says, 'Better to have loved and lost. . .'"

I shrieked. "Don't do that! You *know* that wasn't Milton!"

Sarah threw her head back and cackled. "Ahhh, there's nothing more fun than screwing with your head. All right, interrogation's over for now. We'd better get in there before Mrs. Mara starts getting restless."

"Mmm. She's liable to go on another rampage if we don't keep an eye on her."

"True that." She started to get out of the car, then turned back and caught my hand. "Hey, Faith? I just want to see you happy, you know."

"I know."

"You've never dated or anything—which is totally fine! —but if you've been waiting for the right guy to come along, then you could do way, way worse. Tommy gets the full Sarah Featherstone Seal of Approval.”

I started to say something, but suddenly there was kind of a lump in my throat. I managed to say, “Thanks.” Then we headed for the front doors.

Roy and Tommy were already in homeroom when we got there. They were arguing with Dave Albion about something. Roy nodded to us, and Tommy waved. Dave threw his arms in the air and shouted, “Faith! Sarah! Maybe you can talk some sense into these oafs. Or oaves. Is it oaves? It seems like it should be oaves. What was I saying?”

Sarah smiled. “I think you were babbling, Dave.”

“I get that a lot.”

“Dave here feels that Dracula could take Hercules in a fist fight,” Roy said with deep scorn.

“He can turn into a wolf!”

“Like Hercules can’t beat up a wolf?” Tommy said.

“Dracula’s super-fast.”

Roy scoffed. “Doesn’t matter, Hercules is super-tough. He can take anything that toothy fop can dish out.”

“Taking a beating doesn’t count as winning a fight, you blithering buffoon.”

“It does if you take it till the sun comes up and turns the other guy to ash.”

"Aha! You see?" Dave jabbed a finger in Roy's direction. "I told you, he blithers. Faith, you heard him blither, didn't you?"

"You *are* the resident expert on blithering," I conceded.

"Finally, some respect."

The bell rang. "All right, everyone, let's take our seats," said Mrs. Mara.   I sat down and nursed the cooling dregs of my morning brew. It was nice to see my boys arguing about stupid things; it meant they were getting along.

Algebra, Spanish, English, gym—the first four periods all went by without incident. When lunchtime came around, the three of us gathered outside at Tommy's bench without even discussing it.

"Okay," Tommy said by way of opening the conversation, "so I gotta know—what was so special about that piece of equipment Uncle Syme was holding last night?"

"What did he say about it?" Roy asked.

"He said it was just a stabilizer. He said it was peculiar that you seemed so interested in it."

"It was giving off qi."

I stared at him. "Say what?"

"That stabilizer had an aura, just like a human being. I haven't seen it coming from anything else at all—not animals, or machines, or things being held by people, only from actual live people. I have no idea what this means, not even a clue. But it has to mean something."

Tommy scratched his head. "Yeah, that *is* peculiar."

"Don't suppose you tried any more—poems last night?" Roy asked me. It was sort of cute how he couldn't bring himself to say the word "magic."

"No. But. . ." I hesitated. I didn't want to cloud the already murky situation any further, but I also didn't want to withhold anything from them. "I did have a really weird dream."

"The one about Winston Churchill in a tub of Jell-O again?"

"No, not that one." I told them about the man in blue.

"A bridge," Roy mused. "And three gifts."

"Does that mean anything to you?"

"Nope. Tommy?"

"Nuh-uh. I'll keep it in mind, though."

"I guess that's all we can do for now," I said. "Sooooo—did either of you do the homework for history class?"

The next two periods went by without incident as well. I invited the boys to come over in the evening; I figured we could do some research on James Wingrove, and maybe discuss telling some other people about what was happening to us.

It was warmer out by now, and I felt like stretching my legs, so I headed for home on foot. My head was full of fluttering thoughts, and my heart of hopes and doubts, and I was gazing at the trees and the birds and the clouds and paying no attention whatsoever to my surroundings, when somebody grabbed me from behind.

11

I was parked at the outermost edge of the lot, as was my habit. Longer walk to the front door in the morning, but a shorter wait to get back on the road at the end of the day. When school let out that day, I went sauntering out the front doors in no hurry at all, with nothing much to do and no place in particular to go for the next few hours. I felt about relaxed as I could, considering everything, and my guard was about as low as it gets. I was almost at my car before I noticed a couple of guys lounging on my hood. They were in their thirties, unshaven and dressed in ragged clothes, and they held themselves like men who habitually expected trouble. My qi-sense told me they were at least as tough as they looked. Instantly I felt the tingle in my scalp as my adrenal system went into hyperdrive.

"Hiya, fellas," I said casually. I stopped a few paces away, standing with my weight distributed so I could jump in any direction.

"Heyyy," one of them said. I got the impression he was trying to sound pleasant. He wasn't very good at it. "Your name Belmont by any chance?"

"Who's asking?"

"Why don't you just answer the question, pal?" said the other one.

"I could do that," I said, demonstrating the proper way to sound pleasant under stress. "Or I could make a hood ornament out of your spine. Now why don't you get off my car while I'm still in a good mood?"

I became aware of a third guy approaching from my right. I shuffled a couple of steps to the left, making some space between us, and then a couple of steps backward as the first two guys stopped lounging and started pacing towards me. "No need for all this hostility. We just wanna talk."

"So talk."

"But not here. How's about you come with us?"

I half-turned back toward the school—not to run, but to trick them into thinking I was about to run. As soon as they dropped their guard to come charging after me, I planned to throw a few throat-punches. But as I turned, I spotted yet another guy coming up right behind me. "Let's not make a scene," he said, and caught a hold of my shirt.

I like to think of myself as a well-kempt individual. I dress well, I groom myself, and I have a reasonable awareness of what's considered fashionable in a given year. I do, however, keep my thumbnails perceptibly longer than a gentleman should, and I do it for one reason: to maximize the pain and damage when I shove them into an enemy's eyeball.

The second I jabbed that guy with my thumb, I shook loose and took off for the main road at a dead sprint. The third guy was too close on my right for me to head back toward the school and the other guys were coming too fast for me to have any hope of neutralizing one or two before all four of them were on top of me. Time to make some tracks.

I heard footsteps right behind me, and one of them shouted, "Freeze!" Yeah, sure. At least he didn't say, "Hey, get back here!" As I went tearing down the street with a gang of mysterious neck-wringers on my tail, I suddenly found myself grinning. This right here, the smash and scramble, the broken wall between thought and act, the hinging of your life on being better than the other guy—this was *it*; this was the dream of battle that kept me constantly pushing myself. This was the good stuff.

I kept my lead for a couple of blocks, until I saw my goal: Mount Hope Cemetery. Figured I could lose them in there. The high gates gloomed ahead; their tops wrought with black steel roses; all beyond was wrapped in shade. I leaped onto a nearby fire hydrant at top speed and then sprang across and caught a hold of the gate, swinging my legs up and over in a move I'd been using to get myself in trouble since I started climbing stuff at age zero. Mom used to call me her little monkey. As I hit the turf and rolled to my feet, I spotted one of those ultra-thin slate grave markers a few feet away and threw a flying cross-body block at it, knocking it right out of the ground. I hoisted it over my head just as the first of my pursuers cleared the gate and landed behind me—and, in that perfect moment when both his hands were busy breaking his fall, I swung the stone and shattered it on his astonished face. Two more guys cleared the gate a second later, and I heard the fourth clambering up after them, so I turned again and ran like hell. Not one of them stopped to help their whimpering comrade.

Getting tired now. Always been a good runner. Not Jesse Owens though. Panting for breath, feet pounding the earth. Dodging through gravestones, ducking through ancient elms, hurdling an archangel with a marble sword. Good news was, they weren't Jesse Owens either. I was starting to put some distance between us. Bad news was—they had guns. A chunk of mausoleum exploded, almost in my face, as I plunged around the corner, and I heard the crack of an automatic. Nine-millimeter, most likely. *Hello, Death. Haven't seen you since Monday. How's your week?* I was practically giggling now; adrenaline makes me loopy sometimes.

"Hold your fire, you idiot!" one of them shouted. "We need him alive."

"I'm just gonna kneecap him." Another shot—not a good one. Hit a tree five feet to my left. Someone else fired, the throaty boom of a big caliber—.357, maybe. Blew the wing off another angel. Aiming for the kneecap between my shoulder-blades, apparently. Another shot—even worse, off by ten feet or more. They were too tired to aim by now. Almost in the clear.

Then my foot caught a tree root and I went head over heels. Managed to turn a face-plant into front roll so I didn't knock the wind out of myself (or fracture my clavicles), but I wound up on my back, all momentum gone. Scrambled to my feet— enough of a lead that they weren't quite on top of me yet—but they would be in a second.

"Don't move!" one of them bellowed. Twenty feet away was another mausoleum; I launched myself at it, hurled a flying drop kick with both feet, and knocked the rusty door off its hinges. It was still attached with chains, however, so I barely managed to squeeze through before I heard the footsteps right behind me. This was starting to look pretty grim.

After the autumn sunlight, the tomb was black as pitch. I crawled forward as fast as I could, waving one hand in front of me so I didn't crush my septum on a sarcophagus. I had no plan—just wanted to keep moving. As long as I was still moving, luck might have a chance to turn in my favor. I heard two guys stuffing themselves through the opening behind me; the third must've stayed outside to watch for cops. They got to their feet and didn't advance. No reason to—no way out of here.

"All right, kid, come on out," one of them snarled. "Don't make us pop you."

My hand hit the far wall. No trap door, no secret passage. The deadest of ends. I turned, slowly, and got to my feet. And then I saw something very, very strange.

It was still midnight-dark in here, apart from a tiny puddle of sunlight on the ground where the door had left its moorings. But standing straight in front of me, clear as the feel of the mausoleum stone, were two swirling luminescent figures. It was like someone had cut a pair of man-shaped holes in a wall and I was gazing out at an electrical storm, or a meteor shower, or a distant galaxy of pulsars. At that moment, it was the loveliest thing in all of creation—because now *I* had the advantage. They could barely even hear my movements over the sound of their own panting.

No time to strategize. I crept forward, keeping low and to their left, just one more shadow in a chamber of shadows. One of them was edging forward, cautiously, his gun hand down at his hip and his other hand flailing around in front of him. I could even see the bunching of the qi in his leg muscles, telling me which one his weight was planted on. When he got in range, I took a crow-hop towards him and stomp-kicked the side of his knee, and it snapped like a tree branch. He dropped to the floor with a blood-curdling howl, cradling his leg and writhing on the cold stone. The gun clattered away, and I lost track of it in the dark.

"Barns!" the other guy cried. "What happened? Come out here, you little punk!" He fired off a couple of rounds, randomly, toward the far wall, and the whine of ricochets echoed around the room. And then, stumbling in the direction of his comrade's screams, he brought himself into my reach. Why mess with a winning formula? I reared back and blew his knee out as well.

This guy was better than his pal; he kept a grip on his weapon as he fell. But it didn't matter, I was on him in half a heartbeat. I couldn't see the gun itself, but I could see the tension in his gun hand. I grabbed it, got a hold of the pistol, and twisted it till his trigger finger broke. Then I ripped the gun out of his hand and clubbed him with the butt about a dozen times, feeling the spatter of blood on my face. *They tried to kill me. They tried to kill me!* I'd never been shot at before.

The other one, Barns, was clutching at me from behind. I whirled and pistol-whipped him too.

If I'd let myself, I probably would've beaten them both to death out of sheer blood-rage, but I wasn't quite that far gone yet, and besides, there was still another enemy out there.

I felt around till I found the chain that was holding the door shut. Then I pressed the gun-muzzle against it, turned my face away, and blew the link off. Brandishing my new semi-automatic, I kicked the already loose door and it fell into the grass with a dull boom. I took aim from the shadows, squinting in the sudden glare—but there was no target. I ran forward and took cover behind the nearest tree, peering in every direction, trying to get a glimpse of my adversary.

"Hey, what's the matter?" I roared. "Game's only fun with a stacked deck, is that it?"

Then something occurred to me and the fury turned to fear. The likeliest scenario was that these were Wingrove's men, and that meant—

"Faith." I dug out my phone, already heading back the way I'd come. I was practically exhausted by now, but I pushed myself back into a sprint. The fourth guy didn't resurface; must've taken off when he heard the commotion inside the mausoleum.

I got her voicemail, hung up, tried again. By the time I got back to the school, I'd gotten it three times. Useless. I went to dial Tommy's number, realized I didn't know it, and cursed myself for a fool. That's okay, I know where he lives. Into the car, onto the street, and off to chez Syme with the gas pedal jammed to the floor.

As I skidded into his driveway, I wrenched open the door and leapt out before Betty Lou had even come to a stop.

"Tommy!" I shouted, running towards the front door. But it looked like he was a step ahead of me: a second before I reached it, the door flew open and he came running out.

"Hey, get in the car! Tommy!"

"They just called me!" he cried over his shoulder. "They've got Faith!"

"Well then, get in the—*what are you doing?*" He was already zooming away on foot, and there were cheetahs that would've been impressed at his speed. Only one choice: I hurled myself back into the driver's seat, threw her in reverse, and tromped on the gas. The tires screamed and smoked, and I flew over the curb, shifted into drive, and took off after him.

At high speed on narrow streets, nothing's in the distance; everything explodes in your face, a wailing plummeting kaleidoscope of streaking headlights and swerving grilles, Dopplering horns, shrieking brakes, and the earth-shattering roar of your engine. I shot down the long hill, gathering speed, weaving through single-lane traffic, up on the sidewalks, barreling over medians, crashing through a park bench, barely keeping Tommy in sight.

He was blasting along like a bipedal rocket, scorching the asphalt, oblivious to everything but the thought of Faith in danger. We reached the bottom of the hill and he hooked a left down Main Street; I yanked up my emergency brake and went into a screeching power-slide, two wheels way up in the air, and followed him into the teeth of downtown traffic. An oncoming eighteen-wheeler clipped my rear bumper as I fishtailed crazily up the street, and I caught a flash of it skittering away in my rearview.

As we passed Montmorency Avenue on the left, I glimpsed a pair of cops running for their cruiser. Wonderful. But hey, one miscalculation right now and jail would never be a concern again. Up ahead was a red light; Tommy simply launched himself into the air and went sailing over the intersection in one long impossible bound. I leaned on my horn, gritted my teeth, and aimed for a tiny gap between two cars passing perpendicular to me. Getting lucky, I tore through the needle's eye, leaving a cacophony of brakes and horns in my wake.

Tommy race up the hill, past the farmer's market in midair, and down the far side, going faster and faster and faster. I glanced at my speedometer; dear *God*, we were going over a hundred miles an hour. Good news was, no sirens yet—must've shaken them at the intersection. Bad news was absolutely everything else that was happening. If only I knew where we were going! We seemed to be heading for the south side of town. St. Brendan's Church, maybe? —that seemed like a place that sinister conspirators might choose for a clandestine meeting. But all of a sudden he banged a right down a side street, forcing me to cut through a parking lot, nearly splattering myself all over a telephone pole to remain on his tail. Then he sped into some poor schmoe's front yard and went hurtling over a ten-foot-tall picket fence.

"Aw, come on," I almost whimpered. *Don't think, just move!* As I went careening toward the pine bulwark of death, I leaned over and fumbled in the glove box (Lordy b'Gordy, I didn't even have a seat belt on), dug out one of my butterfly knives, and flipped it open. Then I hit cruise control, pulled up my knees, and went fetal, pointing the tip of the knife at the center of the steering wheel. When we hit the fence, my airbag deployed like a huge nylon fist. Would've blinded me, and probably broken my nose, but when it hit the blade there was a muffled boom like somebody firing a shotgun through a sack of potatoes and the bag deflated into my lap.

The fence wasn't very well-constructed, and it blew apart like a stack of toothpicks.

I veered sickeningly through the backyard and out into the street beyond, and there was Tommy—stopped dead in the middle of the road. I screamed and stomped on the brake with both feet, watched the needle drop to forty, thirty, and then I plowed into the kid and he bounced over my hood, smashed my windshield, and went flying over the roof. I came to a halt about ten feet away and jumped out of the car. He was already back on his feet and dusting himself off.

"Hey, Roy," he said distractedly.

I couldn't even speak; I just flapped my hands and howled at him. He didn't appear to notice.

"This is where they said to meet." He pointed, and I saw my guess hadn't been too far off: it was the town library. Zevon was such a little place that it was only open on Tuesdays, Thursdays, and Saturdays, so we'd have it all to ourselves— assuming our buddies had left the door unlocked.

"Gentlemen," said a familiar voice. "Welcome, ha ha, welcome. Hee hee hee, please come with me, please."

I realized the knife was still in my left hand, and that made me realize something else: the nine-millimeter was still tucked in my waistband. I hauled it out with my right and took aim at Wingrove's forehead.

"Tell you what," I said, shaking with anger and shock and fear and all the many things that drive a man to violence. "You let our friend go by the time I finish this sentence or they'll be mopping your brains out of the gutter, you pathetic little—"

"Drop it." And the click of a gun-hammer pulling back. I knew that voice too: the fourth guy from the graveyard. Wingrove was standing on the sidewalk a few yards from the library; the gunman had just come around the building from the other direction and was aiming his weapon at me. Two others followed him, men I hadn't seen before. All were pointing handguns.

"Okay." Tommy stepped in front of me. Kid wasn't even breathing hard, for pity's sake. I didn't know if he was bulletproof, but at this point it certainly wouldn't surprise me. "I don't want to hurt anyone. Just tell us what you want."

"We merely wish for you to come, ha, to come with us, Mr. Connor. I'm afraid, ha ha, that your friend is not at this, aha, ha ha, this location at, hee, at present, Mr. Connor. But I can guarantee her, ha, her safety, if you'll merely come with us, Mr. Connor."

Tommy and Wingrove were staring at each other, ignoring everything else. I had stepped out from behind him so I could keep a bead on the three gunmen. They might have me beaten in terms of experience, but my edge was that (I hoped) the gathering qi in their gun hands would give me an early warning if they decided to open fire. The guy from the graveyard and one of the others were aiming at me, and the third was still covering Tommy.

"First you have to promise to let Roy go," he was saying.

"Why of course, that's, ha, that's perfectly acceptable, hee. Indeed, if I recall, hee hee, you were explicitly told to come alone."

"Forget it," I growled. "I'm going wherever you go."

"Roy—"

Just then, the sound of sirens became audible. Either they'd picked up the trail of devastation Betty Lou and I had left, or one of the neighbors had called to report six men pointing guns at each other in broad daylight in the middle of the street. No doubt Tommy's instructions had also involved quietly going inside the library, but their plans had gone awry when they failed to capture me as well as Faith.

"Man, this ain't lookin' so good," one of the gunmen said uneasily.

"Buncha small town cops," said graveyard guy. "We can take 'em."

"Like you took me?" I said.

"Better watch your mouth, little man."

"Gentlemen," Wingrove said in his passionless voice, "aha, gentlemen, perhaps it is time that we acquainted our, ha ha, friends with, hee hee, with the gravity of this—"

Then the front door of the library burst open and another goon ran out screaming. His shirt and his hair were on fire. And standing behind him in the doorway, with smoking hands and a look of wrath I'd never seen on her face before, was Faith Avalon.

12

I fought hard when they pulled me into the van. There were two of them holding me, plus a third in the driver's seat, and I bit and scratched and kicked and screamed at the top of my lungs. Dad taught me to go for the eyes, and I almost got one of them, but they were strong, and they had a hold of my arms, so I focused on getting a knee into one of their groins or my teeth into one of their throats. Or something, anything, so if I couldn't escape then at least I'd make them pay for this. But then I felt a cloth over my face and I smelled something sharp and dark and pungent, and everything went fuzzy, as my limbs felt hollow and I floated for a while.

"Ha," I heard him saying when my senses came back online. "So, you failed to capture Mr. Belmont, ha hee ha, that is deeply disappointing. One beardless child with no powers whatsoever, and he defeated three of our, ha ha ha, three of our coldest murderers. And how is it that *you* escaped, Mr. Slade?"

"Okay, look," said a voice I didn't recognize, "the kid was better than we expected, I admit that. He caught Sammy off-guard, and then— I don't know what happened with the other two. They shoulda just shot the chain off the door, but we were in a rush and there wasn't a lotta time to think, so they just squeezed through behind him. And then, I dunno, I guess he just had better night vision than them, or something. After Norris and Zed went down, I figured I better get outta there and report back to you."

"Of course, Mr. Slade, of course. Ha, yes, ha ha, of course, ha ha ha, indeed, of course, yes. No one would want to see you injured or inconvenienced in any way, Mr. Slade."

"Say, how about you creep out someone else, Wingrove. We had two targets and we bagged one of them, so as far as I can see, we're still ahead of the game. This Connor kid'll probably roll over for a chick hostage faster than a guy hostage anyway."

"Mmm, ha, yes, perhaps. Ha, hee, quite so, yes, perhaps. Can I assume that you were at least successful in finding his, ha ha, his phone number, Mr. Slade?"

"Yeah, yeah, I got it. Hold on."

I heard beeps. I stirred, a little, and found that my hands were bound. Not to each other—they were both zip-tied to the arms of a chair. I moved quietly and found that my legs were tied as well. I was sitting in a shadowy room, and I could hear at least three men nearby—Wingrove and Slade and one other. I opened one of my eyes just a crack, but everything was still fuzzy. Involuntarily, I let a small groan escape.

Instantly, someone grabbed me by the hair.

"Good timing, boss," said a third voice. "Looks like she's wakin' up."

"Excellent, ha. Prepare."

"Connor," Slade was saying. "We got someone here—someone you might care about. Hey Mutt, make her talk."

The hand jerked my head back, and I gasped. Dimly, through the phone, I could hear Tommy calling my name.

"Come to the library," Slade growled. "Come alone. I don't need to tell you what happens if you screw around." There was another beep as he hung up his phone. "Arright, he oughtta be on his way."

"Good. Mr. Varris, you will remain here to, ha ha, keep an eye on our guest. If she misbehaves, please feel free to cut her face. Mr. Slade, ha hee, collect the others, hee hee hee. It is time."

Wingrove and Slade left the room, and I was alone with the ape that was yanking my hair. I struggled a little, but my wrists and ankles had clearly been tied by experts. The chair was metal. I wasn't going anywhere.

The ape, Varris, let go of me and started pacing the room. "Just sit tight, chickie. This'll all be over soon, and everyone'll prob'ly be dead. Keep your mouth shut and maybe you'll walk away with just a few scars, huh?"

I glared at him. "So what do you get out of it?"

"Me? Just the cash, little chick, just the cash. Wingrove gets what he wants, me and the boys retire. Got a sweet place in Miami all picked out. Ocean view—nothin' too fancy. Coupla floors. Laundry service."

"You're breaking my heart."

"What'd I say? Shut your mouth."

I fell silent. Varris kept pacing. I could see a gun in his waistband. He was big, dark-haired and pony-tailed, dressed in black leather, a self-made stereotype. The edges of a tattoo showed on his neck above his jacket.

As my head cleared, I started looking around. We were in an office, a cramped little space. Really, it was less of an office and more of a back room. The library, Slade had said. Of course: I recognized the smell now. The dust of old books. The feel of quiet. I realized I'd only been unconscious for a few minutes. From what they'd been saying, they had tried and failed to capture Roy as well. They were using us to get to Tommy. Fear at my predicament was swallowed up in a swiftly rising anger.

Books. I could feel my teeth grinding together as I glared at this pig. From my innermost self, from the very, very bottom of my heart, I wished him misery and pain. I thought of Tommy, and notebooks, and Mr. Jameson's class. I thought of fire.

Unbidden, the words began to congregate in my mind. A lifetime of practice, of playing with rhymes and ideas, guided them as they fell together. Steam began to rise from my fingertips where they gripped the chair. And then I heard the squealing of tires outside, and the voices of my friends. Dimly, through a locked window, I heard Wingrove telling Tommy that I wasn't at this location.

I had no conception of who these people were, The Eye, or what they wanted us for—but I could see his plan, as clear as day, to betray the people I loved and lead them to their deaths. And the smoldering embers inside of me sprang into flame.

Fry the filth and torch the trash,
Choke his screams with smoke and ash,
Blood will bubble, boil, and churn,
Hair will blaze and body burn!

As I spat the last syllable, there was a bright flash like a lightbulb exploding, and Varris' whole torso burst into fire. He shrieked and stumbled into a bookshelf, and half the books caught fire as well. Glowing flames like roses blossomed from my palms and flickered there without harming me. The zip-ties melted and snapped, and I reached down and freed my legs. Varris ran out of the room, trailing smoke, spreading the fire as he went.

I followed him outside. Wingrove, Slade, and two others were standing in the street where Tommy and Roy were facing them. Two police cars were approaching at high speed, sirens wailing.

"Mutt!" one of the henchmen shouted.

"Leave him," Slade hissed. "He's useless now—and so is she." I saw the gun, and I felt my body dropping to the ground and curling into a ball by sheer instinct, even as I heard the smack of a bullet on the brick just inches from my head. I heard Slade howling in surprise and fear, and I heard the howl fading rapidly into the distance as if he'd fallen off a cliff, and then I smelled that happy childhood scent like grass in springtime. Tommy's scent.

"Faith! Are you okay? Faith?"

There were a few more shots, and the sound of running footsteps. I raised my head, slowly, feeling drained.

"Hi there," I said, and smiled.

Tommy smiled back. "Hi."

From inside, I could hear the crackle of flames. A few feet away, Roy was talking to the cops. Of course he knew them, Roy knew everybody. From the next street over, another set of sirens was starting up—the fire department getting mobilized, no doubt. The town planners had wisely plunked the fire station within a stone's throw of the library. Right now it was all background noise.

"Are you hurt?" Tommy was saying.

"Me? No. What about you?"

He shook his head. "Nuh-uh. I think Wingrove got away, though."

"Whatever."

"Heya, sis." That was Roy. "You all right?"

I sat up. "Fine, just tired. How about you? You look kinda rough."

"Aw, just a few scrapes, no big deal. Nice work with the human furnace over there, by the way."

"Oh, God!" I jumped to my feet. "Is he please tell me he's not—"

"Relax, he's alive. Same with the guy Tommy threw across the street. But I tell you what, The Eye is gonna be missing a lotta names at the next roll call. They might think twice before they mess with us again."

One of the cops came trotting over. "Evenin', Ms. Avalon," he said. I recognized him as a friend of my dad's.

"Officer Tooley." I raised a hand and waved, even though he was right in front of us. Obviously Tommy was a bad influence on me.

"There's an ambulance on the way. You should get looked at—all three of you."

We declined. Officer Tooley insisted, and we declined harder. Finally he shrugged and said, "Well, okay, but you'll understand if I strongly advise your parents to get you checked out as soon as possible. Anyways—I'm glad to see you're not seriously injured."

"Thanks, Mr. T."

"Only a few people in this world get to call me that, you know." He winked. "But you're definitely one of them. Come on, let's get you kids home. We do need to take a statement from each of you, but it doesn't have to be tonight."

As we were talking, he steered us gently away from the library. More emergency vehicles were converging—another couple of squad cars, an ambulance, a fire truck. Plus, the neighbors were all out in the street by now, gawking. Nothing like this had happened in Zevon in my lifetime; house fires were thankfully rare, and there hadn't been a shooting here since Old Lady Rutherford killed her husband back in '48. I wouldn't be too surprised if our would-be kidnappers ended up tarred and feathered by the populace.

From what I could gather, only Wingrove and one of his lackeys had escaped. Slade and Varris were on their way to the hospital under heavy guard, along with another henchman who'd been shot in the shoulder by Tooley; apparently, they'd found three men in Mount Hope with their skull's half beaten in. Roy looked quietly smug when they mentioned that. Through some miracle, no one had gotten killed—but Betty Lou had certainly seen better days. The hood was crushed, the windshield was caved in, and the sides and rear looked like the victims of psychopaths with sledgehammers. Even the roof was dented. A tow truck was pulling up to haul her away as the three of us climbed into Tooley's cruiser.

"Sorry about your car, Roy," Tommy said.

"Thanks, man. But she'll get through this. She's a tough old bird."

"So where to?" said Tooley.

"Why don't we all stay at my house tonight," Roy suggested. "Faith's parents are out of town and Tommy's uncle tends to get home late."

"That makes sense. But, can we call the Avalons? I'm sure they'll want to come back right away."

"I'll call them," I said. "And is it okay if Hope stays over too, Roy? If she wants to, I mean."

"'Course. You know my mom, she pines away unless she has people to stuff food into."

As we drove away, the firemen were blasting the library with high-powered streams of water. Smoke was billowing out the windows, but the fire didn't seem to have spread too badly. I hoped they'd be able to contain it. Then I wondered what it said about me that I felt worse for burning books than I did for burning a human being. But then again, as far as I was concerned, Varris was only just *barely* human.

Ma Belmont came running outside when she saw us getting out of the cruiser. Tooley told her what had happened, very concisely and with great emphasis on the fact that none of us were hurt; her lips pressed together in a thin white line like a scar, but otherwise she seemed weirdly calm. She kissed each of us in turn—even Tommy, whom she'd never met before—then she took Tooley by the hands. "Thank you, Officer. God bless you."

"You're very welcome, ma'am. If it's all right with you, we'll keep a patrol out here tonight just to be on the safe side. And I'll be back in the morning to take everyone's statements."

"Of course. Thank you again."

He touched his cap, nodded to the three of us, and drove off.

"Dear Faith," she said, and touched my cheek with the kind of tenderness you only get from a mom. "I am so sorry such a thing happened to you."

"I'm okay, Mama Bear."

"Come in, please. All of you. Tommy, it is lovely to meet you."

"Thanks! You too."

Mama B. was a fantastic cook. The second she had us all sitting comfortably, with soft drinks in our hands, she started making brownies. I didn't really feel like eating at first, but when the aroma from the oven started drifting out into the living room, I realized there was absolutely nothing on earth I would rather do at that moment than eat brownies. Especially because I knew from experience that she had a tendency to melt a thin layer of Andes mints on top of them.

We talked about what had happened for just a minute or two—enough to satisfy her that we really weren't injured or traumatized—and then she let us drift away from that whole subject. Roy mused a bit on the topic of restoring his poor mangled Pontiac.

"Do you know stuff about fixing cars?" Tommy asked, sounding impressed.

"Not a thing. But my buddy Locke does and I've kind of been meaning to learn for a while now."

After a minor eternity of sniffing and yearning, the brownies emerged. I can't even describe them, because I'm not enough of a poet, but they were absolutely the best thing anyone had ever eaten, anywhere, throughout time. I scarfed down about half the pan by myself. Then Mama B. offered us all wine, as she often did at dinnertime. We all accepted.

After a small glass, I borrowed Roy's phone (noticing for the first time that my purse was missing) and called Hope. Mama B. offered to call my parents for me, which I accepted gratefully. I hadn't been looking forward to that. She went in the other room and talked with them for a couple of minutes, then came back out and handed me the phone so I could give them the necessary assurances of being in one piece.

"We'll be on the next flight home, baby," Mom said, her voice trembling.

"You stay close to Roy till we get back," added Dad. "Try and get some rest."

"I will."

"We love you, Faith."

"I love you too. And I really am okay. We all are."

Pretty soon after that, I started feeling sleepy. In retrospect, it might not have been super-smart to drink alcohol after I'd been chloroformed, but I didn't think that was actually the problem. I'd been feeling drained ever since I cast that spell at Varris—as if it somehow sapped my energy to use that much power all at once. Which, after all, made perfect sense. Add that to the stress of the day (and, yes, the wine too), and I found myself nodding off right there on the couch.

"Dear one," Mama B. said sympathetically. "You are exhausted. Come, let us put you to bed."

"Kay." They got me up, and we went to Amarantha's room.

"Sleep as long as you like, Faith. No one will expect you in school tomorrow."

"Hey, how about us?" Roy said. "Because, you know—" he pressed the back of his hand to his forehead "—I don't think I could bear to go back to that terrible place tomorrow, after all the suffering that happened there."

Mama B. rolled her eyes. "*You* would not get a free day so easily, young man. But I want you both here to keep Faith company. Tommy, have you called your uncle?"

"Yes, Mrs. B. I left him a message. He'll probably come by later, if that's all right."

"Of course dear." She turned back to me and kissed me on the forehead. "Rest now, love. You know where the washroom is, if you want to use the shower. We will be just outside the door if you need anything."

"Thanks, Mama."

As soon as they left, I peeled off my clothes and collapsed into bed. Amarantha had voluminous curtains, so it was almost totally dark in there. The bed was soft and fragrant and stocked to capacity with pillows and teddy bears. I could hear the murmur of voices out in the hall for about two seconds before I was out cold.

"Faith."

"Mmm."

"Awaken, Faith Avalon, daughter of my people."

"Mmmmm."

A hand shook my shoulder, lightly. "Don't be alarmed, I'm not your enemy. But we need to talk."

I frowned sleepily and raised my head. It slowly dawned on me that there was someone in the room whose voice I didn't know and I heard myself gasp. I scrambled backwards.

"Peace, little one, peace. I tell you again, we're not enemies." It was a female voice. And somehow, although she was only talking, it sounded like music.

The house was silent, and no more daylight came through the curtains. The clock on the bedside table said 10:23. Squinting in its dim red light, I could just make out her silhouette—and the two long thin shapes rising from her head like antennae.

13

ROY'S MOM WAS a pretty special lady. You could tell she was shaken, but she didn't let it break the flow of her house. She still laughed and scolded and brought us tea and made us scurry around setting the table and straightening the living room—but every few minutes she would glide by and tousle Roy's hair or put a hand on his shoulder. And he didn't seem embarrassed by it, like a lot of guys would. He just responded in kind, and they never spoke about it, like they'd found a way to strengthen each other without admitting weakness. I already liked Roy a lot, but after watching him do this dance with his mom, I liked him even more.

His brother and sister and dad got home shortly after Faith went to bed, and they'd already heard about what happened. There was a lot of hugging. Amarantha clung to Roy a bit, and Mrs. B. kept giving her quick little chores to do in other rooms so he'd have a chance to breathe. Those three had the same eyes, with the same sharpness and the same—I don't know, the same depth—although you could see that he got most of their mother's toughness and Amarantha got most of the gentleness. Mr. Belmont kept shaking my hand, and then hugging me, and then pulling away and harrumphing and shaking my hand again. As for Joseph—he clearly thought this was the coolest thing ever. He kept begging Roy for details, and Roy kept putting him off with stuff like, "The cops did all the work, we barely saw anything". He made a point of mentioning several times that I was with him in the car when we tore through town to get to the library, and I nodded each time so he could be sure I was getting the message.

Now that I had a few minutes to think about it, I was realizing how dumb I'd been to go racing off like that on foot. Roy was right there in the driveway; I should've just gotten in the car like he said. Who knew how many people had seen me doing all that stuff? Right through downtown in the middle of the day. I wondered if *that* might have been part of Wingrove's plan. And Wingrove had gotten away.

There was a crunch, and hot water in my lap. I realized I'd crushed my teacup. Mrs. B. jumped up and gave me a towel and waved off my apologies, and then she went to get me more tea. While she was out of the room, Roy said in a loud whisper, "That's why you hold it by the handle, dude." Joseph giggled, and their father gave them a giant frown with a big smile lurking right underneath it.

"So what's your favorite class, Tommy?" Amarantha asked.

"Oh, um—maybe history? I'm not sure."

"Well, what do you want to do when you graduate?"

"Dunno. I've been thinking I might just go wander around Asia for a while."

"That sounds fun!"

"Just be careful over there, Tommy," said Mrs. B., who had magically re-appeared with my replacement tea. "Do not go looking for trouble, like this one would." She gestured at Roy.

"Aw, he'll be fine," Roy said. "This kid's a lot tougher than he looks."

I mulled that over for a second. "Th... anks?"

Toward the end of dinner, there was a knock on the door. Two policemen were out front, and Uncle Syme was standing right behind them looking impatient.

"Evening, folks, sorry to interrupt," one of the policemen said. "This gentleman says he's looking for his nephew?"

"Hey, Uncle Syme," I said.

"Tommy!" He shouldered his way past the officers and threw his arms around me. "How are you, my boy?"

"I'm fine. Everyone's fine." I patted him on the back and listened to Mrs. B. trying to talk the policemen into coming in for dinner (they said no thanks, but she did get them to take some coffee and pie back to their cruiser with them). Finally, he let go and sort of composed himself.

"Roy!" he said. "So good to see you again. Thank you for watching out for my Tommy." He seized Roy's hand and shook it so hard it almost came off. Roy just grinned. "And—oh my word, please excuse my rudeness. Mr. and Mrs. Belmont, I presume. Wayne Basil Syme, at your service."

We were still making introductions and everything when two more people showed up at the door: Peter Locke from our class and Faith's little sister Hope, who I believe was a sophomore. There was more hugging, and then Mrs. B. started shoveling food into everyone.

Hope wanted to see Faith right away, but Roy thought we should let her sleep for a while. I asked Uncle Syme if I could stay over at the Belmonts' so we could keep the Avalons company, and he said of course.

Roy and Peter bantered about Roy's poor driving, while Hope and Amarantha teased me about my messy hair. Gradually we all relaxed and started to feel at home. My guess was, all visitors to this house felt that way pretty quickly.

Eventually Peter and Uncle Syme had to get going and the younger Belmonts had to go to bed. Mrs. B. put Hope and Amarantha in the guest room, and Roy said I could stay with him. They even had

spare unopened toothbrushes in the bathroom, just
in case of unexpected visitors. I showered and
found some clean pajamas waiting for me. Mrs. B.
kissed me on the cheek before we finally said good
night to everybody and headed into Roy's room.

"Whew," he said, and flopped down on the
bed. I thought that summed it up pretty well. I sank
into the plush spinning chair in front of his desk. He
had a nice big room on the second floor, with a
queen size bed, a couple of bookshelves and a
window looking down at their backyard. The moon
was out. Somehow it was already past ten.

"Your family's really nice," I said.

"Yep, I'm fond of 'em." He sat up. "So.
Now that we've got some privacy—"

I held up my hands. "I know. I'm sorry,
Roy. It was stupid of me, running off like that."

"No—well—yeah, it kinda was, but that's
not what I was going to say. I know you were just
worried about Faith. And you did save her from that
gunman, after all. But unfortunately, now we have
to start thinking about who might've seen you."

"I know, I know. Plus, Wingrove is still out
there somewhere."

"Honestly, I think he's a lesser concern right
now. Whatever's going on with the three of us—
and especially you—there are people who know
about it somehow. And after today, even more
people are likely to find out. And—" he rubbed his

hands across his face "—we *still* don't know any more than we did on Monday."

"Maybe it's time we told the grown-ups. We could use some advice."

He gave me this odd, rueful smile. "I've got to admit, I can't think of a logical reason not to. But it goes against all my instincts. This is *our* mystery. Our adventure." He gestured at the bookshelves. "I grew up idolizing Sherlock Holmes and Allan Quartermain and James Bond—you know, the gentlemen adventurer types. Always suave, always in control. Always the most competent guy in the room. That's the whole reason I got into the martial arts. It sounds—maybe a little silly when I say it out loud, but I just want to go to exotic places and fight spies and, I dunno, discover lost temples and stuff like that. But I *would* prefer to finish high school first."

"You know. . . I bet they've got lost temples in Asia. We could go together, if you want."

He lowered his eyes. "That does sound fun. And—Tommy?"

"Uh-huh?"

"I'm sorry I hit you with my car. That's the second time I would've killed you if you weren't—you know—"

"Oh, *that's* okay. It's not like you meant to. Besides, if I wasn't like this, then we wouldn't have been in those situations in the first place."

There was a knock at the door. Roy raised his head and said, "It's open." The handle turned, and Faith came into the room. We both got up, and we were both smiling—but then we saw the look on her face. She looked half-dazed and half-scared out of her wits. For a second, I wondered if she'd had a nightmare. And then someone else followed her into the room.

Roy said a bunch of things in French that I'm fairly sure were cuss words. As for me, I couldn't seem to speak at all. I just stared.

"Hello, Tommy," she said. And I knew her voice like I'd been hearing it all my life.

I swallowed. "Alyra?"

"The same. Forgive the intrusion, but it's time we all spoke face to face."

Her eyes were purple. Not just the iris, but the white part as well—or what would normally be the white part. There was still an iris, and it was a slightly darker shade, but it was all a really intense violet color, and they were almond-shaped and piercing and just gorgeous to look at, but a little scary too. They almost glowed. Oh, and the rest of her was purple too.

Roy stepped forward and helped Faith to sit down on the bed. I could see him looking Alyra up and down—probably checking her for weapons, judging her stance, that sort of thing. He seemed to have a handle on the situation already. I tried to pull myself together.

She was dressed in a single piece of silver-colored fabric that started up top like a dress, leaving her arms bare but rising all the way up to her chin, and turned into tight-fitting pant-legs that came down to her ankles. She wore sandals, and her hair was long and loose—it didn't look like she was geared up for fighting. Her skin was a soft lavender color, much lighter than her eyes, and her hair was very dark, almost black, but still with a clear violet tone. And I could finally see what the "antennae" really were her ears. They were almost a foot longer than normal, tapering into points over her hair. They were beautiful and strange. She looked like her voice.

"All right, you've got our attention," Roy said. He sounded unusually quiet, like he was trying to restrain himself from shouting. "Now what do you want with my friends?"

"I will answer your questions as best I can, Roy Belmont. First—" she placed her right fist over her heart, covered it with her left palm, and bowed at the waist "—I am Alyra Vauksness of Ardmore, chief city of the land of Faerie. Travel between our realms is difficult, but I have been sent to aid you—and to ask your aid in return."

Faith raised her hand, like we were back in school. Alyra smiled and nodded to her, and she said, "Did you say Faerie? As in, like—actual—Faerie?"

"I did. My people are the elves, and mine is the House of the Moon. I answer directly to Loryk san Varodrim, King of Faerie."

"But, before. . . when you woke me up, you called me. . ."

She nodded again, this time gravely. "I didn't know until this afternoon. But I could sense the weaving of elvish magic in this village, and now I see it in your soul. One of your parents was mortal; the other was one of us."

There was a long silence.

"That's—that's a lot," Roy said finally. It sounded like the belligerence had drained out of him.

"Indeed. And yet, Faith is not the reason I came here." She turned and looked at me. "I came because of you, Tommy."

"Why me?" I said. "What's going on with me, anyway?"

"Do you know of the nephilim?"

I frowned. "Ummm—it sounds familiar."

"Your friends know."

I glanced over at Roy and Faith. They were both staring at me. Roy sat down on the bed with a thump.

"What is it? What does that mean?"

Alyra came forward a couple of paces and took my hand. "You are also the child of two worlds. Your mother was mortal. She bore you and, I believe, gave her life to give you yours. Your father—he was from a realm higher than Faerie."

"Huh?"

"An angel," Faith whispered. "Nephilim were the offspring of humans and angels."

"Precisely—*were*," said Alyra. "The last of that kindred perished nearly five thousand years ago. We don't understand how, or why, another has arisen after all this time. But before we can search into that mystery, we must protect you and those around you. As I told you before, the stirring of your power has been seen by many watchful eyes."

I scratched my head. "So, you're saying I'm half-angel."

She nodded.

"Huh." I thought about it. "Okay."

"Took that pretty well," Roy muttered.

"But what about the other night?" Faith demanded. "What did you do to him?"

"The Moon-elves are most adept at spirit-magic. I simply hastened the awakening of his inner strength. It would have come out soon in any case."

"Spirit-magic?"

"There are five Houses, each with a penchant for a different magic." She smiled slightly. "Judging from your proclivity for fire—as well as your eyes—yours is most likely that of the Wood-elves."

Faith opened her mouth and closed it. Roy was right, this was a lot.

Alyra turned back to me. "Now that you have your full power, you can defend yourself for the time being. But there is a way to hide that power from any gaze, permanently. That is the only way you'll be left in peace."

"Well, how do I do that?"

"Wait—wait." Roy pinched the bridge of his nose. "You're telling me that a half-elf and a half-angel just happened to end up in the same town, in the same grade, at the same time—by *coincidence?*"

"Not remotely. The nephilim have always had a strange effect on the waters of the world. Other supernatural beings are drawn to them, and catalyzed by them, especially during the time of their first awakening."

He got a look of dawning comprehension. "That's why. . . Hey, hold on a sec. What about me?

There's no way either of my parents are supernatural beings."

"No, I sense no magic in you."

"But I can see qi. It just started on Monday, the same as Faith. It's gotta have something to do with all this."

Her brow furrowed. "Perhaps. Some mortals are born with a special gift for perceiving mystic forces without directly sharing them. If you've been in close contact with Tommy this week, it might well have brought forth a dormant ability within you."

"And what about Wingrove? What's his story?"

"*Raakkk.*" Darkness came into her face, and I had to stop myself from taking a step backward. "I have no knowledge of the man who was called Wingrove. But the force which animates that body is no longer human. He is possessed by *raakkk*: the gibbering demons of the Void. They covet Tommy's power."

"Can they do that?" I asked. "Take my power, I mean?"

"They too were angels once—long ago, before the birth of our worlds. If they can cut the beating heart from your body and feast upon it, they will regain their ancient strength. That is why they seek the ones you love. To make you surrender yourself to them."

In my head, I could hear a voice saying, "Connor. We got someone here—someone you might care about." And Faith crying out in the background. I thought about Uncle Syme, and Roy, and then I heard it again: Faith in pain. I felt my hands tightening into fists.

"Uh—Tommy?" That was Roy. "Your qi's kind of spiking, buddy. You wanna take a breath before you wreck my house?"

"How do we kill them?" I asked. It took a lot of effort to talk, and I realized I was clenching my teeth. I did what Roy said and tried to focus on breathing. I didn't want to hurt anyone in this room.

"Peace, peace. First, we have to mask your energy. As long as they can sense you coming, they'll never confront you without hostages."

"Then show me how."

She smiled. "That's why I'm here. To take you to Faerie."

14

This was all a bit much to wake up to. It might sound odd, but I'd never been very curious about my birth parents. Whether they were dead or simply hadn't wanted me, I wished them all the best; I already had a family that loved me, and I loved them back. What else did one need? Of course I had the occasional fantasy about discovering I was the stolen child of a princess or some such thing, but I usually went months at a time without even thinking of Mom and Dad as anything but my parents. And this—all of this—I mean, *elves?*

"What are you talking about?" Roy was saying. "You can't just pop in here and start dragging people away to other realities."

"There is only one reality," Alyra said calmly. "Faerie lies on the border of—"

"I don't care about that," Tommy interrupted. I'd never seen him not being polite before. "If I go with you, what happens next?"

"King Loryk will help you. And there is a task which he will beg of you in exchange."

"What task?"

"I don't know. But he told me to assure you that your stay in our realm will not take more than two or three days."

"Is that two or three days in real time, or politician time?" Roy asked.

Her mouth tightened. "Loryk san Varodrim is not what you people have come to mean when you speak of politicians. And the word of an elf is absolute. Everything that we are comes from our words."

He held her gaze for a moment, and then exhaled through his nose. "I didn't mean any offence."

She nodded, and her shoulders relaxed.

"All right," Tommy said. "Let's get going."

"Whoa!" I exclaimed. "Hold on a minute."

"Yeah, let's not jump into this, dude," Roy said. "You're too mad to think straight right now."

"What is there to think about?"

"Tommy. . ." I got up and put a hand on his arm. "Please, let's just talk about this. At least take a few minutes to calm down before you decide."

He shook his head. "The longer I wait, the longer everyone around me is in danger."

"This isn't your fault."

"It's not about whose fault it is."

"What about your uncle?" Roy said. "He'll be worried sick if you disappear now of all times."

"I'll leave him a note."

"A *note?* What're you gonna say, 'Sleeping over with the fairies, don't wait up'?"

"I don't know. But I'd rather have him angry with me than kidnapped by demons."

Roy and I looked at each other. Sometimes we could have whole conversations that way. After a second, he shrugged. "Yeah, okay. Lemme get my shoes."

"I'm not sure if you guys should come," Tommy said, frowning.

"You're not going without us," I said. "Besides, it turns out I've got family over there."

He turned to Alyra. "Will it be safe for them?"

"The only safe thing in life is death. Still, our kingdom has been at peace for decades. And I think my people will be pleased to meet one of our kindred from afar, as well as a mortal who held his own in battle against one of the nephilim."

I'd forgotten she was there for that fight. Roy didn't respond, but I could see his chest swelling a bit. Great, he'd be insufferable now. I couldn't help wondering if she'd done that on purpose, to put him off his guard. In fact, it occurred to me that she might conceivably be bringing the two of us along for the same reason Wingrove wanted us. We knew *nothing* about this woman. But, it didn't matter. There was absolutely no way I was missing the chance to visit another world. I'd just have to be extra careful.

"So how do we get there?" Tommy asked.

Alyra loosened her collar and pulled out a ring of keys on a chain around her neck. They were tiny, but intricately carved of some iridescent alien metal. "All we need is a door."

"What, any door?" Roy said.

She nodded. "When I open it with these, we will pass into the kairos field. It's the power that binds together the spheres of matter and spirit. Faerie lies on the border in between."

"Nifty."

Tommy glanced down at his PJ's. "Should we bring warmer clothes or anything?"

"There's no need for that. As soon as we arrive, you'll be arrayed in festal garb."

"Do what now?"

"Party clothes," I translated.

"Ohhh."

"Tommy's right, though," Roy said. "We need to do something to let our families know we're safe. Or, you know, safe-ish. Maybe leave out the 'ish' part."

"Yes," I said. "I guess a note will have to do, after all."

He dug out a piece of paper and we wrote something lame about needing to get out of town and being back in a couple of days and being really, *really* sorry. All three of us signed it. And then we turned to Alyra, who was waiting patiently.

"We're ready," I said.

"Very well." She stepped over to the
bedroom door and put one of her keys into the lock.

thing strange. When she opened the door, I
felt something strange. not exactly. Like an echo,
but not exactly. in revereverever Sounds came a
second too soon, like an echo in reverse. reverberate
and now they were starting to reverberate to
reverbereverbereverber

said Tommy. "What's going on?" said
Tommy. "I feel weird
feel weird
feel weird

said Alyra said "Don't be afraid" said Alyra
said "kairos fieldros field perception of time and
spaception of time and spaception of time and space

        time

space

narrow doorway
one still point
looking outwards
spiraling past
everything
tower of stars

of numberless floors
of endless turning stairways
castle of violet light
tolling silent bells forever
endless silence
endless space
the universe is in here with me
road of unreal suns
through haunted emptiness
alone forever in the emptiness
dread of darkness wheeling overhead
coming closer
the never-ending dark and
cold sea without a shore
forsaken void
lost in the silent waters
lost forever in the silent waters
but moving on the face of the deep
A light was glimmering.
somewhere high above and far away
so far away
and long ago
an ancient light, remote, untouchable
but glimmering
glimmering
A secret fire.
It kindled other fires,
And the fires began to sing.
I could feel myself moving once again,

J. B. Toner

Falling,
Falling ever downward through the dark—
And when I'd fallen far enough,
I felt myself falling up.
Falling ever upward toward the lights
And the slowly rising music
Until the void itself began to chime and glow.

Floating in the light
spinning in the song
burning in the flame
but not consumed
no longer seeing or hearing
but one with the wave
I was the music
I am the fire
I will be

and I felt my feet back under me, on solid earth, and
I felt the weight of my limbs and the breath in my
lungs and the fluttering in my breast. The music and
the fire were fading. I was in a
(cottage)
marble hall, a vast and echoing temple of pillars,
cool and white, desolate and yet not lonely, as
though some presence lingered still. Outside were
(evergreens) barren plains, stretching away beneath
a troubled sky. Before me was a cozy hearth—or

rather, not a hearth, but a great empty space under a stone roof twenty stories tall. A giant sun of fire and blood was setting on my left, but on my right a silver moon was climbing, and children were playing in the trees.

I stepped forward, and I blinked and shook my head. I felt as if I'd been swimming for hours. The other three were with me, and we'd all come through Alyra's door together. We were in a little chamber with wooden walls and wooden doors and nothing else, like an anteroom. I closed my eyes and took a breath, returning to myself.

"Whoa," said Roy. "Trippy."

15

Wayne Basil Syme, at your service. Like every man, I am the hero and chosen one of my own modest tales, but for many years now I've been content to define myself as the guardian of Thomas Gabriel Connor. His mother Karen was one of my closest friends in those long-vanished college days, when the valleys and the mountainsides were young. I lost track of her for nearly three years, and then one day she turned up on my doorstep eight and a half months pregnant. Who the father was, where he went, and why she chose me to replace him, are obvious and pressing questions—but I accepted long ago that the answers may well have to wait until she and I can discuss them over good wine in the tavern at the end of the world. In the meantime, I've kept the last promise I made her. Tommy is a good boy, and I know she's proud of her son. I hope she's proud of me as well.

On that particular Wednesday, I was toiling humbly away at my desk in the bowels of Surtex Industries. I fear I'm often less than diligent in checking my messages, and I didn't receive word of the attack on Faith and Roy until two or three hours after it happened; as soon as I did, I headed for the Belmont house at top speed and quite nearly hurled my bulk upon the two pleasant and dutiful officers who momentarily detained me outside (I did remember to apologize and thank them as I departed not long afterward). Even a brief acquaintance with Roy's family satisfied me that my boy was in good hands for the evening and I was not surprised to find Tommy both physically and mentally unscathed by the experience.

Odd things had always tended to happen around him. Bizarre coincidences, strange weather, even one or two episodes of what *appeared* (and I confess myself staunchly agnostic on this topic) to be the visitation of ghosts, all congregated in his presence from the time he was very young. But it never seemed to affect him any more than the daily events of an ordinary life.

When he was twelve, he lifted an entire fallen tree off a classmate who had become pinned under it during a school hiking trip, and he treated the incident as something which, of course, anyone would have done in his place. I had never seen him sick even once; whenever we moved to a new town, I took him to the local doctor for a check-up and was invariably assured that he was perfectly normal. Over the years, I had simply come to believe that some sweet virtue bequeathed him by his mother kept him safe.

I slept fitfully that night. Something very unusual was happening at Surtex—something in the air, something I couldn't put my finger on—and I couldn't shake off the absurd notion that the timing of that man Wingrove's attack was more than mere chance. For the first time in years, I reflected again upon the peculiar circumstances under which I had come to work there in the first place. The phone woke me up before dawn, and Roy's father was on the other end.

". . .and we promise we'll be back in a couple of days, and we're really, *really*, sorry." The note was signed by all three of them.

Standing in the Belmonts' living room with that sheet of paper in my hand, I felt an emotion with which every parent throughout all of time has been familiar: an intense love and protectiveness for my child manifesting itself as a blinding desire to throttle the life out of him. I could see the same fierceness and fear in the eyes of Mr. and Mrs. Belmont—or rather, Roland and Maria, as they insisted I call them. In return, I begged them to call me "Syme"; for whatever reason, I've never much used my Christian name.

"The children will be up soon," Maria said in a low voice. "I wish for some way to keep this from them, but I do not see how we can."

Roland almost smiled. "Joseph will think it grand. Off they go on some wild crusade. He will only be sad he could not come along."

"I don't suppose you've talked with the Avalons," I said.

Maria shook her head. "I hear there are storms out west and their plane is delayed. Perhaps if we find Roy and the others before they arrive, we can spare them knowing of this? At least till after."

"We can certainly try. I'll call Tommy's friends in Boston, and everywhere else I can think of, and perhaps you could do the same with Roy's friends."

"Yes. Now—" she also managed a slight smile "—Syme, will you take some coffee?"

I gave her my courtliest bow. "With honor and thanks, dear lady."

We spent the next twenty minutes or so on our phones, leaving messages and talking to drowsy and occasionally surly young folk or their parents, with the upshot that no one had seen our children but they would call us if they did. By the time we finished, Faith's little sister Hope had come downstairs. We had no choice but to tell her what had happened.

She stomped her foot. "I don't believe it! That is so like her."

"Has she disappeared like this before?" I asked.

"Well, no, but—she's just very unpredictable. It's never much of a shock when she does something crazy."

"Do you have any idea at all where they might have gone?"

"I don't know. . . Have you tried calling Sarah? Sarah Featherstone?"

Maria nodded. "I called her. She has not seen them."

"I'll ask Jason when he comes to pick me up. He and Roy are pretty close."

"I called him as well, dear. He has not seen them either."

"Oh." Her face fell. "I'm not really sure, then."

The younger Belmonts came down a few minutes later, and we went through the unhappy conversation again. No one had any notion of where those three had gone. It was baffling—they seemed like eminently sensible people—but then, teenagers are still teenagers, after all.

We saw the children off to school and talked for a bit longer. I was about to bid my new friends a good day when there was a knock at the door. It turned out to be one Officer Tooley, who I gathered had been present during the showdown with Wingrove and his men. Behind him were two others: a man and a woman, both clad in black suits and ties. The woman wore sunglasses, although it was gloomy and overcast outside.

"Good morning," Tooley said, shaking hands all around. "Allow me to introduce Agents Hyland and Rosaly, FBI." He spoke the three letters with palpable distaste.

"Saul Rosaly," the man said pleasantly, offering his hand. He looked to be somewhere in his fifties—that is, around my own age but as much as ten years older than the Belmonts. He was rail-thin, and rather short, with greying razor-cut hair, and his face was at once affable and weary. "A pleasure. Apologize for intruding. Won't take much of your time."

The woman was tall and fit-looking, and well shy of her thirtieth winter. She had bright, festive-looking orange hair, but her face was severe, even apart from the ominous occlusion of her sunglasses (which, I noted with disapproval, she failed to remove upon entering the house). Her handshake was a single sharp jerk, and she said only, "Jordan Hyland."

Maria's expression was wary, but she waved us all into the living room and bade us sit comfortably. Tooley accepted a cup of coffee, and Rosaly took tea; Agent Hyland shook her head impassively.

"Are the kids up yet?" Tooley asked. "I still need to take a brief statement from each of them."

"And yourself, Agent Rosaly?" I asked. "What sort of statement are you here for?"

He smiled briefly. "The Eye, Mr. Syme—the group known as The Eye—we've been tracking them for quite some time now, quite a few months. Over a year now. We believe they're responsible for a few murders, several murders, around the country. But this incident, this attack, this was out of character for them, from what we've observed of them. We're hoping to gain some insight into their ah, their motivations."

"I see." I glanced at the Belmonts. Roland looked uncertain; Maria looked grim. Something about this visit felt foreboding to me—but there was no sense in trying to conceal the truth. In any case, we could use their help in tracking down our missing ones. "Well, I'm afraid we have unfortunate news," I said after a moment. "See for yourselves." I handed the note to Officer Tooley.

He read it, scowled, and passed it to Rosaly. "Have you tried contacting their friends?"

"Of course," Roland said, a bit querulously. "Our son is missing. We have called everyone we know in the state. No one has seen them, or heard anything from them at all, since they went to bed last night."

Agent Hyland clenched her fist, and the knuckles crunched audibly. "Connor could be halfway across the continent by now."

"Jordan, please," Rosaly murmured.

I rose very slowly to my feet. "What, precisely, was the meaning of that remark, madam?"

"Mr. Syme, please." Rosaly made aimless and placatory gestures. "Please calm yourself, sir. All my colleague meant—"

"What do you know about Tommy, Agent Rosaly? Something, perhaps, that I don't?"

"Only that he appears to be very fleet of foot, Mr. Syme."

I turned my gaze on Tooley. "Officer Tooley, would you please explain?"

He was frowning. "Actually, I'm not sure. We did hear a few accounts from witnesses downtown yesterday that were—a little weird."

"What do you mean by this, 'weird'?" Maria demanded.

"Well—er—a few people have stated that Tommy was not in the car with Roy when it went by. To be specific, we have several accounts that place him out in the lead, on foot. Obviously, I'm assuming there's some kind of misunderstanding here, but—"

"Then you have no interest in The Eye," I said to Rosaly. "You're here for my boy."

"Not at all, sir, no, not at all. I assure you, we came here for no other purpose than the one to which ah, I alluded earlier. But yes, we may have subsequently discovered other data, other facts which are interesting in their own right. But no, I assure you sir, we're only here to help your boy, to keep him safe from James Wingrove."

"But Tommy was never their target. He was only involved because he was trying to help Faith."

"Yes—and, again, we didn't know this until we came here to investigate—but once they had Ms. Avalon, your boy was the first and only person they informed. We traced a call to your house from one of the perpetrators, just a few minutes before the— the incident at the library."

I sat back down, heavily.

"This is madness," said Maria. "Who are these people, Agent Rosaly?"

"They're a cult of some kind, Mrs. Belmont, a cult of—well, devil-worshipers, not to put too fine a point on it. And we honestly don't know why they would be after young adults. As I say, it's not their, well, their usual pattern, their usual *modus operandi*, if you will."

"Perhaps they were not after Tommy, but after Syme," Roland suggested. "Would that not make more sense?"

Rosaly waffled. "Certainly possible. Certainly conceivable, yes. But in that case, wouldn't they have targeted Tommy in the first place, for better leverage? These, at any rate, are my thoughts."

I nodded, slowly. He was perfectly right of course. And if—somehow—that insanity about Tommy keeping pace with a speeding car on foot were true—

"I should go," I said at length. "I have work. Please keep me informed."

Rosaly gave me his card and I accepted the accompanying handshake with some slight reluctance. Hyland didn't offer her hand a second time, nor did I offer mine. Roland shook my hand as well, and Maria gave me an embrace which, I confess, did raise my spirits somewhat. Tooley walked me out to my car.

"Mr. Syme," he said quietly. "I don't know what these feds are up to here in Zevon, but I've gotta tell you, I don't much care for them nosing around my town. Now I promise I will find your Tommy. And when I do, I'll tell you first and then we can decide what to tell them about it. How's that sound to you?"

"Officer Tooley," I said gravely, "that sounds like the word of a good man."

16

THE KAIROS FIELD was both scary and exhilarating. The best I can describe it is that it felt like floating through, not outer space, but whatever it is that outer space *means*. Does that make any sense?

After that, we found ourselves in a plain wooden room with no decorations or furniture at all. Maybe they set it up that way on purpose so you'd have a minute to adjust to seeing things in the normal way again before you had to try and process all the amazing stuff that must be waiting for us outside. Like an airlock for your mind, almost.

"Is everyone all right?" Alyra asked.

"I think so," Faith said. She sounded a little shaky, but she looked more confused than frightened. So did Roy, for that matter. I probably looked the same way myself. "Do you ever get used to that?"

"Not in the slightest, I'm afraid. But at least you'll know what to expect next time."

"Great."

There was a door behind us—must be the one we'd just come through—and another about twenty paces in front of us. As we were standing there getting our bearings, the one in front of us opened up and someone called out, "*Withsif drema?*"

"*Bairka, tulgwa,*" Alyra replied. "Alyra Vauksness, *floma dwenes* Loryk *Chodan.*"

The door opened wider and a guy stepped through it. He was *definitely* an elf: tall and lean, with the same long pointy ears that Alyra had, only he was gold colored. Not like a good healthy tan kind of gold, but actual bright, rich yellow like a sunflower, right down to the "whites" of his eyes. He was also dressed in a single piece of clothing, but it was reddish-brown and tough-looking, almost like some kind of leather, and it left his neck exposed while covering his arms and turning into pant legs like hers. "*Limam serethi nowylan,* Vauksness *afestha,*" he said, and grinned. Once you got used to the ears, their faces were pretty much the same as ours. "*Bairka.*"

She stepped forward and they bowed to each other—that same fist-over-the-heart bow that she gave us earlier.

"*Sruban sithfaas,* Raitah." She gestured at us and added, "*Zithvan sorelsen duur ni stannallat Inolesh.*"

"Ah—yes—of course," he said. "Forgive me." He turned and bowed to us as well. "Welcome, honored guests of our lord King Loryk. I am Shoren Raitah of Windismere, door-warden of Ardmore."

Roy made the same bow back, perfectly, like he'd been doing it all his life. "Roy Belmont of Zevon," he said. Faith and I followed suit, a little uncertainly.

"Um, Faith Avalon of Zevon."

"Hi! I'm Tommy Connor. Of Zevon too."

"Again, welcome. Please follow me." As he turned and led the way out of the room, I noticed there was a sort of scabbard built into the fabric of his outfit and a short sword on his back. I wondered if it was magic.

We followed him out the door as Alyra brought up the rear. Outside was a wide stone corridor, but not like your usual stone corridor. For one thing, it was all one piece. There were no bricks or blocks or anything; it was more like someone had tunneled right through a mountainside. It was perfectly square, rather than round like a tunnel, and the walls were totally smooth to the touch. Also, the stone itself was a cheerful grassy green, and it was bright as daylight even though there weren't any candles or torches on the walls.

"Where's the light coming from?" I asked.

Alyra smiled and reached over and plucked something off the wall. When she held up her hand, I thought for a second that she'd somehow gotten a hole right through her palm. Then I realized she was holding some kind of disc, the same color as the corridor, and it was giving off such a subtle shimmer that you wouldn't even notice it unless you were looking for it.

"Watch." After a couple of seconds, the hole in her palm filled in and turned purple, and it looked like her hand was empty again. "These are *kolmalat*. They blend in with whatever surface they're attached to, and they never grow dim."

"Neat! Can I touch it?"

"Of course." She handed it to me. It wasn't warm like I expected. Honestly, it kind of felt like a dollop of ice cream. I watched it gradually take on the color of my hand. "There—a sample of elvish craft for you. But now we should hasten onwards."

"Oh, right." I reached over and touched it to the wall, and it fastened back on and faded back in.

"Man, Valenzuela would blow his stack over that," Roy murmured.

"How come? I bet we could make stuff like that back on Earth."

"Not the light itself. The part about never growing dim. Second Law of Thermodynamics, you know?"

"Nope."

He cracked a smile. "*Everything* grows dim, is the point. So, are these things elf-science, or elf-magic?"

"We distinguish those ideas very differently than you do," Alyra said. "But all forces are tongues of the one Flame."

"The what?" Faith asked.

"That is what we call the power that forged our worlds and wove the kairos field, that kindled the stars and gave them breath and purpose. Now is not the time to speak of these matters, but I promise you we'll speak of them soon."

We'd gone by a few doors, side passages, and one set of stairs leading down. Now we came to a long stairway leading up that was the end of the corridor. Shoren led the way up the stairs, and we kept on following.

"So what tribe are you from?" Roy asked him as we climbed. "I mean, if it's not rude to ask."

"Not at all, young master. I am of the Mountain-elves. Ours are the peaks and high fastnesses of Faerie, but the great city of Ardmore lies atop the mightiest mountain of all. For my people, it is honor and joy to serve among the king's soldiers in this lofty place."

"You must be a pretty good fighter, then."

"Perhaps I am of some account," Shoren said modestly.

At the top of the stairs there was a big landing and a set of double doors, maybe ten feet tall and eight feet wide, and black as midnight in a sack. I couldn't tell if they were made of metal or stone or what, but they sure looked sturdy. Two more guards were standing in front of them, dressed like Shoren. One was golden—another Mountain-elf, I supposed—and the other was a deep grey color like a wolf. The gold guy was twirling around a couple of short swords like Shoren's. The other one had a spear with a really long blade, and he was basically standing at attention.

"Raitah!" the Mountain-elf said cheerfully. "*Wojand lindros enna, lafis*?" Then he froze and stared at us. The grey guy's eyes widened slightly, but he didn't react beyond that.

Shoren and Alyra talked to them in elvish for a minute or so. Then the gold elf flipped his swords over his shoulders, criss-cross, and slipped them into the back of his shirt. The grey elf twisted the handle of his spear and the blade retracted into the butt. They both did the bow and said, "Welcome." We bowed back and introduced ourselves like before. It felt a bit more natural this time. Then the guards opened the doors for us, and we stepped outside.

It was cold out, but not bitter. The air was clear and frosty, and we could see our breath. The stars were bright, and very close, and I remembered what Shoren said about Ardmore being on top of a mountain. There was quiet music all around us—we were in a huge open space, a city square, and there were elves everywhere, singing softly. We'd come out of a tall stone building that rose in tiers and ended up top in a ring of chimneys putting out long thin lines of blue smoke. Somehow it looked impressive and homey at the same time, like each of those chimneys came from a fireplace where parents were telling stories to their kids. There were similar buildings all around us, but the square was so big that they were hundreds of yards away. The whole place seemed both solemn and happy, and something made it feel like Christmas Eve.

The square was full of trees, and the trees were full of candles. For a second I wondered if that was safe, but then I looked at the nearest tree and I realized it was made of stone. They had built tremendous statues in the shape of oaks and firs. And in the center of the square, rising above the carven treetops, was a mountain made of fallen orange leaves.

"This is the eastern pavilion," Alyra said. "From here it is not far to the Spire of Vissarion, where King Loryk holds court."

"Are those leaves?" I asked, pointing.

She nodded and smiled. "Each year when autumn comes, we gather the leaves in remembrance of summer. The art of the Mountain-elves keeps them untouched by the wind until the first storms of winter—and then we watch them blow away over the high cliffs and the endless river-fall."

The music around us was changing. As more of the passing elves noticed us, the low peaceful melody in the air started to pick up a thread of urgency. It was interesting to see how they sang together—there was no leader, but each elf strolling through the square joined in with a slightly different pitch, so the song kept growing or fading or branching on its own. I couldn't figure out if they were performing some kind of ceremony or just singing for fun, until I realized they were doing both. But now, without ever missing a note or clashing with the overall harmony, the ones closest to us started to vary the tune, and you could hear the new thread rippling outward as the ones farther away picked up on it. More and more elves came drifting over to peer at us—some silent, some humming, some singing aloud. It was eerie, but wonderful too.

"We're in Faerie," Faith whispered.

"Come," said Alyra. "Our king awaits."

"Farewell for now, good guests," Raitah said, bowing. "May our paths soon cross again."

Roy nodded to him. "Peace, brother."

Over to our left was another group of guards. I saw two more Mountain-elves, a couple of grey elves, one guy who was purple like Alyra, and a lady who was a deep blue. It made me feel like I was kind of a boring color. We went over to them and Alyra said some stuff in elvish. In response, they all bowed and said, "Welcome." One of them trotted over to the side of the building and started opening up another door.

"Does everyone here speak English?" Roy asked.

"We have only six languages in Faerie—one for each tribe, and a common tongue. But we dearly love to learn new words and patterns of speech; whenever our agents visit your realm, they try to bring back a new language. Our children play a game called Manspeak, and the object is to hold a normal conversation but switch to a different human tongue with every sentence. If they're clever, it can go on for hours. You people are brilliant at creating new ways to misunderstand each other."

"Gee, thanks."

The guard came trotting back, and five white foxes followed him. One of the others raised her head and whistled, and a whole cloud of ravens came fluttering down from the rooftops.

"Come, please," said the first guy. We followed him back inside and found ourselves in a little space like a garage with a big silver sleigh parked in it. There were cables attached to the front, and a few of the guards came in and carried them outside, and then they started shaking them and the cables frayed into dozens of tiny strands. They laid them on the ground and the ravens dropped down all around us and each bird took a strand in its beak.

"No way," Faith said, breaking into a huge smile.

"This is done only for the highest of dignitaries," Alyra said. "But you are the personal guests of our lord himself—and besides, we rarely get to use the sleigh."

"There's no snow on the ground, though," I said.

She winked. "Just get on board, Tommy."

Once the four of us climbed up, Alyra took the reins and said, "*Skolpsa!*" and the foxes took off running in front of us. Their tails dragged the ground as they went, and wherever they touched, they left a trail of ice. At the same time, the ravens took flight and the sleigh glided into motion behind them like it weighed nothing at all. A second later, we were cruising along in the ice-foxes' wake at what must have been fifty, maybe sixty miles per hour. Elves are awesome.

We left the pavilion and went sledding up a long, broad avenue lined on either side with birch trees (real ones this time). The wind felt clean and fresh. I noticed the moon was out—a waning crescent, just like back home. I was pretty sure the new moon was coming up in another day or two. At least, it was on Earth. And that got me wondering.

"Hey Alyra, do you guys have the same moon as us?"

"Yes and no," she said slowly. "In passing through the kairos field, we didn't move in space or time. It's still Wednesday night, here as in the mortal lands. And our realm is not a planet such as one of your ships or telescopes might someday find. Your moon is an echo, a shadow, of the one true moon that sails the night sky in the highest realm of all; and so is ours. But ours is closer than yours, for Faerie is poised on the very brink of the Firmament."

"The what?"

"The world of the Flame. The world before all worlds. We're so close that we can even glimpse the final truths—sometimes, a little. It is a deep gladness and a deep sorrow to us, to be *nearly* able to touch the things by which, and for which, we were made."

I couldn't think of anything to say. But maybe now I understood why it felt so merry and so grave here, like the whole place was waiting hopefully for its dad to come home.

"Look," she said then.

Ahead of us was a giant river running straight through the middle of town. The rumble of the sleigh had drowned out the sound of it up until now, but as we got closer, it got louder and louder and louder. The avenue led to a bridge, and there were still trees and houses on our right-hand side until we were practically there. And then suddenly, as we came into the open, the city and the earth on that side came to an end. We went about halfway across the bridge and then Alyra pulled the sleigh to a halt. We all stood staring, and nobody spoke.

Not more than a few feet beyond the bridge, the river went tumbling over the edge of a cliff. But it wasn't just a cliff, it was—it was like looking down from an airplane. The river plunged over the edge and fell for thousands and thousands of feet before it passed the starlit clouds. Beyond that, the whole countryside opened up like a distant map. We could see for a hundred miles or more. Way, *way* down below, you could barely make out the tiny line of the river stretching to the horizon. There was a faint, sweet smell like roses in the air.

"My God," Roy said finally. "How high up are we?"

"We don't measure such things. We're as high as the mountain."

"Where does all this water come from?"

"Oh, it isn't water, Roy Belmont. Wait here." She pulled some kind of long stick from the front of the sleigh and stepped down. Then she walked to the edge of the bridge (there were no railings, by the way) and dipped it into the rushing river. When she pulled it back out, I realized it was basically a ladle. She came back and detached the cup on the end from the stick and handed it to Roy. "Try it."

He sniffed it, and his brow furrowed. Then he sipped it, and his brows shot up. "This is *wine!*"

"Indeed. Beneath us flows Lothúrla, River of Roses, and you stand at the precipice of Mellifast, the Great Wine-fall. Welcome to Ardmore, my friends."

Roy handed the cup to Faith, and she hesitated. "This won't make me sleep for twenty years, will it?"

Alyra laughed. "No. I know the tale of Van Winkle, and it does contain a truth—that Faerie can be perilous—but you won't wake up a greybeard, I promise you."

Faith tasted it, and her face lightened. "Wow. You guys must have some great parties." She handed the cup to me.

I held it up to my face, and the rose-like scent got stronger. The wine looked mostly clear, with maybe a very slight pinkish tinge to it. I took a sip, and it tasted like green apples when they're at their best, so tart that you almost can't stand it, and I could feel a tingle going all the way to my toes.

"That's good stuff." I handed it back to Alyra, and she drank the rest.

"Now then." She called something in elvish and we were off again.

"Okay," Roy said, "straight answer? Where in the hell does a gigantic river of wine come from?"

"It comes from the Spring of Miruvel in the hills above the city. As to how and why that spring gives forth wine instead of water, we truly don't know. There are great mysteries within Mount Voor, and the lore of old once said it hides a path that leads to the Firmament itself. But if so, I've never seen it, nor met anyone who has."

Once we crossed the bridge, we entered another big square, and on the far side of it was a huge tower that glittered in the moon. The closer we got, the more I thought it looked like it was made out of diamond. But that seemed a little excessive, even for this place.

"Behold the Spire of Vissarion," Alyra said as we pulled up to the front gate. "Home to our first true king, it was wrought thirty thousand years ago from a single mighty diamond: The Stone of Oth."

A whole platoon of guards came striding over to us. Alyra bowed to them and they bowed back. This time, no one spoke at all. The gates, four stories tall and apparently made of solid diamond, swung open without the slightest sound. The ravens drew us inside, and the gates closed silently behind us.

17

Elves and angels. It was a lot to process, especially when you casually threw in unfading power sources and colossal waterfalls made of wine. I was going to need a few days to sit down and sort through the implications of all this, but I had a strong feeling that we wouldn't be getting much time to ourselves for a while.

For now, it was all I could do to keep from looking like a bumpkin from rural Iowa seeing Manhattan for the first time. Faith was clearly awe-struck by this place, and Tommy had the same look of simple wonder on his face that he got when Coach Strothman turned a cartwheel in gym class. The whole world was astonishing to him. But on the other hand, he certainly had a knack for taking the impossible in stride. Me, I expect things to make sense. It bothers me when they don't.

As an easy example—a tower cut from a single hundred-foot-tall diamond. What did they cut it with? Who cut it? Was there a working class here, supporting the monarchy? Or maybe slaves? If they had diamonds and wine just lying around in the open, then what was the basis of their economy? And how did the existence of magic fit into all this?

Our sleigh pulled into the courtyard and a few dozen more elves gathered around us. Some of them were armed—guards, evidently—and some looked like civilians. They all had a very strong qi, but the quality of it felt the same as that of a human (for that matter, so did Tommy's; he just had more of it). I noticed a couple of green-skinned fellows in the crowd, with eyes very similar to Faith's. Those must be the Wood-elves: fire-casters. They'd be the ones to watch out for in a fight. But then again, I also noticed a disproportionate number of Mountain-elves among the guards. From what Shoren said, these guys probably trained extra hard, so they'd become good enough fighters to get picked to serve here on Mount Voor. Have to keep an eye on them as well.

The courtyard was a wide space with a bonfire in the middle, and the light sparkled and refracted from a million facets on every wall. At each corner they had made an opening in the floor so that trees and grass could grow in here, and the openings were ringed with what appeared to be dandelions cut from the all-encompassing diamond. A lot of the elves were singing that same rippling fugue we heard back in the pavilion. It was pretty—everything was pretty here—and all the vibes I was getting were good ones. But still, this place and these people made me nervous. Not much use scanning for exits; if things turned bad, where could we possibly go?

Apart from the singing, no one was saying anything. I got the impression that everyone already knew about the visiting Earthlings (and man, I never dreamed I'd live long enough to describe myself as an "Earthling" and mean it). I wondered if Alyra's mission had been more or less common knowledge—if they'd been expecting us.

As soon as we stopped, she said something in elvish and our ravens dropped the reins and went flapping away. One of the guards led the ice-foxes out of the courtyard through some inner door to the fox-stables, or whatever they have in Elf-land.

"This way," she said then, and sprang lightly from the sleigh to the diamond floor. We followed, and the crowd parted to let us pass.

We went up a long, very long spiral stairway that rose up a central shaft for what must have been the entire height of the Spire. No windows looked outwards. There were a few landings, each with halls leading to other floors of the tower, each manned (elfed?) by guards with an interesting variety of weapons. I noted that the gold-skinned folk all carried short swords, from which I deduced two things: that Mountain-elves were fond of close-quarters combat, and that Loryk's legionnaires were not issued standardized arms but had a certain freedom to choose their own weaponry.

Their uniforms, on the other hand, were mostly—well, uniform. There were also female guards and they dressed the same way as the male ones. That must mean that Alyra's distinct outfit reflected a difference not in gender but in rank. There were very few Moon-elves among the common soldiery, so maybe her tribe typically served some other function. Spies? Aristocrats? A priesthood of some kind? Spirit-magic, she had said. That was pretty vague.

When we got to the top, we found ourselves on a broad circular landing with a few closed doors around the perimeter. Alyra went over to one of them and opened it. "These will be your quarters. For now, we'll be here only long enough to get you dressed. Preparations for the great feast are already underway."

"What feast?" Tommy asked.

"The feast for you, of course. I hope you're not too tired. I know it's been a long day for you, but we elves tend to be nocturnal."

"I think we're all too wired to sleep right now anyway," Faith said.

The room inside was spacious—almost as big as the whole bottom floor of my house—but arranged in such a way that it still felt cozy. They had a knack for that here. There were long vines of grapes and chrysanthemums growing along the walls like ivy, and the unbreakable floor was comfortably clothed in soft azure rugs. There were marble statues of birds perching in the corners, a fireplace, and even a window looking out over the titanic cliffs and the Great Wine-fall itself. There were also a couple of blue-skinned people in fluffy robes waiting for us. One elf, two elf, red elf, blue elf.

"Greetings, guests!" the guy said happily. "We are to attire you in fitting raiment. I am Ajuth, and this is Ashaka, my wife." They bowed; it was a different bow than the one we'd been seeing up till now, with the right palm against the stomach and the left hand covering. Totally guessing, but— maybe the bow of a servant, as opposed to a soldier? These two had no weapons, and they didn't carry themselves like fighters.

"So, what kind of elves are you?" Tommy asked. He had the exact same tone as Ajuth: instantly friendly. It's easier to be trusting when you can bench-press a station wagon.

"We are Sea-elves," Ashaka replied. "And you are the nephil, are you not?"

"Alyra pronounced it 'nephilim'."

"Actually, 'nephilim' is plural," Faith said. "Like 'cherubim' and 'seraphim.' I think she's right, 'nephil' would be the singular."

"Leave it to you to know something like that," I murmured. She smiled and punched me on the shoulder.

"And this is the mortal, and this the *meldilanafa*," Alyra said, indicating me and Faith.

"That's a lot of syllables," Faith said.

"It's our word for half-elven humans. There have been very few *meldilanafa*, but some of them were great heroes among our people. Now come, let's make you presentable."

Twenty minutes later, we were elfed up and lookin' fly. They put Tommy in a long silver robe with no adornment but a mark on the left shoulder like a dim golden sun, dark in the center but ringed with brightening rays.

My get-up was surprisingly similar to my karate gi, an open blue tunic and black breeches, soft as silk but, upon inspection, tough as rubber. They also looped a necklace over my head, a strange multi-faced crystal on a vermilion thread.

As for Faith—when she stepped out from behind the screen where she and Ashaka had been conspiring, I remembered abruptly just how beautiful that girl really was. She wore a green dress, hemmed with glistening emeralds, that fell to her knees. It covered her right shoulder like a toga and her right arm like a sleeve, but her left arm and shoulder were bare; her hair was bound in a long braid that fell over her left side and ended in a tiny flashing ruby.

"Wow!" Tommy said. "You look—elvish."

She lowered her eyes, not shyly but demurely. And for the first time in my life, I found myself thinking of her not as a girl but a woman. I couldn't find a single thing to say.

"You all look perfect," Alyra said. "Ajuth, Ashaka—many thanks." They bowed to her, and to us. "And now it's time to meet the king. Are you ready, my friends?"

We assented, and she led us back down the stairs. When we reached the bottom, there was another long passageway and more guards and doors, and then a big chamber with some kind of trench running along the walls with scarlet fire burning within it. The room was full of tables and the tables were full of food, and a hundred elves were singing something that sounded a bit like the "Hallelujah Chorus." All that was for us, apparently. Top of the world, Ma.

At the far end of the chamber was a raised platform with a simple chair. As we entered, the occupant rose and everyone fell silent. Alyra led us through the smiling crowd to the figure on the dais. He wore a silver robe like Tommy's, but open at the chest and displaying a necklace like mine. His eyes and his skin were dark purple, and he was unusually broad-shouldered. His qi was strong, and it had a coiled quality as if constantly ready to strike. There was a thin blue circlet in his hair, a crown of sorts, and his face was alert like a young man's but wise like an elder's. No one doubted that this was the king of the elves.

Alyra bowed low. "Loryk *Chodan, zotana riyu.*"

He bowed to all of us, with his hands straight at his sides. "Hail and well met. I am Loryk san Varodrim, King of Faerie."

I bowed back the same way. If that was the king's bow, it was probably not appropriate for me to use it, but—whatever. I'm an American. The other two watched me and did the same thing, and I realized a bit late that I'd just volunteered myself as our spokesman by pretending to be the most confident person in the group. I cleared my throat.

"Hello, on behalf of our country. I'm Roy Belmont of Zevon and these are my friends. It's an honor to be guests at your—court."

He didn't quite smile, but his face lightened. "And it is with honor that we receive you, Roy Belmont of Zevon. Likewise, Faith Avalon and Thomas Connor of Zevon. Will you break bread with us?"

I glanced at the other two, and they made covert little "I dunno" shrugs at me, so I said, "Absolutely. Thank you."

And the crowd burst into song, like I'd said the greatest thing ever.

A second later, we were seated at the table closest to the throne, and Loryk had stepped down to sit at the head of it. He put Tommy on his right hand and Alyra on his left, with me next to Alyra and across from Faith. A bunch of elves in long flowing costumes came cartwheeling through the aisles and filled our cups with rose-scented wine, and Loryk raised his glass and bellowed something in elvish. Everyone cheered and stomped their feet, and we all drank. Archers came running in and started firing arrows at our plates, and the arrows were shish kebabs loaded with vegetables and meat, dripping with spices and sauce. Jugglers ran across the tables throwing loaves of sweet, steaming bread to each other from across the room and plunking them down in front of us. The revelers tore into the food like they hadn't eaten in decades, but everyone managed to keep singing in between bites and swallows. Every few minutes, someone from every table would get up and dance a sort of hornpipe with someone from another table and then they'd switch seats, so everybody ended up sitting everywhere and drinking with everyone in the room. Faith was right—these people knew how to party.

The music was fantastic, the food beyond delicious, and everybody was in such high spirits that you couldn't help laughing even when you didn't get the jokes. I gathered we were sitting with the royalty of the realm, but I didn't sense any meanness or snobbery at all. They told us a dozen stories of their land and people, funny and sad and exciting, and everything I heard and saw gave me the impression that they really weren't that different from ourselves. Except the part about never aging. There was a Sea-elf sitting near me, and he nodded when I brought that up.

"Yes, the fell gift of death. We often envy you. How precious it must make your days!"

"I guess. We don't generally look at it that way."

"Of course. You envy us in turn. What magnificent folly, that the gull should long to be a dolphin and the dolphin long to be a gull! Yet such is the way of things."

"We may not age," said one of the Mountain-elves, "but at least we can still die in battle."

I took another sip of wine. "I gotta be honest, I'd *love* to have a match with one of you guys."

"Roy," Faith said in a warning tone. "We didn't come here to start brawls."

But my buddy the elf looked intrigued. "It would be a privilege to cross fists with you, Roy Belmont. Perhaps we can do so after the meal, if our king allows it."

"Um. . . are you sure that's a good idea?" Tommy asked me.

"Nephil, please. I can handle myself in a scrap."

"No, I mean, what if it's not polite?"

"Well, it can't hurt to ask." I leaned towards Loryk and raised my voice over the clamor in the room. "Say, Your Highness, is it cool if I have a friendly sparring session with uh, this guy over here?"

He raised his eyebrows. "By all means, if you wish it. But know that Ishten Raunos is one of our best fighters."

"Sweeeeeet."

"The repast will soon draw to a close. There will be an exhibition of our craft, and after that you may have your match if that is your desire."

A few minutes later, the cartwheelers came cartwheeling through the aisles again to clear away our plates and refill our cups. And a minute after that, four elves got up and stood at the corners of the room. For the first time, silence fell. The crackling of the fire in the trench was the only sound. We waited. Then one of the elves in the corners, a Wood-elf maiden, began to chant.

By dancing lightning-light we dance our dance,
Rejoicing rushing cosmos-kindling flame—
Now join the joyous romps and revel-rants
And leap with life as when first summer came!

The fire exploded upwards, blazing to the heights of the walls, rising to a great roar, and licked at the diamond ceiling. It bent over us, embracing the entire chamber, folding itself down from above, and stopped just a couple of yards above our heads. Then all at once it subsided, and everybody drank and applauded.

"That was intense," Faith muttered.

Another chant began, from a Sea-elf this time. It went:

A leaf upon the river flows by many shores,
By shores of peaceful and of warring lands, by
glory and by havoc,
But the river is always one, and there all shores
meet
In the fall of rain from heaven and the waiting seas
beyond,
And all times and all sorrows and all hopes are one
in the river,

*And we drink of it and dance, that tonight's bliss
may touch
The days of sorrow by which we also flow,
So, fall and flow and dance with us tonight.*

And the wine in our glasses sprang into the air like a hundred mini-geysers, swirled around for a moment, and then dropped back into our cups without spilling a single drop. We clapped again, and the next chant started. This time it was one of the grey-skinned folk. I'd learned they were called Deep-elves and dwelt in the caverns and subterranean tunnels of Faerie, so I wasn't surprised by the subject matter:

*When winter cloaks the stone in mournful slumber
deep,
When war and edge of blade bring quiet to our
groans,
Then life and motion sleep in stillness and in
shade—
Yet though the world may weep, its spinning does
not fade,
And those in tombs now laid shall one day claim
their bones
And dance where hawks have flown, and earth itself
shall leap!*

The floor rippled underneath us in a long smooth wave, as if we were on a ship. We rose and fell and rose again, swiftly yet comfortably, a roller coaster made of rock. And when that finished, the last chanter—a Mountain-elf, of course—began:

With the breath in our bodies we have danced, we have sung,
With the breath in our bodies we will sing.
We will dance once again when another evening comes,
But for now let the gentle zephyr spring—
Let it breathe peace upon us, and all things.

A cool breeze came whispering through the room, an exhalation from the elven hills, to soothe our fevered brows. We drank again, one last time, and I suspected on a normal night that would have concluded the festivities.

Tonight, however, things were different. Loryk raised his hands and shouted something, and everyone stomped their feet as if a second feast were starting. Ishten Raunos got up from our table and walked to the center of the room.

"Just be careful," Faith said tightly.

"I got this." I rose and followed Ishten to the open space in the middle. All eyes followed us and silence fell once more.

Ishten was an inch or two taller than me and maybe five or ten pounds heavier. He was dressed like me, in a suit that was nearly a gi. I took off my necklace and set it down on one of the tables nearby, and then walked towards him. He bowed, but this time his left palm covered his heart and his right fist was on the outside. I assumed that meant, "I will now punch you." I bowed back the same way, and then we started to circle.

Now, I know what you're thinking. But you're wrong this time. I wasn't drunk, and I wasn't trying to pick a fight to gratify my pride. I won't say that I had some larger strategy in mind, like assessing their potential combat capabilities or some-such, although I could probably make it sound convincing. I was doing this partly because, elf or human, dudes are dudes, and I knew this would be a quick way to bond and win some respect; and partly because I was way out of my depth here, and it made me scared, which made me angry, and this was the best way I knew how to deal with it.

His stance was low and highly mobile, with his right hand out toward me and his left hovering near his hip as if he were about to draw a blade. I formed the assumption that as a member of a tribe associated with air and wind, he would favor speed over power, and instinctively adopted a boxing stance in order to counter him with a little brute force.

We circled a couple of times, and then he came at me, staying low, moving with rapid shuffling steps. I was expecting him to close in and throw a series of quick hand-strikes, but he surprised me. Once he got in range, he made an incredible leap into the air and threw a spectacular flying back kick at my head. The only thing that saved me was the split-second warning I got from his surge of qi. As his foot scraped past my jaw, I caught him around the waist and lofted him into a full-body suplex, dumping him shoulder-first onto the diamond floor.

I could hear the wind leave his lungs, but he rolled out of the impact, bounced back to his feet, and threw an axe kick that clipped the very tip of my nose; another half-inch and it would've knocked me out. I tried taking out his other leg with a sweep, but he was miles ahead of me—rather than re-planting his kicking leg as it came down, he used the momentum to launch himself into a mid-air barrel roll, and my leg passed harmlessly underneath.

I closed on him and started throwing punches. He traded a few blows with me, but gave ground fast, and finally pushed me back with a front kick. I absorbed that one, hopped back a couple of paces, and threw a high kick of my own, a heavy left roundhouse aimed straight for his neck—but he got his hands up there in time and took most of the impact on his forearms. We both dropped back another pace, breathing hard.

I realized two things. First, my initial analysis of the Mountain-elves had been lacking. They favored light, maneuverable blades not because they wanted to *start* a fight at close quarters, but because they wanted to end it there. What they really wanted to do was rattle your skull with kicks, and then dart in while you were stunned and finish you off with their short swords. That meant they were most comfortable fighting at long range—i.e., kicking range—or in close, at stabbing range. That was confirmed by the fact that he hadn't wanted to slug with me, as punching happens in the middle range. The other thing I realized was that I was having a blast. I grinned at Ishten, and he grinned back. Then we lunged at each other again.

He could tell I'd picked up on the weak spot in his style. He came straight at me with a jumping double front kick, then peeled away and stayed well out of punching distance. I tried trading kicks for a few seconds, but after he caught me in the floating ribs and almost dropped me, I could see I didn't have a chance against him that way.

In a fight like that, there's no time to think sequentially; you bypass reason and act directly from will alone, taking in the whole situation as if from some higher dimension beyond time, seeing everything at once and blending decision with movement. In the gap between eye-blinks, I decided that if I couldn't out-kick him and he was too fast for me to crowd in and out-punch him, then I'd have to out-grapple him. His instinct to close after landing a solid kick might help me there. Even as this non-thought crossed my consciousness, he started to throw another kick which my qi-sense told me was a feint: he wasn't committing to this kick but hoping to draw out my guard so he could catch me with his other leg. I feigned blundering towards the incoming kick as if I was trying to land a lucky punch, and it took me hard in the face; but I'd been ready for it, and it hadn't carried its full power since it was meant as a feint. I shook it off, grabbed him, and took us both to the ground. Time to see if elves knew Jiu-jutsu.

Turned out they did! Or some equivalent, anyhow. We rolled across the floor, struggling to wrap each other's limbs and throats, and bashed into the nearest table, knocking it over. The elves all jumped up, laughing and yelling, and gathered in close around us as we came down to the final moments. A hard match is unbelievably exhausting, and I was already feeling it; I could tell Ishten had more gas left in his tank than I did, so I'd have to finish this fast if I was going to have any hope at all.

Unfortunately, grappling is a patient man's game. You have to bide your time and wind around your enemy like a chess-playing boa constrictor, reading his moves and blocking them one at a time as you tighten the net of your own master plan. But I didn't have enough stamina left for that, so I opted for the quick and dirty approach: I got my feet under me, knotted my fists into Ishten's tunic, and lifted him high in the air, intending to slam him down onto the overturned table. He twisted his body and managed to get a foot on the ground, thus breaking my body-slam and my last hope at the same time. Then he shoved me, and I stumbled backwards with my dukes still up in blind reflex—the other elves came swarming between us, cheering us both, slapping us on the backs, pressing drinks into our hands. At this point, I was happy to call it a draw.

Ishten raised his glass toward me, drained it, and shattered it on the floor. I did likewise. Blood was running from his nose, red like mine, and he was laughing. We bowed, and then he came forward and caught me in a bear hug. I heard myself laughing too. Looks like I'd made my first elvish friend.

18

I woke up early Thursday afternoon in a strange bed with no idea how I'd gotten there. For a second I panicked, fighting off the blankets as if they were throttling me, and sat up with a gasp—Tommy was there, sticking his head through the curtains around my bed and smiling his smile at me. I still didn't remember where we were, but all the fear left me instantly.

"Hey, Faith," he said in a stage whisper. "Roy's not up yet. How'd you sleep?"

"Okay? I guess? Where—" Then it came back. "Oh my God, we're in Faerie, aren't we?"

His smile got bigger. "Yep!"

I flopped back down on my pillow. This was really happening. Up till now we hadn't gotten a minute to ourselves to stop and think about everything, but—this was really happening.

"You hungry?"

"Not yet, but. . . I don't suppose elves drink coffee, do they?"

"You know, they brought in a cart with a bunch of food, and one of the pitchers smelled like it might have coffee in it. I haven't tried it, I'm not a big coffee guy."

"Even after we composed our ode together?"

"Yeah, that was fun."

I sat up and got my feet on the floor. I was wearing a pale green nightgown made of some amazingly soft and comfortable material which I spontaneously dubbed "fairy silk." Tommy was in a sort of fluffy brown robe, the sort of thing you might very well see back home but probably wouldn't have in your closet unless you were a duke or an earl or something. Impulsively, I reached over and stroked one of the sleeves. He gave me his hand and helped me to my feet, and I stood facing him for a moment. Our fingers interlaced.

"Hi," I said quietly.

I could feel the pulse in his fingertips.

"Hi."

One moment. Then Roy groaning in his bed. We stepped apart.

"Oh Lord, please tell me elves have ibuprofen," Roy croaked, shuffling off his covers. "I haven't been this sore since—well—since I fought Tommy."

I grabbed a pillow and threw it at him. "Maybe you should stop trying to beat up everyone you meet, *Roy*."

"I was bonding, *Faith*. It's something *men* do."

"Like you'd know."

"Actually, there's something on the cart for you," Tommy said. He went over and handed Roy a tiny glass vial. "They said Alyra had it sent up."

"Gimme." Roy pulled out the stopper and upended the vial over his tongue. Only a few drops fell out, but whatever it was sent a shiver through him. "Ye gods, that'll wake you up in the morning. Tastes like biting into a lemon." Then he shivered again. "Whoa."

"You okay?" I asked.

"Yeah, no, I feel good. It's like all the aches just got warm and fuzzy. This stuff's fantastic."

I checked out the cart for myself and discovered the pitcher Tommy was talking about. It turned out to contain a thick, steaming brew that tasted like the strongest coffee you've ever had but without the slightest trace of bitterness. Just the thing to counter-act elvish wine. I'd probably be awake for twenty years now.

After that, I stepped into the bathroom. I don't wish to be indelicate, but I have to take a minute to talk about the bathroom. There was no sink, no tub, no toilet. Instead there was a deep pool in the center of the floor with diamond gratings on either end, and through some ingenuity of engineering, the rose-wine of the River Lothúrla was flowing right through our room at the top of the Spire of Vissarion. There were towels and sweet-smelling soap, and even toothbrushes provided for us. The idea of bathing in wine might sound odd, but this was no ordinary wine; it was invigorating and cleansing, and it toweled off like water but left a faint lingering perfume in its wake. As I stepped out and began to dress myself, I felt as if the elven side of my nature was beginning to stir.

And that was something else I hadn't had time to think about. "One of your parents was mortal," Alyra said; "the other was one of us." It certainly explained the magic. But it didn't explain why I was left on Earth and raised by parents who weren't my own. *Meldilanafa*, she called me. Maybe for all their friendliness, these people weren't prepared to accept half-breeds here.

But no point in worrying about that yet. We still had no idea why we were even here; might as well deal with one intractable problem at a time. I pulled on my outfit: a single piece like Alyra's that covered my neck and bared my arms, except that mine turned into a skirt above the knees rather than splitting into pant-legs. It was a soft white color shaded with an almost imperceptible tinge of crimson. I dried my hair and let it hang loose around my shoulders. Another cup of coffee and some breakfast, and I'd be ready for whatever this place could throw at me. Well—maybe two cups.

Roy and Tommy were devouring a platter of eggs and sausage when I came out. I pulled up a chair and tucked in alongside, and for the next ten minutes there was very little conversation besides the sound of slavering and mastication. Traveling to higher planes of existence is hungry work.

"Ahhh, dat's da stuff," Roy said finally, pushing back his chair. "I feel like a hundred and fifty million bucks."

I finished my second cup and debated pouring a third. Then I realized I could feel my scalp tingling and decided to play it safe for now. Who knew if they had defibrillators in Faerie?

"So," said Tommy. "You think they'll tell us about Wingrove today? It's nice that they're so welcoming and everything, but we did come here for a reason."

"I'm sure they will," I said. "They know why we're here."

"I'll be interested to see about this task they have in store for Tommy," Roy said. "Must be something pretty hefty, if they need a nephil to do it."

The door opened a crack, and Alyra's head peeked through. "My friends? You're all awake?"

"Yeah, come on in," Roy called. Then she stepped into the room and he added, "Oh! —uh— hey. What's up?"

Today she was clad in a long silver skirt that fell to her ankles, and a golden top that covered her arms but left her slender midriff bare. Her hair was bound in a long braid and woven around her neck like a choker. We all stared for a few seconds longer than was appropriate, and she finally laughed at us. "Please, blink. Your eyes will dry out."

"You look great, Alyra," I said.

"Thank you, Faith. You look wonderful as well. But I see the men have yet to dress themselves."

"It doesn't take us as long," Roy said, getting his bravado back. "Thanks for that elixir, by the way."

"You're welcome. The juice of the Luna-fruit can heal almost any injury, but it's extremely rare. It blossoms once every hundred years in the Weeping Groves of Kalamorn and must be harvested with many songs and spells or its virtue will be lost forever."

He looked taken aback. "Jeez, you know—I wasn't really injured. Just a little sore."

"It's all right, Roy. You're the first mortal to feast with King Loryk in many years, and you gave us all an impressive show last night. We're happy to offer you a few gifts in return."

"Alyra?" Tommy said. She nodded to him. "Can we talk to King Loryk now? About Wingrove and the demons and all that stuff?"

"Yes, we can. That is why I've come to summon you. Have you breakfasted?"

"Yeah, we just finished."

"Excellent. Then let's get dressed and be on our way."

They both pulled on vaguely monastic-looking robes—dark red for Tommy and sky-blue for Roy—and we headed out to the landing. There she led us through another door and up a short flight of steps that brought us up onto the roof of the tower. A great open terrace looked out over the endless falls and the wild beauty of the country below. It was even more breath-taking in the daylight—but I could see black storm clouds rolling in from the east. Thunder muttered in the distance.

Loryk san Varodrim was standing on the far side of the terrace, gazing into the west. On that side the city of Ardmore stretched away for miles, green and vibrant, and the river went all the way back to a shelf of hills rising above the edge of town. The sun was beginning to sink; here, like back home, the days were getting shorter. We walked over to the king, and he bowed gravely to us.

"Good day, my friends. I trust you slept well." He was clad in a simple tunic and breeches today, but he wore a long scarlet cape that I can only describe as regal. The same blue circlet from yesterday rested on his brow, the crown of Faerie.

We bowed back and thanked him, and he offered us chairs. The terrace was lined with trees and fountains, and a handful of elves were moving about the place, some singing, some talking, some just sitting in the shade. Over on the eastern corner there were a couple of Mountain-elves sparring with wooden swords. Where we were standing, there were a number of chairs and couple of tables holding jugs and glasses. We sat, and Loryk offered us wine, which we all declined.

"Little early for me, thanks," Roy said.

Loryk sat facing us, and Alyra joined him. Standing to our left was a stocky Deep elf with a spear and a dour expression. "This is Zoras Ganarlaith, my Captain of the Guard," said Loryk. "He has been with me for a very long time."

Ganarlaith sketched a bow and said nothing. I was getting the impression that the Deep elves were generally a taciturn bunch.

"Your Highness," Tommy said, "Alyra told us you could help me hide my presence from the demons. I forget what she called them."

"The *raakkk*," he said in a low voice. It sounded like "rack," but it also sounded like he was hacking up venom from the pit of his guts. It was all the more disconcerting since most of their words were so lyrical. "Yes. It was they who split the cosmos in twain. In the early days of creation, matter and spirit were wedded together, distinct but inseparable, like the warmth and the light arising from a flame. When the dark ones rebelled, they sundered that original unity and tore the Vale and Firmament apart from one another."

"Sorry, what's the Vale?" I asked.

"That's what we call your realm," Alyra said. "Vale as in valley, not as in veil of illusion."

"Gotcha."

Loryk poured himself some wine and continued. "Your world—not merely your planet, but all of space—has been slowly pulling farther and farther apart from the Firmament throughout the ages. Even Faerie is beginning to sink into the Void, the non-space between the realms. When the split is complete, the lights of the universe will go out one by one."

"Yeesh," Roy said, almost inaudibly.

"Do not fear, my friends. This process has been underway for aeons and will likely go on for aeons more. But even within the short history of your own civilization, the effects have been felt. It was merely five millennia ago that the angels ceased from walking openly among your people. They still appear in the Vale from time to time, as do we, but only in secret or when there is dire need. And that is why, as Alyra has told you, there have been no nephilim in the cosmos for all that time."

"So nephilim are the offspring of good angels, not fallen ones?" I said. "Because I always kind of thought it was the other way around." I glanced at Tommy. "Sorry, I don't mean—you know—"

"'Sokay."

Loryk shook his head. "That is a garbling of old legends. When the dark angels fell, they forever lost the power to take corporeal form. That is why demons must take possession of the living in order to work their evil in the world. And even then, an unclean spirit cannot possess any intelligent being unless that being foolishly opens the door of his own free will."

"Why would anyone do that?" Roy asked.

"Because they are deceived. Because they think it will grant them wisdom, or power, or purpose. Even elves can fall under their sway, if they are weak or harbor foulness in their souls. But by the same token, elves too can walk with angels from time to time. Indeed, it is not only with the daughters of men that the sons of heaven once had congress."

My eyebrows shot up. "You mean there are elven nephilim too?"

"They were known as the lyrilim. But that was long ago, and there were only eight of them in all of history. Those eight are now lost to black days and treachery. However—they left behind a mighty gift for our people. It was the lyrilim who forged the keys that allow us to walk between worlds."

"Oh yeah, I was wondering about that," Roy said.

"You see, their power was different in kind from that of the nephilim. They did not inherit great strength or invulnerability, like Thomas here. Instead they gained the ability to pass through the kairos field at will. They traveled through many realms and revealed many secrets to us before they were destroyed."

"What happened to them?" Tommy asked.

He shook his head. "That is a long tale—indeed, eight long tales—and it does not bear upon our present business. What matters is that they created eight sets of enchanted keys with which the bearer may visit any place in the universe—as long as that place may be reached through a door."

"What, like an actual physical door?" Roy said skeptically. "That seems kind of arbitrary."

The elf-king smiled. "The longer you spend among us, Roy Belmont, the more you will come to see that magic has many limits. Some are imposed by the very mind of the wielder. A door is two things: a portal between places and a symbol of transition. So, it is with every object in the material world. Magic functions by making the symbol become one with the literal object."

"You can just call me Roy."

"Of course. Forgive me. In any case, here is the crucial thing: in our explorations with the keys, we discovered that yours is not the only inhabited planet in the Vale. It was less than two centuries ago that we first encountered—"

"Whoooooa," I said, raising my hands in extreme slow motion. "Whoa, whoa, whoa. What did you just say?"

Alyra gave me an impish smile. "Welcome to the cosmos, little sister."

"There is a sphere known as Xaxos, so far from the Earth that the light of today's dawn will not be seen there for over a billion years. I myself have trodden that alien soil, and at one time there were Xaxons whom I called friends."

Roy sagged in his chair. "Oh man, that's a lot. That is one hell of a lot."

"What do they look like?" Tommy asked curiously. He didn't even miss a beat.

"They are not fearsome to the eye. In truth, they might easily have existed on your planet, or you on theirs, had the Flame wrought differently. They stand perhaps four feet in height, and are swathed in fur, and winged."

"Wait, they're bipedal *and* flighted?" Roy asked, sitting up. You could see the scientist in him taking over. "No terrestrial species has ever achieved that mix of traits."

"Yes, they are altogether a remarkable race. They have enormous intelligence and physical strength, and their knowledge of the sciences is truly astounding."

"Do they—do they know about us?" I asked. "Humans, I mean?"

He nodded gravely. "They are aware of your existence. I fear they learned of that through their dealings with us. However, despite their advanced technology, they do not yet have the capacity to travel the stars."

"So what happened? You said you *called* some of them friends—why the past tense?"

He and Alyra exchanged glances, and his face became graver still. "War," he said quietly.

We fell silent. I became aware that the thunderclouds were nearer than before, and the rumbling was louder. Miles away, out across the open plains below, I saw the first flicker of lightning.

"Lemme get this straight," Roy said finally. "There was an inter-dimensional war between elves and space aliens, and we never heard a single thing about it on Earth."

"Why would you have?" Alyra said.

"Well. . . I don't know, it just seems. . ."

"You know," Tommy remarked, "it's not like we don't know about this stuff. Almost everybody has a story. Everybody's seen a ghost, or an angel, or a UFO. Except we're really good at telling ourselves it must've been a dream or a trick or something."

"That's true," Roy admitted.

"The Faerie-Xaxon War began twelve decades ago," said Loryk. "It was brief—we have now been at peace for a hundred years—but it was brutal, and a great many of my people perished."

"What started it?" I asked.

"The keys. They coveted our power to travel through the worlds, and at last one of their people murdered a kinsman of mine and stole one of the eight sets of keys. Then there was bloody conflict, and in the end they destroyed every door on their planet. Now there is no passage between their sphere and ours. But—in all this time, we have not recovered the stolen keys."

"So they could come pouring through any one of your doors at any time."

"No. We have worked powerful magic upon every door in Faerie, so that the keys of the lyrilim will not gain entry there without my personal leave. There is only one door through which our agents may freely come and go, and it is the one by which you yourselves arrived here yesternight."

"Um—no offense?" Roy said. "But that door had only one guard on it. If the Xaxons are smart—"

Alyra smiled faintly. "Relax, Roy. There are Moon-elves monitoring the door at all times through spirit-magic. When it opens, they can sense the energy of whomever passes through it, and they will raise the alarm if those persons carry hostile intent."

"Cool beans."

"Now," said Loryk. "The task which I beg of you, Thomas Connor, is this. In the final days of the great war, we seized an unknown artifact treasured by our enemies. Zoras?"

The Deep elf stepped forward and produced a short metal rod that looked like a scepter of some kind. It was dull and unadorned, nothing much to look at—but Roy gave a slight start when he saw it, and his eyes widened briefly. Then he resumed his tranquil expression. I couldn't tell if the others had noticed.

"I sought hidden knowledge for many years, and among many strange counselors, before I discovered this object's true purpose. It is a torch; a torch capable of withstanding the Flame itself and bearing a spark of that all-creating fire back into the Vale. I do not know how they forged this instrument, nor what they meant to do with it. As far as we know, they have no means of entering the Firmament—and more to the point, no one but an angel can approach the Flame without being consumed."

"So you want me to go fetch the fire for you guys," Tommy said immediately.

The king looked surprised. Tommy was so earnest that he sometimes came across as simple-minded, but I was learning that he was a lot sharper than he seemed.

Loryk nodded and smiled. "Yes, that is my hope. With that light, perhaps I can begin to mend some of the damage the Xaxons have done to my land and my people."

"Okay, we can talk about that. But first I want to know about hiding my energy. That's what Alyra promised and it's the only reason we came here."

"Very well. As I mentioned, our realms were nearer to one another in bygone days, and there were many comings and goings. The nephilim of those times learned of a way to conceal themselves by visiting the land of the elves, and that method is still possible today. To mask your life-force from all eyes forevermore, you need only one thing: the breath of a dragon."

There was another long silence.

Finally, Tommy scratched his head. "Do. . . do what now?"

19

The storm broke as the sun was setting over the western hills. I was relieved to see that it didn't rain alcohol here—but like everything else in Faerie, a thunderstorm was a lot bigger and more intense than anything we're used to back home. No wonder they needed to make the palace out of diamond. The rain came driving down like a million lashing whips as lightning scorched the skies. The wind shrieked through the streets like a stampede of banshees. For a mortal caught outside in this, it was even odds on whether you'd live till dawn.

Like Alyra said before, these folks were mostly nocturnal. As the storm got up to speed, the Spire began to stir and come to life. Faith and I followed Tommy as far as we could on his little journey to the lowest chambers of the tower, and we passed elves of every tribe and vocation on the way down. I imagined that, this being the capital city, it was more cosmopolitan than most places in Faerie; if you happened to visit the northern caves, for example, you'd probably see almost nothing but grey elves doing grey things. I wasn't getting a very good vibe from this Ganarlaith cat, but Tommy needed his guidance in the tunnels below Ardmore.

Kid had stones, you had to give him that. When Loryk explained the process for camouflaging his qi, he didn't hesitate. It didn't even seem to *occur* to him to hesitate. I'm not ashamed to say that in his place I would've wanted some time to work myself up to it, but Tommy was on his way down the stairs within sixty seconds, with Faith at his side trying to think of something encouraging to say and me trailing behind, trying to let him know by my mute presence that I had his back even if I thought he was crazy. We hadn't known him long, but we already both knew it was pointless trying to talk him out of this.

Before long, the five of us—me and Faith, Tommy, Ganarlaith, and Alyra—arrived in a tiny stone room at the bottom of the stairway. Another Deep-elf stood guard in front of a narrow door, clutching a staff and looking dour. When he saw Ganarlaith, he bowed and opened the door without a word.

"From here the nephil and I go on alone," Ganarlaith said. His voice was quiet, and a little grim.

"The nephil's got a name, the Captain of the Guard," I said. He ignored me.

Tommy smiled at us. "Okay, guys. I guess I'll see you in a few hours."

"Good luck, man," I told him, and we bumped fists.

Faith threw her arms around him. "Please be careful, Tommy."

"I will." He held her close, and she kissed him on the cheek. Then he and Ganarlaith disappeared through the door, and the guard closed it behind them.

I turned toward Alyra. "So, run this by me one more time. In order to hide his qi, our boy's gotta travel to a forbidden cavern deep inside Mount Voor, wake up a sleeping dragon, and ask it to breathe all over him. And after that, the demons won't be able to sense him anymore."

"Succinctly put," she replied.

"And it won't just incinerate him, because. . .?"

"The dragons and the nephilim were allies long ago. Some of the dragons still remember. They live for a very long time. Besides, not all of them breathe fire. There are frost dragons, poison dragons, and lightning dragons as well."

"Oh, good! That's *way* better!"

"You don't have to worry. Even if the worm bathes him in its hottest fire, it won't kill him. Nephilim are practically indestructible."

I thought about what Betty Lou's hood looked like after I crashed into Tommy outside the library. "Yeah. . . maybe." I glanced at Faith, who was being unusually quiet. "You okay, sis?"

She didn't answer.

"My friends," Alyra said then. "I had planned to offer you a tour of Ardmore while

Tommy was on his quest, but with the storm coming through, it's best that we stay inside for now. So I've come up with something even better to help us pass the time. Please, come with me."

Once again we followed her up the stairs and through the winding halls. Eventually we came to a big open room full of people beating the crap out of each other. I realized it was an elven dojo, and all at once I felt my mood skyrocketing.

"This is a *keet*, a training room. I've asked a couple of friends to meet us here."

A tall Mountain-elf came walking toward us and bowed. "Ishten!" I said. "Hey, good to see you again."

"And you, Roy," he replied, grinning. "Perhaps today we can learn from each other instead of trying to beat each other senseless."

"Sounds like a plan."

Then a slim green-skinned lady joined us.

"Greetings," she said, and I recognized her voice. It took me a second to place her, but I was pretty sure she was the Wood-elf who was weaving fire-magic at the banquet last night.

"This is Vala Farlonn," Alyra said. "I made some inquires this morning and found that one of our agents disappeared in the Vale eighteen years ago. That agent was a Wood-elf named Sulora Tulurieth, and Vala was a friend of hers."

Faith opened her mouth and closed it. Then she opened it again and stood staring. "Do you—do you mean—"

Vala bowed low. "I would know your mother's face anywhere, Faith Avalon, and you wear it beautifully. It is a deep gladness to meet you."

I peered at her—Faith, I mean—trying to get my head around the whole thing. One of my oldest and dearest friends: half human and half—immortal magic person from another world.

For a few moments no one spoke. Then Alyra said gently, "I thought you might like to learn about our magic, Faith. *Your* magic. Vala has offered to teach you, if you wish."

Faith nodded slowly. "I think I'd like that. Thank you."

Vala took her hand. "Come, little daughter. We will find a place of solitude."

"Wait." Faith looked at me. "I'm not sure we should split up."

"Yeah, I thought of that. But you know, it's only for a few hours. I think at this point, we kinda have to trust them."

"All right. I'll see you soon. Work hard."

"You too."

She and Vala went off hand in hand and I was left with a room full of elves curious to see how tough the Earthling really was. "You gonna stick around?" I asked Alyra.

She laughed. "I wouldn't miss it. Are you ready to start?"

"Born ready, baby. Let's do this."

Ishten kicked things off. It turned out each tribe of elves had its own distinct martial style, which came as no big surprise. As I had surmised earlier, the mountain folk were partial to a high-flying acrobatic approach to combat. Ishten gave a brief demonstration of his style, which he called *vergelsi*, and it looked a lot like a Brazilian art called capoeira. I'd picked up a trick or two here and there, but I had no real experience with this level of athleticism.

They gave me a close-fitting outfit like the one Alyra wore yesterday and then introduced me to a mat of spongy material called *dulitim* that you could fall neck-first onto from ten feet up and bounce right back to your feet without a scratch; we spent about half an hour practicing front flips and back flips. It was a good thing I'd started the day with some Luna-fruit.

It wasn't long before I started getting the hang of the more complicated maneuvers. I was already plenty agile, and I learn fast. By the end of an hour, Ishten and I were practicing a two-man form together that was essentially a dance in which each person alternated throwing and dodging spin-kicks, and I was having the time of my life. These elves were cool guys.

After that, a Sea-elf stepped in and showed me some of their style, *haradir*. It was a more defensive, fluid style that used the opponent's momentum against him. He invited me to charge and throw a punch, and a second later I was hurtling through the air and slamming onto the *dulitim*.

"Nice move," I gasped.

They laughed. "Try again," said the blue guy, smiling.

I got back up and dusted myself off. At my age, I'm hardly a master of anything, but I've been studying the arts for almost as long as I could walk, and I can at least grasp the core concepts of a given style even if I haven't formally trained in it. I saw now that this *haradir* was essentially aikido, and that meant it was non-aggressive, designed to subdue without injury as much as possible. I could keep my feet as long as I didn't try to win by overpowering him.

This time I shuffled in cautiously, throwing out jabs, and he gave ground. I waited. What happens if I just don't attack, I wondered? After a second, he came edging back toward me with his hands relaxed and low. I eased forward and threw another jab, not committing my weight to it—and he promptly caught my wrist and threw a ridge-hand strike at my windpipe. Probably would've killed me if he'd struck full force.

"That was better," he said. "Patience is good, but do not confuse it with complacency."

I cleared my throat a couple of times. "Right. Got it."

He showed me how to manipulate the opponent's body by controlling his wrist. It was startling how much you could make a guy do—coming up on his toes, dropping at the knees, bending backwards or forwards at the waist, even flinging himself onto his head—just by what you did to his hand. Finally he taught me a couple of basic throws. I'd seen some of this stuff before, but it was nice to have a teacher who'd been doing it for centuries.

Sensei Avalon once said that old warriors learn to rely on their minds, partly because they have gained wisdom, and partly because they're too old to rely on their bodies anymore. But here we had warriors with the wisdom of age and the vigor of youth. There was so much I could learn.

Next a female Deep elf showed me some of their art, *krokolokorak*. It was an extremely close-quarters method, relying on the assumption that you were fighting in a tunnel with little room to move around. It started with knees and elbows, sort of like muay Thai, and then moved right into some seriously hard-core grappling. Luckily, Jiu-jutsu is one of my favorite things, so I was able to do fairly well this time around. She still beat me pretty fast, though. At the end of the day, it's hard to argue with decades of experience—plus, that chick was not shy about biting and eye-gouging. We had a few matches, and each time she would beat me with a different technique and then we'd do drills until I understood how she'd done it.

"So tell me something," I said after awhile. "If *krokolokorak* is all about fighting in narrow tunnels, then how come whenever I see a Deep-elf guard, they're carrying long spears or staffs? Wouldn't you want a small weapon like a Mountain-elf sword?"

She shrugged. "In narrow passageways, it is good to strike at a distance, and in a straight line."

"Makes sense."

Then one of the Wood-elves showed me some *roongaj*, which was a lot like kenpo karate: fast, powerful mid-range strikes. By this time I was getting tired, so we only sparred a little and then he showed me a quick drill to improve my hand speed. I thanked him, and we both bowed.

Alyra had been there watching and encouraging me with all the others, but she hadn't taken part in the training. After I went over my *roongaj* drill until I was sure I'd retain it, I slumped down in the corner to catch my breath, and she came over and sat beside me.

"They're impressed with you, Roy. You're very dedicated."

"Thanks."

"You seem more comfortable here than Faith."

"Yeah, well, I grew up as one of about ten black kids in a town full of Learys and O'Hanrahans. You get used to looking different. Besides, I know who I am and where I come from. Faith's finding out that she doesn't."

"But now she does."

"I guess so. It's gonna take her some time to adjust, that's all."

She nodded. "She has a good heart."

"Yup. So hey, can I ask you something?"

"Anything you like."

"Who exactly are you? They've got you out running around the Earth like a covert operative, but then you keep sitting right next to the king like you're royalty. And how come you didn't sing at the feast? And how come there's no Moon-elf martial art?"

"Peace, peace. One question at a time. I am Loryk's niece, his sister's daughter. He did not happily consent to my becoming an agent in the Vale, but I pleaded until he grew weary of it—and also, I happen to be the most gifted weaver of spirit-magic in the realm, apart from the king himself."

"Wow. So you're—you're an actual fairy princess."

She smiled. "I suppose I am."

"Does the king not have kids of his own?"

"He has a son, Prince Gaelric, who is away studying with the Sea-elves. His wife, Queen Hyloria, perished in the Xaxon War."

"How long has he been king, anyway?"

"Eight hundred years."

"And he's only had one son in all that time?"

"Ours is not a fertile race, I'm afraid. When we have children, it's a cause for great celebration, but it happens rarely. The sages tell us the Flame fashioned our people thus to balance our immortality, so we would not overrun the world."

"Huh." We sat quietly for a minute. "I'm sorry about your aunt."

"Thank you, Roy."

"So how about the Moon-elf martial arts?"

She laughed and shook her head. "You don't give up easily, do you?"

"Wouldn't be here if I did."

"True enough. We don't sing at the feasts because our magic is mostly internal, and no use for dazzling the eye. And we do have a fighting style, but it's strictly defensive—even more so than *haradir*—and not much fun to watch."

"I'd still like to see it. If you don't mind teaching me."

She put her hand on mine. "I don't mind. Come."

We got up and moved back out onto the floor. The others gave us some space. "Are you sure you can fight in that dress?" I asked.

"*Len-fa* uses as little movement as possible. I've been trained in the arts of all five tribes, but I won't be throwing any flying kicks today." She exhaled and stood facing me with her hands at her sides and an air of total, untroubled serenity. "Whenever you're ready."

"Uh—is that your on-guard stance?"

"Yes."

"What if I don't attack?"

"Then we go our separate ways. As I said, this style is entirely defensive."

"All right." I raised my fists. "Let's say I'm a dangerous psychopath." She held my gaze, still emanating calm. I took a step forward and made as if to throw a punch. She didn't move. I swung my fist at her head and stopped an inch shy of her jaw. "Is this your whole strategy?"

"So far I haven't needed a strategy. Your heart clearly wasn't in that punch."

"Well—I can't hit you if you're just standing there."

"Then we have no quarrel."

"Oh, for Pete's sake. All right, I'm really gonna swing this time."

"As you will."

I *really* didn't want to hit her, but I couldn't have her thinking I didn't respect her as a warrior. And I figured she must have *something* up her sleeve. So—I stepped back, hauled off, and launched a right cross at her head. And just as I was planting my weight to swing, she gave an ear-splitting, blood-curdling scream at the absolute top of her lungs. Have you ever had someone scream dead into your face when you weren't expecting it? Your whole body turns to jelly. And then, as I was right in the middle of jumping about fifteen feet in the air, she took a step forward and kicked me square in the balls.

Luckily, the floor in that particular spot was warm and comfortable. As I lay there in a crumpled heap, I reflected clinically that *len-fa* was not without its terrestrial analogue. Many martial artists believe that the *kiai*, or spirit-shout, can be used as a weapon to unnerve or even physically weaken the opponent, and I could now attest to that from personal experience. Mind you, I didn't say any of this out loud. What I said was, "*Urrrrrg*."

All the elves crowded around me, slapping me on the back and roaring with laughter. I didn't mind—it was good-natured, the way we laugh at the new guy when he makes the same dumb mistake we all made on our first day. Even Alyra was giggling, which was a little out of character but oddly fetching. "I'm sorry, Roy. Are you all right?"

"'Course," I wheezed. "Why wouldn't I be?"

She leaned down and kissed me softly on the forehead. "Come on, let's get you cleaned up. It'll be time for dinner soon."

I looked up and saw her smiling at me with her strange piercing otherworldly eyes, and a thought came into my head unbidden: *Oh, crap. I think I'm in love.*

20

Vala led me up to a small chamber overlooking the courtyard. There were no furnishings but a couple of diamond chairs that were actually part of the floor; they must have cut *around* those shapes while they were carving out this room. There was no one in here, and no sound but the drumming of the rain outside. She shut the door softly behind us and gestured me to a chair.

"This is a keet for our people to practice our weaving when we visit the palace." She gave me a faint smile. "There is nothing here that can burn."

The chair was hard, obviously, but it was somehow contoured in such a way that it was still reasonably comfortable. "So..." I didn't feel like talking about my—Sulora yet. "You don't live here?"

She sat across from me and leaned all the way forward to keep us close. "I am an officer in the garrison at Uruvyrda, the great forest of our people. I was sent here three years ago to study spirit-magic."

"The elves are pretty egalitarian, huh?"

"Egal—? Forgive me, I do not know this word."

"Sorry, just babbling. I mean they don't discriminate based on gender."

She looked confused. "Women tend to be better at spirit-magic. And as your friend Roy will be discovering, we tend to be better at krokolokorak, the fighting style of the Deep elves, because our hips are stronger. When it comes to earth-magic, or roongaj, the male is often better suited. But all depends ultimately upon the individual."

"What's roongaj?"

"Our style of combat; the Wood-elf style. It relies more on brute force than the others. For my part, I favor the Sea-elf style."

"So, every tribe gets to learn the magic and martial arts of the other four tribes?"

"It was not always so. There have been many wars of elf against elf over the long, long years. But Faerie had been at peace for centuries—since the time of King Loryk's father—until the Xaxon War began." Her smile faltered before returning. "When it comes to the magic of the Wood-elves, however, it is not a matter of training or preference. You see, we did not choose the fire: the fire chose us. The other tribes can wield its power, but never as well as we can."

I gazed at her—her pale green skin, her blond-green hair, so lovely but so foreign—and for the first time I felt a kinship. I knew those eyes, glittering, green-in-green, from my own mirror;

although my whites and pupils were those of an Earth-born girl. I saw now that I'd always known my irises were a little too bright, too green, too fiery, for a human being. *Never as well as we can. . . .* Suddenly I felt like burning something. Roy would've understood.

"How does it work?" I asked, feeling my fists clench.

"Each of the elements responds to a different state of soul. The winds come most readily to a joyful heart, the waters to a peaceful one, and so on. For us, it is anger that calls forth our power."

Varris.

"From what Lady Alyra has told me, your magic awoke because of your proximity to the young nephil, Thomas. She also said that you struck down an enemy who foolishly underestimated you."

"I didn't kill him. But I—I wouldn't be sorry if I had."

"That is good, Faith. Life is war."

"But I tried doing a spell to find Alyra, and it didn't work at all."

"That is spirit-magic, which does not come easily to our people. On that first day in your classroom, when your powers had just been catalyzed, you might have done many things spontaneously; hereafter, you will have to learn to control what lies within you."

I nodded. "I'm ready."

"Come, then." She got up and walked to the center of the room, and I followed her. "As you know, there are two worlds—one of matter and one of spirit. The beasts belong to one and the angels to the other, but men and elves have feet in both. When those worlds collide in us, there are sparks, and those sparks are *words*. It is therefore through words that we call forth the power of the spirit into the physical realm. Even mortals can do this, in a way; but because we elves are poised upon the cusp of both spheres, that power is far more acute in us. Do you understand so far?"

"Um, yes? I think so."

"The experience of the soul manifests itself as thought within your mind and as emotion within your body. You must use your thoughts to draw the forces within your soul into your body, and from there they will become incarnate in the outer world. We use poetry because it is the truest words in the truest order: it provides the most direct route from the soul to the universe."

"Okay, yes. I get that."

"Good. Then make fire, little daughter. Do it now."

She sounded like my dad, telling me to punch through a board. Hope was better at punching stuff, but I'd had a knack for weaving words for longer than I could remember. Fire, fire. Poetry and fire. It worked better when I didn't try to overthink it—just let it flow. What rhymes with fire? No, more important: what pisses me off? Poetry and *anger*, and then fire.

"Lashed to a chair, helpless and scared, a pawn in a game, till I bring in the flame!"

And tongues of fire blossomed from my palms. It wasn't much: a blazing crimson wreath around my hands. But it was flame, and it was magic. I held them up, enraptured. Vala beamed at me. I held onto it for as long as I could, through sheer willpower, but after about thirty seconds it faded away. Wisps of smoke floated up from my fingers, and I felt tired.

Vala took my face in her hands and pressed our foreheads together. "That was fantastic, Faith. How do you feel?"

"Good. A bit drained, but good." I found myself chuckling for no reason. If I'd had more energy, I would've laughed out loud.

"You are truly your mother's daughter. It's not for nothing that she was chosen to hold one of the seven remaining sets of keys."

I pulled back a little and took her hands in mine. "Vala—what happened to my mother?"

"We don't know, darling. Every few decades we send an agent into the Vale to see what the humans are up to, and Sulora was one of the best fire-weavers in all of Faerie. She went to Earth nineteen years ago, and we lost communication with her a year later."

"And she didn't—she never said anything about falling in love with a human?"

Vala held my eyes for a moment, and then sighed. "Faith. . . her last report said that she'd been in contact with a mortal named Jason Morrison. Then we lost touch with her for months. Finally, we sent a team to track her down, and we found this Morrison's body. He had been murdered, and her keys were discarded by his corpse. We reclaimed them, but we never discovered what happened to her. It wasn't until this very week that we suspected there was any trace of Sulora Tulurieth left in the cosmos."

I pulled away and turned my back. "So she's dead."

"No. We don't know what happened to her. And we don't know for sure that Jason Morrison was your father."

"But it's been so long."

Very gently, she put her hands on my shoulders. "Eighteen years is such a short time for our people. She could be anywhere. She could be in hiding, or in captivity somewhere. We don't know. But we do know that she loved you enough to endure whatever destroyed Morrison, bring you into the universe alive, and find you a home."

"I already have a mother."

"The lady Avalon. I have no doubt that she is a wonderful woman. But surely it is no disloyalty to her to honor the one who bore you."

I felt tears starting in my eyes. "What if she *is* dead?"

"Then we will find the ones responsible, no matter what it takes. But think—if the body of a Wood-elf had been found on your Earth, in your America, would it not be a matter of much public discussion? More likely Sulora is still alive somewhere, imprisoned by whomever slew Jason Morrison."

I turned back around to face her. "Who was she to you, Vala?"

"Your mother was ahead of me in the classes of the fire and she helped me to learn, although she was never named a teacher among our folk. That is how our friendship began. We have climbed a thousand trees together and shared a thousand dreams. I loved her dearly, Faith. I love her still. And I do not doubt that it is by the will of the Flame that I should happen to be here in Ardmore at the moment of her daughter's arrival."

I closed my eyes and felt a single tear run down my cheek. "If this Flame really runs the whole of creation—and if we're the ones most in touch with fire and flame—then how come the Moon-elves are in charge of Faerie, instead of us?"

She put a hand on my cheek and wiped away the tear with her thumb. "Because the Wood-elves are too passionate. Too governed by anger and affection. The Moon-elves have wisdom that eludes us. Our forefathers accepted that millennia ago, and there has been peace between our kindreds throughout the endless fallings of the leaves since then."

"I'm not tired anymore."

Her smile came back. "Good. But remember—any given line of poetry can work only once. It is the moment of inspiration that kindles the inferno within you."

"Got it."

I took a step back and squeezed my eyes shut again. It was hard. It was really hard. You had to call up the most intense emotion, yet balance it with extremely precise intellectual articulation. At this moment I was practically afloat on a maelstrom of inner turmoil, swirling through parts of my heart and soul I'd barely touched before, so accessing the raw passion was not a problem; but forming it into words was more and more difficult the more I allowed the passion to dominate. And if I pushed it all down and focused on verbiage, then the feelings began to fade.

Vala was so patient with me. I realized that five or six minutes had gone by in silence. It was time to try something, even if I failed utterly. I couldn't think of any words of my own, but the words of another poet burst into my brain, and I cried them aloud:

O for a Muse of fire, that would ascend
The brightest heaven of invention,
A kingdom for a stage, princes to act
And monarchs to behold the swelling scene!

And I burst into flame. A raging aura of fire enveloped me from head to toe, just for a moment, and then extinguished itself without leaving a single mark on my skin or clothes. I stood there panting, with steam rising from my body, and Vala stared in disbelief.

"Faith—were those words your own?"

"No, that was Shakespeare. I couldn't think of anything."

There was a long pause. "I had forgotten. For our—for the elves, it is impossible to call forth our inner power with the words of another. But the old legends whisper that the meldilanafa have abilities beyond those of elves and men alike. Perhaps. . ." She trailed off.

"Vala?"

"Sweet sister. Perhaps you harbor a power that neither your father's people, nor your mother's, could ever have imagined."

Good, I thought. Good. Because whatever insanity Tommy was suffering right now, I had a feeling that sooner or later he was going to need my help.

21

IT WAS DARK in the caves. Ganarlaith had a kolmalat, but it only shed enough light for us to see a few feet ahead. He seemed to know where he was going, though.

The passage we were following went down sharply for a long way and then branched and kept going down. After a while we came to some rough steps that went down even more sharply, and then another series of branches. Ganarlaith never hesitated, and every fork we took led us more steeply downward. Eventually we ran out of steps and found ourselves half-scrambling, half-sliding down a long crumbly tunnel that went around in spirals. It was hard to say for sure in the dark, but I felt like we were still more or less directly under the palace.

"So what kind of rock is this?" I asked. We hadn't spoken for about an hour, and I was getting sort of antsy. "Seems like we left the diamond behind us back at the palace. Is it like, igneous? Or maybe, you know, metamorphic? Or, or, that other kind? Shale? No, not shale. What's the other kind?"

He didn't answer.

"Kay, well, whatever. Just rock then, I guess."

And we were quiet for another half an hour or so.

"So how far down are we going?" I asked finally. "Coupla miles at least, huh? Seems like we ran outta stairs awhile back. I guess nobody comes down here much, huh? Nobody wants to wake up the dragons, prob'ly."

No answer.

"Do you guys have dragons back home? In the Deep-elf caves? Hey, um—can you hear me?"

"It is best not to speak in the tunnels."

His voice was gravelly and hard, but quiet. It sounded like a whisper was his normal speaking voice, but you got the feeling that people still shut up and listened when he did talk. I didn't say anything else.

We went on for another half an hour or so, and it was starting to get cold. The air felt clammy, and the walls were starting to be slightly moist. Maybe it was limestone, I thought. I realized I could see the walls a lot more clearly than before. At first, I figured it was just my eyes adjusting to the dark, but then Ganarlaith went around a corner ahead of me and I was in total darkness for a second, but I could still see. It must be a nephil thing, like super-vision.

I wonder if I have eye-lasers! I thought. I squinted at the ceiling, trying to shoot heat rays, but nothing happened. I kept at it. At least it was something to keep my mind occupied.

So, dragons. I always thought dragons were cool. I never thought I'd meet one, though. And I *definitely* never thought I'd be asking one to breathe on me. Loryk said it wouldn't be ice or fire, just some kind of mystical fog—unless I caught one of them in a bad mood. I was feeling pretty nervous.

As we kept going down, Ganarlaith kept going slower, and I could feel my heart starting to pound in my ears. I tried to focus on the eye-laser thing, but then I started worrying about hitting Ganarlaith with it, and that got me wondering if I could possibly find the way back up on my own, and *that* got me thinking about being trapped down here, alone in the dark and surrounded by hungry dragons.

"Hey!" I hissed. "How much farther?"

"We are come to the Worm-halls." He was even quieter than before. But it wasn't an edgy quiet, like he was afraid of being overheard—it was more of a solemn quiet, like in a cathedral. "The rest of the journey is yours to make." He offered me the kolmalat.

"Keep it," I said. My throat was tight, and I sounded strange to myself. I stepped past him and went onward.

With the light gone, my vision actually got sharper. I guess it just needed a challenge. The tunnel went on for a few more yards, running straight ahead instead of down, and then I passed under a high stone arch and found myself in a huge open space. I still couldn't see much, except giant shadows looming up in every direction, but I could hear the distant echoes of my own footsteps. On either side big shelves of rock rose up from the floor, and stalagmites stretched up from the shelves like giant spikes. I could hear a fluttering above me, too high up to see, but it sounded like dozing bats. The air was cool and still.

I didn't really know what I was looking for, so I just kept walking in a straight line. I figured if I bumped into a dragon, I'd probably know it.

After a few minutes, I started hearing a dim rumbling sound from up ahead, and my whole body tensed up. *That must be them. They must be snoring. How do you wake up a dragon? What if I startle it? What if I make it mad? My God, what am I doing? This is nuts!*

And for a second, I froze. Then I thought about Wingrove coming after Faith. I gritted my teeth and kept going.

After another few minutes, I decided the rumbling wasn't snoring. It was too regular. And it was too familiar. I'd heard this before somewhere, plenty of times. Finally I realized what it was: a waterfall. Or more likely, the Great Wine-fall going past the cliffs outside. So I must be getting close to the outer walls of the mountain, and I still hadn't seen any worms in the Worm-hall. I have to admit, I was a tiny bit relieved at the thought that there might not be anything in here after all.

Then I heard something else. It was only a soft rustling, like curtains, but somehow it made my hair stand up on end. This time I *really* froze. I strained my eyes peering into the dimness, but all I could see was shadow and rock. The rustling got closer.

I cleared my throat. "Um. . . hello?"

Now here's a pretty morsel.

It sounded like my own voice in my head. But I wouldn't say something like that to myself, especially right now. Maybe dragons were telepathic?

"Hi, I'm Tommy," I said out loud. I thought it might get confusing if we both talked inside my thoughts. I wouldn't want to lose track of who was speaking.

A man of Earth! How comest thou here? It sounded amused, almost playful, but the rustling had gotten behind me now. I turned and saw something moving in the dark, before it was behind me again. I tried not to picture a giant serpent slowly coiling in on me. I hoped it couldn't see what I was trying not to picture in my head.

"I, uh, I came here with an elf. Do you know King Loryk?"

Ah, does that one rule still? It is many a day since I have stirred from sleep. Not yet ruined by his own duplicities, then. Was it he who sent thee to my bower, little one?

"Yeah, he—he told me you could help me." I didn't understand what it was implying. Maybe it was just kidding around with me.

Indeed? And he sought a favor of thee in return—some trifle, perhaps, a generous rate of exchange for the kingly gesture of sending a boy into a dragon's den unarmed.

"Do they even make weapons for fighting dragons with?"

There was a bubbling hiss like hot iron plunging into cold water—not in my mind this time, but out loud in the cave, somewhere over to my left. I'm pretty sure it was laughter.

What a precious plaything Loryk has sent us. I shall have to thank him with a swift death when the time comes.

"Say what? I thought you guys were at peace!"

Oh, we are, Tommy dearest—for now, until the elves break the treaty. We're merely waiting till that day. But how rude of me, I haven't introduced myself. I am Ka, frost dragoness of Loth. What an exquisite delight to make the acquaintance of so polite a young man. It's a life-age of the cosmos since I last spoke with a mortal.

"Hi, Ka. It's nice to meet you too. So, hey—I thought elves never lied."

She rustled around behind me again. *They don't...not directly. Not honestly. They lie with the truth. But come, thou hast traveled far in the darkness and I burden thee with my own paltry troubles. Tell me what brings thee hither.*

"Well. . ." I realized I hadn't stopped to think about how to bring this up. "I need you to breathe on me."

Silence.

"See, it turns out I'm one of the nephilim. I didn't know that myself until yesterday, but Alyra—she's an elf—she came and told me, and that's why I'm here. There are these demons that want to eat my heart, and they're gonna hurt the people I care about to get to me, so I want to get to them first, but they can sense me coming unless I mask my qi, and to do that, I need to get a dragon to breathe on me." It actually sounded simpler than I expected when I summed it all up like that. "So do you think you could help me out, Ka? Please."

The silence went on. Slowly—very slowly—a big tapered thing like the head of a snake rose from the ground and came closer and closer to my face. I couldn't make out any features except for two tiny pinpricks of cold grey light. Her head was almost as big as my whole body, and it was amazing that she could move around so fast and quietly. But right now it didn't feel like she was playing with me anymore. I started to get afraid again.

One of the nephilim, thou sayest. She was only a foot or two away from me now.

"Yes, ma'am."

Did this Alyra tell thee how many millennia have passed since a nephil last walked the Vale?

"Yes ma'am, she said five thousand years."

Hold thy hand out, mortal man. Yep, the playful tone was definitely gone.

"Yes, ma'am." I swallowed hard and raised my hand. Her head dipped closer, and I felt a very slight pinch like a needle in my fingertip.

There was another pause. *I know this blood,* she said finally. *So, thou speakest truth, Tommy of the Vale. Tell me what Loryk asked of thee in return for his counsel.*

"He wants me to go the Firmament and bring back some of the Flame." No one had told me to keep that a secret, but I hoped I wasn't starting a supernatural inter-species political incident by telling her. I was getting the impression that there was way, way more going on here than we knew about.

Ah yes, of course. His mind would turn to the increase of his power. But the more power he gains, the more swiftly he will violate our pact of peace—so I think perhaps I shall aid thee, and speed that end.

"You mean you *want* to fight the elves?"

There was war between us for endless centuries. At last both races grew weary of it, and we reached an accord. My people have mostly slumbered in the deep places of the world since then. But now our strength is returning, and a bloody fray is just the thing to shake off our lassitude. Dragons, however, do not violate our pacts. So we will await Loryk's treachery, and then arise to avenge ourselves upon his people once again.

". . .Okay? That doesn't really make sense to me, but I guess you know what you're doing."

Loryk knows our devices as we know his. None of this will be a surprise to him. He would not have sent thee into the forbidden cavern if he feared anything thou mightest learn from us. At first I thought he had merely dispatched some poor human fool, deemed expendable, to see if we were even awake at all.

"How come they built their city right on top of your caves, if you guys hate each other so much?"

We care nothing for the peaks and the open air. As long as they do not disturb us, they may raise their fragile citadels wherever they like. Besides, the Spire of Vissarion was here before we made our homes in these caverns. The city merely grew around it like a fungus.

"Oh."

Now—as the elf-king no doubt told thee, my people had allies amongst the nephilim in the yore-times. There are some in this very cave, like myself, who keep thy kindred in living memory. They were a strong and proud people, and often cruel, but they knew the honor of warriors. Wilt thou make a pact with me, angel's son?

That sounded ominous. But after all, I was in her home uninvited and asking for a favor. She was already being at least as friendly as I had any right to expect from a legendary killing machine. "I will, if I can. What's the pact?"

Nothing that need vex a gentle spirit, such as I sense in thee. I ask only thy word not to raise arms against any dragon on behalf of the elves. If one of my kind should assail thee or thy loved ones, thou mayest defend thyself, but never shalt thou seek out strife with us unprovoked. Is that agreeable to thee?

I nodded. "I'm okay with that. You've got my word."

Then close thine eyes.

I did what she said, and I heard a sound like a rushing wind as she inhaled. I braced myself for a hurricane of ice—but when it came, it was soft as an autumn breeze. It was cold, but not freezing, and it smelled like morning frost on the last few blades of grass. I could feel it tingling all over me, and then a deeper chill as it sank in through my pores. I shivered for a moment, and then it was over. My body warmed back up right away.

"Is that it?"

That it is, young Tommy. Nevermore shall any demon sense thy presence, in this realm or any other. Go thy way in peace, for now. I have no doubt we will meet again.

"Thank you, Ka. I hope you guys can work out your problems without anyone getting hurt."

We shall see.

I headed back the way I came. My eyesight was getting even sharper, but when I turned to look back, there was no sign of her. The sound of the falls grew fainter behind me, and eventually I found my way back to the arch where I'd parted ways with Ganarlaith. He was still waiting outside in the passageway with his kolmalat in hand.

"What luck, nephil?" he asked.

"Best not to talk in the tunnels."

He gazed at me without expression for a few seconds, and then turned and led the way back up the mountain.

22

Bathing in wine turns out to get you just as clean as using water (assuming you have access to magical elvish rose-wine, obviously), and it has the major added benefit of anesthetizing any aches and pains you may be carrying around. The trick is not to let too much of it into your mouth—otherwise you end up drunk and your whole day is wasted. That's what Alyra told me, anyway, so I just lay there in the shallow end of the bath and let the river run over me, soaking and soothing my battered body. The same clever plumbers who routed the wine-flow up to the top of the tower had found a way to heat it too; it wasn't as hot as I'm used to, but it was warm and comfortable. I could've lain there all night, except I was starting to get hungry. I hadn't realized how much time was passing in the keet. It was already almost midnight: lunchtime for the elves.

Faith came into the room about one second too late to see me with my pants off. "Hey there!" I said, tightening my belt. "How's the magic lesson coming along?"

She brushed hair out of her eyes and gave me a tired smile. "Better than I expected, actually. How's the inter-dimensional martial arts lesson?"

"Painful, but fun. You comin' to dinner?"

"Yep. Starving." She went over to her bed and picked up a clean shirt. "Turn your head, pervert."

I clapped my hands over my eyes. "Lemme know when it's safe."

". . .All right, I'm decent. You look nice, by the way."

"I always look nice. It's my curse."

She crossed her eyes at me.

"So—are you okay? Did you find out anything about. . . you know. . ."?

She nodded. "A little. Do you mind if I don't talk about it right now?"

"Sure, of course. I, uh—I don't suppose you've heard anything about Tommy."

She shook her head. "Not yet. Vala said they should be coming back up in another hour or two. Might as well get some grub."

"Sounds like a plan." I offered her my arm with a show of gallantry, but instead of accepting it she slumped against my chest. I put my arms around her. "Hey, babe. Everything's gonna be fine. The world's a lot bigger than we thought, that's all."

"And full of dragons," she mumbled into my shirt.

"We always knew that, Faith." I smoothed her hair. "That's why we've gotta be knights."

"...Yeah." She sighed and pulled away, and then she dug up a little smile and punched me on the arm. "Thanks."

"For what?" I punched her back. "Come on, let's eat."

"Right."

Ishten was waiting outside our door as we emerged. "My friends! I'm here to guide you to the dining hall. The meal will be a bit more modest than last night's banquet, and I fear His Majesty will not be joining us. But—" he grinned at me "—if you need entertainment, I'm sure we can find someone for you to fight with."

"Thanks all the same, brother mine, but I think I've had enough for one night. Where's Alyra?"

"She'll meet us there. Miss Avalon, you look lovely."

She actually curtseyed. I didn't even know she knew how to curtsy. "Why thank you, good sir. Shall we?" She offered an arm to each of us.

"We shall," said Ishten, and the three of us headed down the stairs arm in arm. "So Roy, how are you? Still speaking in a manly baritone, I see."

"If you're referring to the len-fa incident— I'm perfectly fine. A little discomfort is a small price to pay for learning a valuable technique."

"What technique?" Faith asked.

"I'm sure Ishten here will be happy to tell you all about it later. For now, let's just focus on eating as much as we possibly can. I'm about to fall over."

"Me too. Remind me to have a bigger breakfast tomorrow."

"The air of Faerie has an invigorating effect on mortals," Ishten said, smiling. "However, it does tend to be taxing for the first few days."

"Hey, that's a thought," I said. "Isn't Faith technically half immortal now?"

She shuddered. "I hope not. I want to grow old and be surrounded by grandkids and all that normal human stuff."

Roy, you idiot. I'd said it lightly, without stopping to think that it was a pretty heavy topic. And her comment reminded me of what Alyra said about elvish fertility. God, what if Faith was cursed to outlive everyone she loved? And, say—what about Tommy?

"I don't know much about the meldilanafa," Ishten said. "I believe they tend to live longer than humans, but I have heard that their attributes vary enormously from one to another."

"You get that with hybrids," she said in a neutral tone. I couldn't quite pick up on her mood. I hoped I hadn't just spoiled her dinner.

This dining hall was a good deal smaller than the one from last night and not nearly as crowded. My guess was that each floor of the tower had one or two halls like this for the people stationed on that floor. As we entered, Faith's new friend Vala came over to us and they embraced like long-lost sisters. I guess in a way they were. "Hey," I said, offering Vala my hand. "We didn't really get to meet before, I'm Roy."

"Of course!" She took my hand in both of hers. "Vala Farlonn of Uruvyrda. It is an honor to meet such a brave Earth-man."

I grinned. "Thanks." The whole thing was worth it, just to be called an Earthman.

Alyra joined us a minute later, once again clad in her silver fighting outfit, but now she wore a blue circlet in her hair like Loryk's. We all bowed to each other, and then she led the way to a table where we all sat on a long pine bench. Servers came out and started placing fragrant dishes in front of us. No cartwheeling or arrow-kebabs tonight, sadly.

"So I want to hear about this incident Roy mentioned," Faith said. "What was the word you said, len-fa?"

I grumbled, and the others laughed.

"Len-fa is the Moon-elf fighting style," Alyra said, positively twinkling at me. "It's based on avoidance and deception. I merely gave Roy a demonstration."

"Right in the little Belmonts," I added.

Faith looked half shocked and half amused. "Oh, my gosh—are you okay?"

"Eh." I shrugged. "It was a rough thirty or forty seconds, but I'm over it."

"He took it like a true champion," Ishten said, and raised his glass to me.

I raised mine back and smiled. Always nice to earn the praise of a fellow fighter. On the other hand, I was ready to talk about something else now.

"So Vala, that was pretty impressive last night with the fire and everything. How long till Faith can do that kinda stuff?"

"Not so long, perhaps. She is very gifted."

I gave Faith a little congratulatory nudge with my elbow, and she batted her eyelashes as if to say, "I know, I'm awesome."

"Did you make up that rhyme on the spot?" I asked Vala. "Or do you have a bunch of them stored up in your head?"

"Both, in a way. We were asked to weave our spells in your language, to show you courtesy, and we had two or three hours in which to compose the words. I was still composing up until a moment before I got up to chant, and that often makes for the best magic. The great difficulty is to discipline the words while still leaving them free to dance."

Alyra nodded gravely. "A spell prepared too far in advance tends to leak potency over time, as the moment of inspiration grows more distant. It's a good idea to have several fragments of potential spells in readiness but leave room to adapt them to a given situation."

"Unless one has the Pen of the Varodrim, of course," Ishten said cheerfully.

I raised my eyebrows. "What's that?"

"There are no spell-books in Faerie," Alyra said, "because writing down the words calls forth their power as surely as speaking them aloud, and then the power is spent. There's only one exception: an enchanted pen forged by King Loryk's grandfather in the depths of time. With it, the king can write down a score of spells and keep them in reserve, at full power, for as long as he likes—and then invoke them at will from within the pen itself."

"No kidding! I wonder if that's where the whole idea of magic wands came from back on Earth."

"Probably. You people garble everything."

"You garble everything."

"So how old is the oldest elf?" Faith asked.

Ishten beamed. "The Ancient One! I met him once. He dwells at the peak of Mount Erevoth and holds council with the eagles. They say he's breathed the air of the living for over twenty thousand years."

"*Man*, that's a long time," I said. "Did he tell you the secret of life?"

"No, we skipped stones on his pond. He could skip a stone over sixty times before it sank."

"Lotta practice, I imagine."

We ate and drank and shot the breeze for awhile, and then the servers drifted back in and started clearing the plates away. Elven society appeared to be pretty laid-back, which made sense; removing the specter of death by old age was bound to remove a lot of urgency from daily life. It was interesting that they kept the same basic pattern of eating and sleeping over twenty-four hours that we do: a day was still a day to them, and a year was a year. But there was nothing in the back of their minds forever whispering that their time was running out. If nobody happened to stab an elf to death, he or she could live longer than the entire recorded history of my species. There was no way I could ever relate to that.

Faith had been drinking elvish coffee again, and she now sat drumming her feet and fiddling with her cup. "What time is it? Shouldn't they be back by now?"

Alyra glanced around. Most of the other elves had wandered off to go do whatever elves do. "We don't use clocks here, but it feels like about an hour past midnight." Ishten nodded.

"TGIF," Faith said, and finished her coffee. "Friday was named for Freya, you know. Goddess of love and war. The Greeks had two separate gods for that, but the Norse knew what was up. You do not wanna mess with a Norse chick. She will love and war you right in the *face*."

"Say, maybe you should slow down with the java," I suggested.

"I'm fine, I'm just worried about him."

"I know. He'll be all right. Kid outran a speeding car the other day."

"Check out Mr. Methuselah here. You guys are the same age, Roy."

"No need to get snippy, missy."

"I'll get snippy if I want to get snippy."

"Faith," Vala gently interceded, "perhaps we could put in a bit more practice before Tommy returns?"

"I don't know if I can concentrate right now."

"That is good. Learning to focus your energy in times of stress is critical for warriors and poets alike."

Faith smiled wanly. "Fair enough." She turned to Alyra. "Promise you'll come get me the second he's back?"

"I promise, Faith."

"Thank you." She jostled me with her shoulder by way of farewell, bowed to the others, and went off somewhere with Vala. Ishten excused himself as well. Alyra and I were left sitting alone in the deserted dining hall.

"So," she said.

"So."

We both smiled. What do you say to an attractive stranger from another world? I hesitated for a second, then figured aw heck, why not go with the direct approach.

"So, is there a Mr. Vauksness?"

Her smile widened. "'Fraid not." Was she picking up my speech patterns? "It seems I haven't met the right elf yet."

"You get to choose for yourself, then? I was wondering if you guys had arranged marriages."

"It happens, but not often—especially in times of inter-tribal peace. Lifelong matrimony is quite a commitment for our people."

"I'll bet. But how do your people feel about people who don't live quite so long? Everyone's been really nice to Faith, mixed parentage notwithstanding."

And the smile faded. It was like watching the sun fading into mist. "We don't treat the meldilanafa with contempt, but we do tend to view them with pity. They belong to no realm and can never be fully at home anywhere."

"Alyra—is she going to live forever?"

"I don't know. Our races can interbreed, but our traits become jumbled. The children of such unions can look like elves but age like men, or age like elves but lack our powers, or look and age like men while keeping the power of an elf. Sometimes they look like us but with the ears and eyes of mortals, or vice versa. Sometimes they lack true immortality but age much more slowly than your people. It's impossible to say."

"How long do nephilim live for?"

"Longer than men. Centuries, if they're not killed. But they do age."

"I guess I'll be in the ground long before anyone else in this crew of ours."

"Don't count on it. Now that there's a nephil abroad in the universe once more, times of turmoil are coming for everyone. As I told you back on Earth, their mere presence tends to attract and excite the supernatural. The fact that Tommy was even conceived at all means that things are moving in the Firmament."

"*Carpe diem*, then."

"Roy. . ." She reached across the table and took my hand. "I'm truly glad that I got to meet you."

"But?"

"But, I'm too old for you."

"How old? I know I shouldn't ask but humor me."

"I'm twenty-six."

"Oh, psssh, that's not such a big—"

"And we measure age in decades."

". . .Oh."

It kind of hit me again, all of a sudden. These were actual elves, from Elf-land, and I was in actual Elf-land, surrounded by elves. This whole thing was insane.

She squeezed my hand. "Are you all right?"

"Yeah, I—no. Not really. You know, older doesn't always mean wiser. As you get older, you get more and more set in your ways, less and less open to change and improvement. I mean, look at this place, for Pete's sake, you don't even have electricity."

"It was I who brought the first light bulb back to Faerie," she said. "I walked your world in Tesla's time." She didn't let go of me, but her tone was different, elevated—the voice of a princess. "We have machines of Earth here, and weapons of Xaxos as well, but we use them only in dire need. We've seen how such possessions enslave their possessors."

I let out a breath. "I'm sorry. I shouldn't have said that." I started to pull away. "I'm sorry."

But she held onto me. "Wait—wait. There's truth in what you said. And I *have* grown stubborn, and proud, with the years."

"Whereas I was like that from the get-go."

"I've noticed." We smiled at each other again, for a moment, and then she gave out a sigh that sounded like a groan and covered her face with her other hand. "Dark days are coming."

"So I gather."

"There's no time for star-crossed love right now."

"Prob'ly right."

"This is asinine! I barely know you."

"Ain't life funny."

She reached over and touched the scruff on my cheek. "You need a shave, Roy Belmont."

"Never kissed a guy with a beard?"

"Not yet."

Then some pointy-eared motherless wretch of a messenger came running into the hall. "Vauksness *afestha!* Ganarlaith *culurmawa vessoth.*"

She jumped up. "Tommy's back. Let's go get Faith."

"Right." I got up and followed her out of the hall. Right. Great. Damn everything anyway.

23

FAITH HELD ME for so long I was starting to think she might not let go. And you know, honestly, I was very okay with that. But, eventually she did let go, and I waved to Alyra, bumped fists with Roy, met a Wood-elf lady called Vala, and looked around and saw that Ganarlaith had already taken off. I didn't feel tired, even after all that walking, but as soon as Alyra asked if I was hungry, my stomach woke up and started rumbling at me.

"The king has food in his chambers. He'll want to see you immediately."

"I remember." I had promised to check in as soon as I got back. I had also promised that, if it worked, I would take his torch and get him his piece of the Flame. "Can you see me?"

She smiled. "With my eyes, yes. But with spirit-magic—well, let's find out. Vala, Faith—would you care to corroborate?"

Vala nodded. Faith looked surprised, but she nodded too. The elf-ladies both murmured some words in elvish and then peered intently at me. Faith took longer to think of a spell, but finally she whispered something—it sounded like English, but I couldn't catch the words—and peered at me as well. Then they all looked at each other and shrugged.

"If you are truly of angel's blood, it is well hidden," Vala said. "Your aura is that of a mortal man."

Roy frowned heavily. "Are you guys sure? He looks exactly the same as before to me."

"Say what?" Faith said sharply.

"Yeah, no difference at all. He's still got a qi like a tank."

"That doesn't make any sense," I said. "Ka breathed magic fog all over me."

"Who's Ka?"

"Wait," Alyra said. "It's not fitting that I should hear this tale before the king does. Come. I think I know why Roy's vision wasn't affected." She led the way back up the stairs from the basement, and we followed. "Roy—when we cast our spells, did you see any change in our auras?"

"Nope."

"Faith, what about you?"

Faith nodded. "I did see kind of a shimmer around you two, after I cast my own spell. Like heat waves."

"I thought as much. What you call qi is the force that binds together the body and the soul, just as the kairos field binds the Vale and the Firmament. Magic is a separate force, arising within the spirit alone and then emanating out through the body. The *raakkk* are forever cut off from the physical world: they have no perception of it whatsoever. All they can see are the souls they wish to corrupt and devour. They can see the power within a nephilic soul like a fire on a dark plain, but the dragon-breath cloaks that power for good, and qi is invisible to them. They have no way of picking Tommy out of a crowd now."

"If they can't see anything but souls, then how does Wingrove get around?" Roy asked.

"When they possess a body, they can use its faculties—clumsily, and temporarily. But their true method of navigation is to sniff out the hidden darkness within the heart of their quarry. Demons hunt by sin."

We all fell silent for a minute or two. By the time I felt like talking again, she was knocking at a big black door and a voice was bidding us to enter. We headed inside, bowed past a couple of guards, and found ourselves in a big suite full of flowers and tapestries. The windows were open, and the rainclouds were drifting away. The moon was a pale, dim fingernail in the sky. Tomorrow it would be gone.

Loryk came toward us, looking tired. "Thomas, my friend. Welcome back to the world above. Zoras has already spoken to me of what little he observed, but I hope to hear a full account from you. Will you take refreshment?"

"Hi, King. Yeah, some food would be great, thank you."

So we all sat down, and I started telling my story, and of course whenever I stopped they would all sit on the edges of their seats and stare at me, so I didn't get to eat until I'd told them everything I could remember about my conversation with Ka. Then they asked me a bunch of questions, and I sat munching away and trying to answer as much as I could with nods and headshakes. Like Ka predicted, Loryk didn't seem surprised by the fact that the dragons were waiting to pick up the old feud right where they left off.

"The worms have no craft," he said. "They keep all thought and memory locked away within their minds—unsung, unetched, unwritten. Therefore, their view of the world is simplistic in the extreme. They have no patience for subtleties. But the minds and hearts of elves delight in subtlety, and thus are laid the seeds of dispute between our peoples. This gap between us could be overcome with patience, but both races are proud and stubborn."

I noticed Roy and Alyra glance at each other when he said that.

"In any case," Loryk concluded, "these burdens are not yours to bear. For the dragon-folk, as for us, a swift response is one that happens within the decade. This matter will not reach its crisis for many years yet. My concern today is for my realm and my people. Will you fulfill the pact we made between us, Thomas Connor?"

"And then Alyra will take us home?" I asked.

"She will. But you will be ever welcome here, as honored guests of Ardmore."

I nodded slowly. "Okay then. Bring me the torch and let's do this thing."

"*Dwenes!*" Loryk called. "*Hulath du samatas.*"

An oddly hunched Mountain-elf came limping out from a nearby room, carrying the Xaxon torch. "*Timoray,*" he said in a low voice.

Loryk stopped when he saw him. "Koshin," he said. "I—did not realize you were here."

Roy gave the Mountain-elf a casual once-over, then shook his head violently before he jumped to his feet and got in front of Faith.

"Demon!" he shouted. "That thing's a demon!"

Everyone got up in a hurry, and the guards came running over with weapons drawn. Loryk stepped toward the guy with the torch—Koshin, I guess—and Alyra stepped in front of him.

"Roy, what are you doing?" she demanded.

"Alyra, that's not an elf. I've seen this energy before, in Wingrove. It's one of *them.*"

"That's impossible. You don't think we scan everyone in this palace for malignant energies before we let them near our king?"

"*What?* Alyra, wake up! It's barely been ten minutes since we established the fact that I can see things you can't."

"Don't be a fool. No dragon would grace a devil with its breath, and there's nothing else that could hide such an obscene power from my sight. Nothing but the spell of a stronger Moon-elf, and only the king himself is stronger in spirit-magic than I am."

There was a sudden pause when she said that. Then Faith raised her hand.

"Your Majesty, you never did tell us how you found out about Tommy. Or the Xaxon torch. Just that you consulted—how did you put it? — 'many strange counselors.' That's a pretty ambiguous phrase."

"Faith," Alyra hissed. "How dare you? Are you all insane?"

"Loryk *Chodan*," said a voice. We all spun toward the door, and there was Zoras Ganarlaith with an iron stick in either hand. He started to say something else in elvish, but I was getting tired of not knowing what was going on. I stomped a foot as hard as I could, and the whole room shook, and a vase fell off a shelf with a shattering crash.

"English," I said. "You wanna speak around me, you speak English."

Ganarlaith's eyes flicked down to the floor at my foot. The diamond was cracked. "King Loryk," he said. "As you know, I have no gift for the weavings of the spirit. If Lady Alyra sees no demon, then I am content that no demon is here. However—this Mountain-elf, Koshin Varaukos, has greatly changed in these past few weeks. I know my soldiers, and he was once a stalwart fighter. His only fault, if fault you call it, was too great a yearning for strength and glory in combat. But lately, since the turning of the leaves, he has grown slothful and bitter, and yet stronger in body than ever before. Could it not be possible—."

"Peace, old friend," Loryk interrupted. "Koshin has been aiding me of late in a clandestine project. Perhaps the labor has taken its toll on him. But this is no time to discuss such matters. As to your question, Faith—I have indeed consulted many sources, and many of them are beyond your knowledge and perhaps beyond your very comprehension. Because you are my guest, I will not take your implication as a deliberate insult, but I ask you to remember your place while in my house."

She scowled at him. "That's a lot different from saying, 'No, I haven't spoken with any demons.' Ka said you won't lie but you'll still deceive. Is she right?"

Loryk's voice got louder, and Ganarlaith's got quieter, and they both started berating Faith for her rudeness, but I missed the next few sentences because Koshin was staring at me while licking his lips. Something about the guy sent a weird shiver down my spine. I held his gaze, and his lips slowly pulled back from his teeth.

"Ha," he said. "Ha, Your Majesty, it may be that I have, ha ha, disconcerted your guests. I shall withdraw. Here is the hee hee, the torch of the Xaxon folk."

"You're not going anywhere, pal," Roy said grimly.

"Do not even think to threaten violence in the king's chambers, creature of dust," Ganarlaith practically whispered.

Koshin passed the torch to King Loryk and slunk out of the room. Roy glared after him, then jabbed a finger at the torch. "And *that* thing. That thing's giving off qi, just like that stabilizer from Surtex that your uncle was waving around." He turned and gave me an accusing look. "I don't think the elves are the only ones that aren't playing it straight with us."

That came all the way out of left field. I gaped at him. "Huh? You think Uncle Syme is mixed up in this?"

"I don't know what to think. Everything made sense until you showed up."

"Hey, this isn't Tommy's fault," Faith said angrily. "You're just looking for some reason to blame him."

"What's that supposed to mean?"

"I've known you my whole life. You think I can't tell when you're jealous of someone?"

"I'm not—" He stopped. "You know what, fine, maybe I am. I've worked my *ass* off for the skills I have, and then this guy comes along ten times stronger than I'll ever be, without even doing a single push-up. It's not fair."

"And what good would all that hard work have done, if you just happened to be born with cerebral palsy? Or no legs? Or parents who didn't support you in everything you do? You started out with advantages too."

"My advantages didn't bring down murderers on our heads."

"Um, no offense taken," I said.

"Look, I'm sorry, but the first time you went all angelic, you nearly ripped me limb from limb. You know in the Bible, every time an angel appears to a human being, the first thing it has to say is, 'Don't be afraid.' Now why do you think that is?"

"Okay, now I'm starting to take offense. You think I don't remember the clock tower? The only reason I attacked you is because you kept running after me and kicking me in the face."

"What?" Faith shouted. "Gee, Roy, you never mentioned that part of the story."

"He was tearing the whole building down!"

"Like you really care about town landmarks. You were looking for a fight, weren't you? You want to know what my dad says about you?"

"Oh yeah, what's that?"

"He says you're the best fighter he's ever seen, but you'll never be a true warrior until you learn to fight for something bigger than your own ego."

"Sounds like his usual Zen crap."

She went from angry to furious. "Oh, you mean like the existence of qi? *That* kind of Zen crap? If it weren't for my dad—"

From out in the hallway there came the blast of an explosion. The door rattled in its frame, and the sound of screams came pouring into the room. There was a rush of feet and the roar of more explosions, and a voice cried, "*Xaxoné! Xaxoné filiu* Vissarion *Severothis!*"

Didn't need to know elvish to get that. Xaxons in the Spire of Vissarion.

24

I love Roy, but right then I could have cheerfully pulled his head off his neck. I'd never been so angry with him in my life. To be fair, it was a stressful situation and everybody's tempers were pretty high—but the "Zen crap" remark put me way past the point of being fair. I was just about to go from shouting into all-out screaming when sudden chaos erupted in the hall.

Ganarlaith and the guards lunged past me and clustered around the king like Secret Service agents, babbling in elvish. Roy and Tommy stepped between me and the door. Vala, who had been present but very silent during all the yelling, ran over and stood next to me. Alyra darted into an adjacent room. And while all that was happening— it only took a second or two—I was getting hit with a revelation.

"Koshin," I said. "He let them in."

"Too bad we let him leave, *Zoras*," Roy said.

The elves ignored him. They were brandishing their weapons at the door, waiting for something to come barreling through. Loryk had no sword, but I noticed a short silver stylus in his hand. *The Pen of the Varodrim, I presume.*

There was a crash at the door, and it staggered open a little ways. A pair of gleaming white eyes appeared in the gap, staring at us. My head stayed clear, but a scalding rush of fear swept up from my feet through my body. I ignored it and began to summon up a spell of fire.

"Roy!" Alyra's voice called from behind us. He turned and she tossed him a two-foot metal rod with a handle and trigger on the end. "Only in dire need, remember?"

"I'm holding a space gun," he said under his breath. It looked very similar to the sort of thing you might see any human soldier carrying back on Earth. He raised it and took aim at the eyes in the doorway.

"Wait," Loryk commanded. Then he drew himself up and called out to the—to whatever was on the other side of the door. It was in a strange, furry, chittering kind of language. The thing with the eyes responded with a series of clicks and squeals and gnashing teeth. It made me feel like rats were scurrying up my pant legs. "They will not negotiate. They demand our immediate surrender."

"*Thevis taa*," Vala muttered, and flexed her hands into claws. No one seemed to feel inclined to surrender.

A second later, a blinding white flash came through the door and hit Tommy right in the chest. I screamed, Roy opened fire, and Tommy said,

"Ow." Vala and two of the guards started hurling balls of flame, and another guard took a running step forward and hurled a javelin through the widening gap. The Xaxons fired another bolt at us; this time Loryk himself somehow smothered it in midair with a wave of his pen.

Then Ganarlaith started chanting, and the floor swirled around us like a diamond whirlpool. We all dropped through to the room below, and the ceiling re-solidified above us. "They will be upon us again in moments," he said. "Nephil, I must protect my king. Will you hold this floor behind us?"

Tommy turned and looked him in the eye. There was a smoking hole in the middle of his shirt, but his skin was unmarked. "Your king's more important than my friends?"

"My king cannot survive their weapons. You can. If you wish, your friends can come with us."

In the same breath, Roy and I said, "Forget it."

"I ask only that you win us one or two minutes," Ganarlaith said, ignoring us. "Tommy— this is my duty. Is there nothing for which you would give your own life?"

Somehow, they seemed to understand each other. "Go. I'll slow them down."

"Thank you." He chanted again, and the floor began to swirl.

"Alyra," said Loryk. "*Azhasa Xaxoné lak, astatha* Thomas *giyas fenneth* Voor."

She looked confused, but she nodded. "*Sa, Loryk Chodan.*" She took a step toward us as the king and his guards dropped through to the next room down, and the floor hardened behind her. Vala stayed with us as well, so that made five of us against who knew how many aliens.

"Is there any way we can get back up there and shut their door?" Roy asked.

Alyra shook her head. "Let the legions worry about that. They'll be coming shortly. Our job is to buy time for Loryk. Come on." She led the way into the hall. "Only one staircase leads down from the floor above. We can hold them here." She and Vala nodded to each other. "Faith—are you ready to weave?"

"Yeah."

"Good, then open your mind to me. I can strengthen the spells that you and Vala cast."

"Okay?"

"You'll feel it happening. Just don't fight it."

"Okay."

Footsteps on the stairs. Roy dropped to a knee and took aim with his Xaxon rifle. My elves and I pressed back against the walls and started mumbling magic words. Tommy just stood there in the middle of the hall with his hands at his sides. *Please, God*, I thought, and then there were Xaxons.

They were small in stature, not more than four feet tall, and they wore no clothes or armor. They looked a bit like bears, but even more like giant squirrels on their hind legs. If I'd seen a picture of them, I might have called them cute, but in person there was might and dignity in them that even the elves could scarcely match.

The first one down the stairs paused when he saw us and chittered something. Alyra chittered back, and the Xaxon slowly spread a huge pair of wings from his back, raised his weapon, and took aim. We were less than thirty feet away, and I had a fleeting memory of old Civil War pictures I'd seen: boys, children, standing out in the open and firing muskets into each other's teeth.

Then Tommy lunged forward. The hallway lit up with the blasts of their rifles. This time I didn't scream; I stepped up and howled words of inferno, and Vala with me. Alyra put her hands on our shoulders and sang out in her sweet elvish tongue, and I could feel the force doubling and tripling inside of me. I opened myself to her, my sister from beyond the universe. Her energy was kerosene on my soul. The fear was gone: I was power and rage and fire.

Tommy pushed his way up the wide staircase, simply grabbing the Xaxons and throwing them back the way they'd come. Vala and I launched twin columns of flame past him on either side as Roy continued blasting away. After a few seconds, the Xaxons pulled back and there was a tense lull in the fighting. Tommy came back down and stood with us again. His entire shirt was gone now, and steam was rising from his lean torso. His fists were clenched, and he was breathing hard; I'd never seen him angry before.

"Are you okay?"

"I'm fine," he said through his teeth. "I don't like these guys."

We heard trampling footsteps behind us and whirled around. Loryk's legionnaires were coming down the hall, bristling with swords and spears and Xaxon rifles. Alyra called out in elvish and pointed up the stairs. They nodded to her and went rumbling by us.

"Can the soldiers hold them off?" I asked.

Alyra's face was grim. "They can keep them from following us down the stairs. But if the Xaxons want to invade Ardmore, all they need is a window."

Right—wings.

"They've got the high ground now," Roy said harshly. "They can bottleneck your men just like we did to them."

"No," Vala said. "You saw what Captain Ganarlaith did to the floor. Our soldiers can attack them from a hundred directions at once."

"So, it comes down to how many of their people can get into the air before the guards find their door and close it," I said.

Alyra closed her eyes. "No enemy from the Vale has invaded Faerie since. . ."

"Since what?"

"Since the last of the nephilim perished."

"Dark days," Roy muttered.

There was another explosion in the distance. "That came from outside," I said.

"They're on the ground," Tommy said. "We should get down there."

More explosions from below. We raced down the stairs, passing more and more soldiers on their way up. At one point we passed a window, and I could see hundreds of winged forms sailing down from the tower above us. The city beyond was on fire.

As we came out into the courtyard, Alyra pointed toward the open gates. "We have to get to the boats. Follow me." We sprinted for the exit.

A titanic serpent landed in front of us. It was coiled in on itself, but it must have been fifty feet long, and it had six pairs of wings along the length of its undulating body. It was a pale, dusty no-color, and its eyes were grey pinpoints; but when it grinned at us, its fangs were scarlet. I could hear it in my head, but it wasn't talking to me.

Hello again, Tommy.

"Ka? What are you doing?"

I truly did not expect matters to erupt so quickly. Even thy bloodiest ancestors did not stir up warfare with such speed. I'm impressed.

"What? This isn't me. This is the Xaxons."

We know nothing of Xaxons.

"What is the meaning of this?" Alyra shouted. "How dare you enter Ardmore unbidden?"

The giant head swiveled toward her, and a long pink tongue flickered out. *Hast thou forgotten our treaty, elf maid? Thy king has vowed that he shall raise no strife upon this mountain. Didst thou think we would not hear the clamor of battle in our caves?*

"This strife is no doing of ours, idiot reptile! We are attacked!"

Indeed thou art.

Roy took aim at the dragon's head. "Maybe you should get out of our way. Thou knowest not with whom thou messest."

Ka hunched in on herself and then streaked into the air, rising hundreds of feet in the blink of an eye. Far above, she circled once and then headed out over the city. Xaxons were still pouring from the Spire overhead, and more dragons went sailing by as we stood gazing upwards. One of them, a jet-black worm as big as a freight train, opened its mouth and scorched the citadel with lightning.

"This is their excuse," Alyra said quietly. "They'll blame Loryk for bringing war to Mount Voor and that's all they need to justify attacking us."

"The boats," said Vala. "Come, Lady Alyra, the king gave us orders."

She nodded slowly. "Yes."

We headed out through the gate and found raging bedlam in the streets beyond. There were Xaxons everywhere, wielding rifles and rocket launchers, blowing holes in every house they came to. Elves were swarming out of the surrounding buildings, slinging spells of ice and flame and rock, weaving gales out of the still air, swinging blades and staffs or returning fire with Xaxon guns. A few of them were even firing what looked like American M-16s.

In the air above us, Xaxon raiders were swooping by and hurling explosives at the elven heads below, and above them, the night sky was filling up with dragons. Fire and lightning and boiling venom rained down indiscriminately, slaughtering elf and alien alike. Smoke filled the air, and twisted corpses littered the earth.

"This way," Alyra said, and led us right into the thick of the fray. Vala wove a roof of billowing flames over our heads, and Roy laid down suppressing fire. Tommy went ahead of us with his forearms crossed over his face, absorbing stray blasts from passing Xaxons. With all the combat happening around us, no one paid our group any special attention. We ran and ducked and fought our way through about half a mile of the city, and then we were at our destination.

It was a squat, two-story building right on the edge of the river, and like every other building in every direction, it was burning. Alyra dashed inside with us at her heels, and we saw that the floor was only a series of walkways over a large eddying tidal pool filled with boats. They were long and slender, azure and carven with swan-like figureheads. They had neither sails nor oarlocks; I wondered how we were supposed to steer them upriver.

Alyra jumped into the nearest boat. "Tommy!" she shouted, pointing at the outer doors. He ran over and shoved them open—it must have ordinarily taken at least ten people to do that—and then leapt back into the boat with the rest of us. Vala drew a short blade and severed the mooring rope, and we drifted out into the current.

"Now let's hope they don't spot us for the next sixty seconds," Alyra said.

The River of Roses swept us along and the battle unrolled all around us on the nearby banks. One of the dragons wheeled overhead and came soaring down at us, breathing out a long pillar of frost that turned the wine at our stern into drifting shelves of ice. Just before its breath caught up with us, Roy blew a hole in its skull. The vast slithering bulk crashed into the river a few yards behind our boat and came floating after us as if the dragon's corpse now sought revenge. Ahead of us loomed Mellifast, the Great Wine-fall.

"Hey, Alyra?" Tommy said in a very calm voice. "Did you notice that we're going the wrong way?"

"We're going the right way, my friend. Hang on."

Roy squeezed his eyes shut. "Ohhhhh, crap."

I had just enough time to drop and curl into a ball on the deck. And then we went hurtling over the falls and plunging into the empty air beyond.

25

Surtex Industries opened its doors in 1965. Back then, it was just one man: Norman Grey, founder and CEO of what has since become a multi-national, multi-billion-dollar corporation. We started out designing airplane parts for other companies, and rapidly expanded to handling our own distribution and finally our own manufacturing. The first plant still stands in Vigrid, North Carolina. The real breakthrough came in the '70s when we began consulting for NASA. We're now one of the chief global authorities on space-craft design.

When Karen Connor came to me with her child, I was nearly thirty-five and still had no path in life. I had gone to school for philosophy, switched majors once or twice, and ended up teaching high school literature in Connecticut. It was a reasonably fulfilling station in the world, and I had no clear ideas on what else one would do with oneself; it did trouble me somewhat that I hadn't chosen the teacher's life but had simply washed up on the shore of it. Still, I might have done a great deal worse. But when Tommy came into my life, I suddenly needed a much more lucrative job and had no especially "grown-up" notions about how to find one. I had about three weeks of mounting anxiety as

I scrabbled through phone books and newspapers in search of someone looking to pay a princely sum to the least qualified man they could find. An employer with a free day care in the back room would also have been acceptable.

Then one day, two men in suits came to my front door. They said they represented Surtex Industries and were looking to hire an efficiency manager, and that my name had come up. Now, I had heard the name Surtex once or twice and had some vague conception of what they did, but I had absolutely no connection with anyone associated with that company. I pressed them for details on how they had heard of me, and they eventually divulged that one of my students was related to a Surtex higher-up and had spoken so favorably of me that the higher-up in question had decided to offer me a job. However—he wished to remain anonymous.

Please believe that I was as skeptical of this tale as you. It wasn't until they explained the salary and benefits of the position that my doubts began to fade.

"This position opened up quite unexpectedly," one of the men said. "It's a once-in-a-lifetime chance."

Perhaps? Perhaps some benevolent power had taken a moment to bless with me with a much-needed lucky break. I overcame my suspicions and signed with them that same week; I've been with Surtex ever since. I turned out to be surprisingly good at my job and I take pride in it. I've even met Mr. Grey a few times at luncheons and seminars around the country. I laid my suspicions to rest a long time ago, and I consider myself a company man.

On Friday morning, the day after the children disappeared, I was sitting at my desk. I was tapping a pencil on a pad on paper, and every few minutes I would check my phone. I'd had a sleepless night and it looked like being an unproductive day.

But Tommy could take care of himself. He was a strong one, that boy. Strong in his will and that uncanny innocence of his. Whatever came at him, he'd wade through it somehow. And he'd watch over his friends, too. They would be fine. I could still finish the forms for the new modem upgrades. No use in worrying. Tommy could take care of himself.

And so it went, in circles in my head. I leaned back, sipped my coffee and gazed at the ceiling in wordless supplication. And at that moment, the door of my office opened.

"Hard at work, I see," said a frail, feathery voice.

I looked over, and then jumped to my feet. "Mr. Grey! Please, come in."

He shuffled over to my desk and sat down across from me. Outside in the hall I could see the hulking forms of his two bodyguards, reputedly ex-Israeli special forces.

Grey himself was a small, birdlike fellow in his early eighties, given to long pauses and sudden movements. He didn't smile or shake hands, but he was still a commanding presence in a room. You could feel the dynamic quality that had made him such a force in his chosen field, even though he was so spectrally thin that you could almost see the light through his neck.

He peered at me. "It's been a few years, hasn't it, Syme?"

I sat back down. "I believe so, sir. We last spoke in person at the unveiling of the new plant in Texas."

"Quite right. Quite right. Well. I was in the neighborhood on business, and I've just heard the news about your boy Tommy. Wanted to say I'm sorry."

"Oh! —thank you, sir." Who in the world would have mentioned such a thing to Norman Grey? "I'm sure they'll be fine."

"Let us hope so. A man's life means nothing without a legacy."

"Yes."

"About Tommy. He's a senior this year, isn't he?"

"He's a junior, sir."

"Ah yes, of course. Has he given any thought to what he'll be doing after high school?"

"No more than the usual amount," I said, and smiled slightly. "Possibly even less. I believe he plans to go on to college and trip over his destiny there."

He gave a sharp nod. "You see too much of that these days, don't you? Young people leaving everything to chance. Not considering the future."

"I'm sure that's nothing new to this generation. And Tommy always lands on his feet."

"Again, let us hope. That's a talented boy. It would be a shame if he squandered himself on an ordinary path."

I could feel my brow furrowing. Grey had never met Tommy. And the few times he'd met me, we had talked mostly of corporate strategies and baseball scores. "Well, ah—I do appreciate that."

"Indeed. Perhaps once he's home safe again, you might mention to him that a number of intern positions have been opening up. He might enjoy some part-time work, and if he distinguishes himself, he might also have a salaried job waiting for him once he graduates. I need hardly tell you what a rare opportunity that is for a young man, Syme. The chance of a lifetime."

"That is very generous, Mr. Grey. I don't suppose you extend such courtesy to every employee of this corporation."

"No, I don't."

"I wonder what specific qualities about Tommy caught your eye. He's a bright young man, but not a phenomenal student."

Grey leaned forward so quickly that it looked as if he'd been hit with a cattle prod. His face was intent, but not threateningly so. "I assure you that I want only the best for your nephew. He has extraordinary capabilities, and we can help him to develop them to their fullest. If you haven't yet seen what I'm speaking of, then I suspect you soon will."

I leaned forward as well, slowly, and held his eyes across the desk. "You will please tell me from whom you received these reports."

His hand snapped up over his shoulder, as if tossing the whole subject away. "I have many eyes. We take care of our own here, Syme. You've been with us seventeen years, and that earns you some personal attention in a time of stress."

When he said, "We take care of our own," the serene intensity of his tone—the tone of a man stating a conviction too profound for momentary agitations—convinced me that *that* part, at least, was the truth. And in my experience, Surtex was quite generous with its workers. But now the old doubts were beginning to percolate once again: why was *I* one of their workers? I had no more prior knowledge of my own field than Tommy would have of whatever field they wanted him for. Their pursuit of me made as little sense as their pursuit of him. Unless he was somehow the reason, all the way back then, that I had ended up here in the first place.

"Well," said Grey. I realized I'd been staring silently at him for longer than a conversational pause allows. "It's up to you, of course. Deal's on the table." He got up shakily, and I stood up as well. I couldn't think of anything to say. "I'm sure he'll be home before you know it. We'll talk later."

"Yes, sir," I said, and he made his way out of the room. I lowered myself back into my chair and rubbed my hands over my face.

What in the fires of Hell is going on here?

26

I WASN'T AFRAID of heights until the moment we went over the falls. But in that second, when the whole of Faerie opened up below and I saw the far-off clouds come rushing up at us, I discovered that being high up was the worst possible thing in the universe. The roar of the wind and the roar of the wine filled my head, and I couldn't even hear myself screaming.

Reflexively, I grabbed the side of the boat, even though it was falling as fast as I was. My hand crushed the dense wood into splinters as I hung there in the rushing air with my feet barely brushing the deck. The fog of the clouds was all around us, whipping by, and then we were falling and falling toward the distant countryside beneath. I saw an eagle's nest on an outcropping as we shot past at terminal velocity. Above us, plummeting grimly along, was the dragon Roy had killed. Our prow touched the wine from time to time, kicking up spray, as if we were a stone that someone had skipped vertically down the falls.

I ran out of air to scream with, but we were still falling. I struggled to take a breath from the howling winds. The ground was getting close now, and I'd run out of panic. I looked over and saw Faith curled up on the deck, though it was now almost perpendicular to her and she was just floating alongside. I hurled myself on top of her and covered her body with my own. She clutched at me, and I held her as close as I could. I knew that even if I survived this, she wouldn't.

Then the angle of our fall started to change. More wine-spray came flying over the sides than before, and our descent became a very, very gradual curve. After a moment, I stuck my head up and squinted into the driving foam coming over the prow. We were going down an incline, a smooth slow incline over a mile long, and I could see ahead that it continued in an easy curve way out into the plains. Instead of falling straight downwards and smashing onto the rocks at the bottom, we were coming out of freefall and sliding down a stretch of river like a ramp that would put us back on a horizontal setting without splattering us across the foot of Mount Voor.

We kept flying downhill, but the wind got slower and the ride got smoother, and the deck got more and more solid underneath us. A minute later, we were gliding down the final curve and splashing into level fluid. The boat slowed, and the clamor of the rapids faded behind us. A minute after that, we all started breathing again.

"How's about," Roy gasped, "how's about next time you give us a little warning, huh?"

"Yeah," I wheezed.

"Forgive me, my friends," Alyra panted. "There wasn't time to explain. The ground at the foot of Mellifast is made of diamond and has never been worn away by the falls. Our earth-weavers were able to fashion it into a chute so that we could sail our ships down the Wine-fall if we had to escape from Ardmore. It's been many years since we last needed it."

Faith sat up. "Is everyone okay?" she asked.

We all patted ourselves down. Vala had bumped her head and was bleeding a bit, but the rest of us were unhurt apart from scrapes and bruises. Faith reached outside the boat and wetted her sleeve and dabbed at Vala's forehead with it.

"Okay," Roy said. "So, we're out of the city. What's next? Is there a plan? What did Loryk say to you back there before we split up?"

"Peace," Alyra said. "He told me to take Tommy to the foot of Mount Voor. There's an old Sea-elf named Ratoska who lives by the falls, and Loryk sometimes goes to him for advice. The king will meet us there."

"We should disembark soon, Lady Alyra," Vala said.

"Yes." She leaned over the side of the boat, dipped her hands into the flowing wine and sang awhile in elvish. The boat started to drift in the direction of her hands, like she was pulling us by an invisible cable to the shore, and after a minute or so we ran aground on the riverbank. As we got out, I went to a knee and dug my fingers into the earth. Roy and Faith did the same.

"Come," Alyra said. "The sooner we find Ratoska, the better."

We headed back toward Voor on foot. Because of the length of the ramp and the speed of the current, we'd been carried two or three miles away from the mountain. No one spoke as we walked along. I tried to process everything that had happened in the last hour, and I decided I'd need to take some time later on, when the shock wore off a bit. I hated fighting with Roy.

The terrain got steeper, and much harder, as we came to the diamond ramp. Alyra brought us all the way up to the last point where the falls were coming straight down, just as the long curve began. There, on a wide shelf of diamond, a simple straw hut stood an arm's length from the great crash of falling wine. As we approached, the front door opened and a blue-skinned elf in a robe walked out. He didn't look old, but he was leaning on a staff. I wondered if elves got arthritis after a few thousand years.

"*Bairka*, Vauksness *afestha*," said the Sea-elf. His voice sounded kindly but grave.

She dipped her head in a quick bow. "*Bairka*, Ratoska *floma*. These are my friends from

Earth—Tommy, Roy, and Faith—and this my kinswoman, Vala Farlonn. Has the king arrived?"

"Not yet. But the Wine-fall has brought me tidings of the battle overhead." Even as he said that, a body went tumbling by. "Come—let us step inside."

We followed him into his circular hut. It was a small space, maybe twenty feet around, with a simple mat on the floor and a small stack of books next to it. Leaning against one wall was another, shorter staff, and a spare robe was neatly folded at the foot of the bed. That was it. I guess if you wanted a place to be alone and meditate, the bottom of a super-giant waterfall was as good a spot as any.

"Why did we split up with the king if we're just meeting him here anyway?" Roy asked.

"He didn't say. My guess is that he was heading for the Fane. It's a vault in the depths of the keep, where we store our greatest treasures when they're not being used. One such treasure is the king's keys. He can open doors that no one else can."

"Why didn't you just zap us down here with *your* keys?" Faith demanded.

"First of all, I don't have them on me. Mine, like Loryk's, rest in the Fane when I'm not using them. And secondly, I can only open the door that we came through on Wednesday night. I don't have the power to open any door in Faerie unless the king lifts the spell that protects us from—Xaxon invasion."

"So, they couldn't have gotten in without his help," Roy said. "Just like the demon inside of Koshin couldn't have stayed hidden without his help."

Alyra breathed very deeply. "Roy, what you're saying is absurd. Apart from the fact that Loryk has far more honor than to deal in such a way, it doesn't make sense for him to harm his own kingdom."

"Unless he was trying to help the kingdom," Faith said. "Maybe he was getting secret information from a demon. Maybe he gave it a set of keys and a door that no one else in Faerie could open. A private door just outside the king's own chambers. But when Koshin saw that Tommy's aura had been cloaked, he realized Loryk had double-crossed him, and *that's* why he let in the aliens."

"Nice." Roy offered a fist, and she bumped it with her own.

"This is madness!" Alyra shouted.

"My lady," Vala said quietly. "Is there any chance, however small, that what they say could be true?"

"No. Never."

The door opened again, and Loryk walked into the hut. Behind him were Ganarlaith and three guards, and behind them were flames and the sounds of battle. The noise cut off instantly when he closed the door.

"Ratoska *floma*," he said, bowing slightly.

"Loryk *Chodan*."

"My friends, I'm pleased to see you all made it here unscathed."

"Vala hit her head," Faith said.

"I see. Forgive me. It would have been safer for you if we could have stayed in one group, but I had to obtain my keys. Tommy—I fear that our time has run out. We must go into the Firmament immediately."

"My lord," Ratoska said. "Is this a proper time to sail the Shoreless Sea?"

"The what?" I asked.

"It's what Sea-elves call the kairos field," Alyra said.

"Oh. I think I like their way better."

"We have no choice, Ratoska," Loryk said. "Our land is assailed. Only with the power of the Flame itself can we withstand our enemies."

"But we do not know how long the passage will take. The city could be rubble by the time you return."

"What do you mean?" Roy asked. "How long could it possibly take to run in, stick the torch in the fire, and run back out?"

"Remember when we crossed over from the Vale?" Alyra said. "Travel within a given realm—say, from here to Windismere—is instantaneous; but when you pass between worlds, you step out of the flow of time. If we spend five minutes crossing into the Firmament, hours or even days might be passing here in Faerie."

"Our fighters have seized the door by which the invaders entered our realm," Ganarlaith put in. "That threat is ended for now or will be once we round up all the enemy soldiers still at large."

"Why would the Xaxons send in such a small force?" Roy said. "They must have known you guys would be able to shut the door on them."

"It was not a conquering army," Loryk replied. "Perhaps they hoped to re-take their torch. Or perhaps they simply wished to sow terror among us."

"What about the dragons?" I said.

"We have dealt with them before," said Ganarlaith. "Their attacks are destructive, but haphazard. They lack discipline. Our soldiers can hold Mount Voor without reinforcements for an entire year if necessary."

"Great!" Faith said in a chipper voice. "I guess that answers all our questions. Oh, wait, there was just one other little thing, Your Highness: how's your deal with the *raakkk* working out for you?"

The guards bristled and fingered their weapons. But I noticed that Ganarlaith turned and looked at Loryk instead of glaring at Faith like the others. His expression was neutral (like always), but he did seem interested in hearing a response. There was a long pause.

"Loryk," Alyra said softly. "Loryk *Chodan, utuvien salthor*—"

The king held up a hand for silence.

"It may be that I have done ill. I knew the worms were stirring once again from their slumber. I knew the Xaxons were edging closer to our borders. I knew that strange powers were abroad in the universe. And I was desperate for my people." He met Alyra's gaze. "Yes, I sought knowledge among the fallen ones. It was they who taught me the purpose of the Xaxon torch."

Her eyes closed.

"In return, I promised them a boon at some future time. And then, only last week, the Seer of Kalamorn contacted me and told me she had sensed the presence of a nephil in the Vale. The one who was Koshin Varaukos came to me that same day and demanded his boon. I vowed to lead the nephil to the edges of their domain so they would have a chance to capture him; and that vow I shall keep, for the outer gate of the Firmament lies at the very brink of the Void. However—I never promised that

I would not help you as well, Tommy. Now that you have been bathed in dragon's breath, you can dance at the boundaries of their place of exile and they will never be able to sense you. Koshin saw this, and that is why he betrayed me and let the Xaxons into my city."

"Called it," Faith said under her breath.

"Come on, you weren't helping Tommy," Roy said. "You just didn't want him to get eaten by demons before he had a chance to come back with your precious Flame."

"My soul bears the weight of every life in this world, Belmont," the king said darkly. "You cannot imagine such a burden. I alone am responsible for the elvish race, and I will not let them suffer. If I have erred, it is because I sought a way out of the stalemates that entangle us—a way to bring true peace to my land. Such things cannot be achieved without cost."

"Aw, you're breakin' my heart. It's like a friggin' telethon in here."

"My king," Alyra said, almost pleading. "The oath of the throne—you have sworn never to consort with unclean spirits."

"I have sworn never to *summon* such spirits. Koshin came to me on his own initiative."

"Wow," I said. "Ka was right about you. I'm not sure I'm comfortable handing you the power of creation, or whatever this torch thing does."

"You made a promise of your own, Thomas Connor. All this ruin has come down upon my land because I kept my pact with you—because I taught you to shield yourself from the sight of the darkness. Now you will honor your end of the bargain."

"Or what?"

"Or nothing. We will raise no hand against you. You and your friends will be free to walk out of this hut and wander the trackless wilderness of Faerie, hunted by demons and abandoned by the elves, until death finds you in whatever form it chooses."

"So that *is* why you brought me and Roy," Faith said. "As leverage on Tommy."

Alyra stared at her. "What? No! Roy, please—I swear to you, I knew nothing of this."

Roy gazed at the ground. "Whatever. I'm tired of this place. Let's just get the stupid Flame and go home."

"Sure," I said. "But there's one other thing first." With one hand, I grabbed Loryk by the collar and lofted him into the air. The guards hustled forward and started pricking me with spearpoints, shouting at me to put him down. I ignored them. "The next time you threaten my friends, I will personally hand you to over to the frost dragons. Do you understand?" He didn't answer, so I shook him. I was really mad. "Do you understand?!"

"I do," he said. His voice was totally even, like he was accepting an offer of tea.

"Fine." I dropped him back on his feet. "Then let's finish this."

"King Loryk," Ratoska said, "I ask you to re-consider your course. If the darkness suggested this plan to you, then it must be bent in some way, and sure to lead you to an abyss."

"Their knowledge is great," Loryk said, just a bit sharply, "but their wit has limits. They did not reckon with dragon's breath. If we act quickly, we can pass over the Void and be gone before they ever have a chance to distinguish us from the marching dead."

"And what is that?" asked Ganarlaith. He still didn't show much on his face, but he was radiating disapproval. I suspected that Loryk would have some explaining to do when this was all over.

"The lyrilim believed that the marching dead are the souls of all who have perished in recent days. They find themselves at the near side of the Great Bridge over the Void and must cross it to reach the Firmament. At the far side, they shall pass through the Flame and be purified for whatever eternity awaits them. We who still draw breath will stop there only for a moment, and the nephil will fulfill his covenant with us. Then we will return and end this war."

"You have a key to the Firmament itself," Alyra said. "In all these years, you've never told me."

"There are two keys," Loryk said. He didn't sound apologetic. "They must be used in conjunction or the door will shatter. Ratoska has guarded the second key for many winters."

Ratoska clung to his staff as if his knees were failing him. "Please, Your Majesty—"

"Enough! Ardmore is *burning!* If ever you loved this land, heed me now. Open the door, Ratoska."

The old elf gave such a long sigh that it sounded like he was deflating.

"I cannot refuse my king," he said wearily. He glanced at us. "Be prepared, friends. When you set foot upon the Great Bridge, you will be directly over the Void, and you will hear its call in your inmost hearts. Hearken not to its voice." Then he muttered a few words and passed his hands over the earth.

The diamond floor opened, and he pulled out a small ebony box. Inside was a ring with just three keys on it, and a tiny bundle like a crumpled-up napkin. He gave the bundle to Alyra, then headed outside with the keys and closed the door behind him.

Loryk produced a keyring of his own, with way more keys than Alyra's had. He handed the torch to Ganarlaith and then stepped over and inserted a key into the lock. We heard a rattle from outside as Ratoska did the same. "Prepare," Loryk said loudly. "Let us turn them—*now*."

The door opened. Beyond it was nothing but a dark space; it was tough to tell if there was even a ground. Not that it mattered at this point. The dark space was growing all around us, and that dizzy echoing sensation was starting up again. At least this time I was ready for it.

Right before everything went fuzzy, Roy heaved a reverberating sigh. "Hey, Tommy? I take back what I said up there. None of this is your fault."

"Thanks, Roy."

I think he said something else, but I couldn't hear anymore. I couldn't see. Couldn't feel. Back in the dark again, floating. And then it started whispering inside me.

27

Roy Belmont: Get out of my head.

The Voice of the Void: Your doors are open. We waited for you.

RB: You don't know me.

VV: We smell the blood. We taste the blood.

RB: What blood?

VV: You killed today. First kill. Not your last.

RB: The dragon. It would have—I was protecting my friends. I know it was a person. I didn't want to kill it.

VV: Of course you did. Crush the enemy. Kill the enemy.

RB: I don't have any enemies.

VV: Yes. Lie more to us. We chew on lies. We gnaw, gnaw forever on lies.

RB: I don't have enemies! None of us do. Everyone wants us dead, and we haven't done anything.

VV: To exist is to feed on others. To live is to kill. Why do you fear to kill? You have strength. Strength is crushing others.

RB: Yeah? Because a lot of people I trust have told me that real strength is helping others. 'Matter of fact, my sensei says that moderate strength is shown in violence, but supreme strength in levity. Makes a lot of sense to me.

VV: Sensei's daughter will be tied down by your enemies. Pretty little Faith, tied down and cut with blades of steel, cut till she screams, cut till she weeps blood. And then the rape and the screaming and the blood and the laughing enemies that rape and rape and rape. You could have stopped all that. You could have killed them before.

RB: You don't know what you're talking about. No one cares about me or Faith. They're after someone else.

VV: Angel man. Steel man. Steel blades won't cut him. Have to cut little Faith instead. Sweet Faith, pretty Faith. Screaming Faith, begging Faith, raping Faith, breaking Faith forever. Everyone will cut her. Everyone will rape her.

RB: You bastards, if anyone touches her—

VV: Yes, kill for us. Crush them. Spill them. Lap their spurting marrow.

RB: I'll do nothing for you. And believe this: if I get a chance to touch any of you, I will crush you into absolute nothingness.

VV: We *are* nothingness. We fear nothing now. We have endured death and Hell and oblivion. We are eternity. Eternity is nothingness. Eternity is Hell. Behold, you pass into the higher realms and what do you find? You find us. Can you doubt that Hell is forever and ever and everywhere?

RB: I doubt anything you say. My mom told me about you. She said there's no such thing as pure Evil.

VV: We know her. We remember her. She was pretty once. The machetes changed her. The guns and the men with guns made her less than she was. She escaped that country, that country where we roamed free, but we will find her again. She will welcome us. Welcome the cutting and the cutting and the cutting. Just like her sister did.

RB: You. . . I swear to God I will find a way to kill you.

VV: There is no death. There is only suffering. She will not die. Faith will not die. Their bodies will die. Then the screaming will begin. They will scream forever. You will watch. You will die, and watch, and scream as well. Forever.

RB: This is crap. You've got no power. If you could touch me, you would've done it by now.

VV: Can't touch you here, no. Noooooo. Won't be here long though, will we. Soon emerging onto the bridge. Into the desert. Out on the plain. You think someone out there cares for you? Cares for your souls? It's empty there. You'll see. Hell is power, Hell is truth. Hell is all there is. No one cares for you. No one comes for you.

RB: Okay, well, worst case scenario is you're right—everything sucks and the best I can hope for

is to go down swinging. You want truth? Truth is,
I've wanted this all my life. A chance to die fighting
impossible odds, to grin at Death and see him nod
back at me. You think I'm afraid, you spineless
shadows? You don't even know what courage is,
how could you possibly expect to know it when you
see it. Think whatever you want.

VV: There are no heroes. We have been in the
camps. We were there when you threw each other in
the ovens. We have fed there and rolled in the filth
of your dying reeking crying puking bodies, rolled
in your weakness and despair, watched your
strongest and your purest crack and break beneath
the cudgels and starvation of regimes that
worshiped us yet never knew our names. They
knew enough: they knew that courage breaks. Hope
breaks, faith breaks, truth breaks. Suffering endures.
Suffering is eternal.

RB: Good. If I can't destroy you, at least I can be
sure you're miserable.

VV: You blame us. You made your own choices.
You opened your doors.

RB: Well, consider this one closed.

VV: Too late too late too late. The doors of others.
So many others. Wide as the gates of the Void.
Open to us. Bound to us. So many killers. Like you.

RB: You think I care what you say? I know who I
am. I fight things like you. Maybe up till now I've

been fighting for the wrong reasons. But if I do kill again, it'll be to protect my friends.

VV: Can't. Not strong enough. Others are coming, coming for you. They will slice her and gash her and use her and make her beg for death. You're too weak to stop them.

RB: We'll see.

VV: Unless. Unless you let us in. With our strength, you will be invincible.

RB: Forget it.

VV: You need our power. We can make you stronger than the angel man. The strongest one of all.

RB: Get stuffed. I'm not talking to you anymore.

VV: Let us in, Roy. Let us in. Let us in let us in let us in let us in let us in let us in let us in let us in let us in let us in let us in

RB: *SHUT UP!*

VV: Will you let us in?

RB: What, are you in third grade? No, I won't let you in. And what's happening to my feet? I can feel my feet again.

VV: You should have let us in. You should have let us in.

RB: Hey, I'm getting my vision back. I can see the bridge. Looks like this is where we part ways, the Void. It's been real. Catch ya on the flip side.

VV: You should have let us in.

28

The voices were ugly, and cruel, and I shut them out with everything that I had. I knew what they wanted: to get inside of me, a swarm of flies wearing my body like a husk to spread their lies and murder. I didn't even bother speaking to them; I spent that time outside of time, that kairos time, singing aloud. I couldn't think of anything else on the spur of the moment, so I just sang Christmas carols. It wasn't even Thanksgiving yet. But it worked pretty well for distracting me from the voice of the Void. Toward the end, all I could hear was "Let us in", over and over and over again.

And then at last, like a fading nightmare, the voices grew faint and weak, and I felt something solid under my feet. I realized I was walking, and had been walking, and shapes and colors began to leak back into my field of vision from the corners of the universal darkness. I felt others walking beside me and I heard their steps and smelled the air again. It smelled like Easter somehow.

I let my feet keep walking, and slowly raised my head to look around. There were strangers on either side of me, looking weary but hopeful. We were on a path of white stones, wide enough for three to walk abreast. Beyond the path was blackness. All around us was a thin grey fog. I heard my own voice whisper, "Tommy?"

The fog thinned as we marched along, and I realized I was in a giant crowd. Before me were hundreds—no, thousands—of walking strangers, and I could hear the shuffling of thousands more behind. The dreamlike quality was almost gone now, and I was beginning to ask myself rational questions. Where were we? Who were these people? Loryk said something about the marching dead—were these the souls of the recently departed, seeking whatever lay beyond? And what became of those who happened to fall off the path?

"Tommy!" I shouted. "Roy? Hey!"

One of the men next to me turned his head, slowly, and smiled a sad, kind smile.

"Long time on the Bridge," he said, croaking, as if he hadn't spoken in years. "Long time since I heard a voice with love in it. We must be getting close."

"Who are you?" I asked him.

"I can't remember anymore. I'm sure it'll come back to me. Look ahead." He pointed. "We're almost there."

Beyond the fog and the Bridge and the line of marching souls, I could see a broad shelf of rock stretching away in either direction as far as I could see. Just as Mellifast dwarfed Niagara Falls, this chasm made the Grand Canyon look like a faint and far-off echo. To my right and left, beyond the edges of our narrow path, the awful abyss of the Void gaped forever like a scar on the face of Creation. All around us the marching dead were raising their heads and looking around as if awakening from an endless daze. Where the Bridge ended at the rock shelf, there was a short open space and then beyond that. . .

Beyond that was. . .

"Dear God," I whispered. It had been there the whole time, looming over us, towering over everything, blazing to the distant purple sky. As the mists cleared away from the titanic vistas around us, it slowly came to fill my whole perspective. A wall of fire, horizon to horizon, a hundred stories tall, roaring and burning for eternity. Nothing I'd ever imagined looked like this, and yet—and yet in some dim way it felt familiar, as if I'd glimpsed it long before my oldest memories began.

"Yes," the man beside me murmured. "Yes, that's it. That's what I was trying to remember all my life."

We were almost there. The Flame was stirring things inside me I can't name: great awe, great hope, and overwhelming fear. Not of burning, not of pain—but of what it must mean, and of what must lie beyond it. I kept on walking; in fact I walked even faster, as if I were finally, finally coming home; but at the same time, I started yelling louder and louder, "Tommy! *Tommy!*"

Up ahead I saw a waving hand in the crowd. "Faith! Hey!"

My whole body lit up, as if I hadn't seen him in fifty years. I jumped up and down and screamed his name. The man beside me laughed and put a hand on my shoulder. "Calm down, love. We're almost there."

A few minutes later, we were off the Bridge and standing on level, rocky ground, and Tommy was holding me in his arms. I knew there were dark things behind us and before us, but for that one eternal moment, everything was okay again.

"Hi," I said quietly into his ear, and felt his fingers running through my hair.

"Hi."

Roy came pacing toward us, looking grim. "Hey, guys. Looks like we all made it."

"Roy!" I leapt at him and hugged him as hard as I could. "Are you all right?"

"Will be. Lotta voices in my head."

"Same here," said Tommy. He looked serious, but there was still a smile fluttering in the crinkles of his eyes. "They promised me some pretty silly things."

"All the power in the world?" Roy asked.

"Yeah, stuff like that. Anyway, I don't think they can bother us anymore. Not here."

"Maybe. Any sign of Loryk?"

"Nope."

"Let's get out of the way," I said, still keeping an arm around both of my boys. We drew apart from the crowd and let the marching dead go by. There was a ledge, maybe forty feet long, between the Flame and the Void. The Bridge-farers crossed it calmly, one by one, and walked directly into the fire with growing smiles. None of them came back out.

Roy watched tensely. "What do you think. . . you know. . ."

"Dunno," Tommy said. "But I guess I'm supposed to go in there, so I'll let you know what I find."

A couple of marchers peeled away from the crowd and came toward us. I recognized Ganarlaith and one of the soldiers. "How is it with you, Earthlings?" Ganarlaith asked. The torch was in his hand.

"Been worse," Roy said. "How's yourself?"

"I have been better. Have you seen our king?"

"Not yet."

Another soldier came drifting toward us a moment later, and Vala was right behind him. I waved to her, and she came over and embraced me. We waited another couple of minutes, and Alyra and the last soldier showed up. There was still no sign of Loryk.

A Moon-elf maiden stepped off the Bridge and headed for the fire with the rest of the yearning dead. Alyra called out to her in elvish, and I caught the name "Loryk" in her cry. The maiden turned and smiled at us, not breaking stride, and said (and somehow I understood her), "I remember that name, my sister. But he is no longer my lord. Good luck to you." Then she vanished into the Flame.

It was hot on the ledge, but not nearly as hot as you would expect from the vast inferno a stone's toss away from us. I edged closer, wondering if we could simply stick in the torch and be done here; but at about ten feet away, the heat abruptly became so overwhelming that it was almost metaphysical. I could sense that I didn't belong here, not yet, and that to trespass any further would be to accept the full intensity of the fires. From the looks on the others' faces, they were getting the same message. Only an angel or a naked soul could pass.

We kept waiting. Time went by, and more time.

"Well?" Roy said eventually. "What's the plan now, Captain?"

Ganarlaith scowled deeply. "None of this is to my liking. If our king has fallen into the Void, who among the living has the wisdom or the power to set him free?"

"And who'd want to? If he's gone, I say we give Alyra the throne and call it a day. But I doubt we're that lucky. He'll show up sooner or later. Question is, how long do we have to stand here and wait for him?"

One of the soldiers, a Deep elf, brandished a spear. "We will wait as long as it takes boy."

"Hey, ears. In case you ever visit Earth, you oughtta know brothers don't much like it when you call us boy."

"What do I care what mortals choose to call themselves? Devastation has come down on our heads because we let your kind into our city. And you two—" the soldier stabbed a finger at me and Tommy "—a wingless mongrel and a round-eared freak! At least the human belongs to an actual species, even if it's inferior."

My own reaction surprised me: I burst out laughing. It was oddly refreshing to encounter a form of racism that lumped all human beings together.

Tommy just smiled at the guy, and Roy said, "Nice delivery, ears. Now call me a low-born dog. Or no, wait—how about infidel swine?"

The elf took a step forward, raising his weapon, but Ganarlaith put a hand on his shoulder. "Karmata," he said quietly. "*Ilatoth myst.*"

"*Sa*, Ganarlaith *Vortah*." The soldier reluctantly stepped back, still glaring.

"Enough of this," Alyra said. Her voice was tight, and her face inscrutable. "Only one of us can enter the Flame in any case. The rest of us will stay here and await King Loryk, but there is no reason to delay Tommy's mission. Captain Ganarlaith, please give him the torch and let us proceed."

"As you say, Lady Alyra." He bowed slightly to her, then paced over and held out the torch.

Tommy glanced at me. "You'll be okay?"

"We'll be fine," I promised. "Go get 'em."

He took the torch from Ganarlaith, nodded to me and Roy, and started to turn away. Then he turned back and cupped my face with his free hand and kissed me on the mouth. My eyelids fluttered and closed, and when I opened them again he was gone—into the wall of fire.

"'Bout time," Roy said. I could hear him grinning.

"Just shut it," I muttered. There was a big goofy smile on my face that I couldn't wipe off no matter how hard I tried.

"Lady Alyra," Vala said, "how long do you think it will take for Tommy to return?"

Alyra shook her head. "I have no idea, Vala. It could be moments or years."

Roy made a show of looking around. "Don't suppose they've got any concessions stands around here."

"No, we have no food. Or bedding, or spare weapons, or incoming allies. This whole operation was pitifully planned."

"Our king did not reckon with a double invasion, my lady," Ganarlaith said.

"There are many things with which our king failed to reckon, old friend."

He didn't answer.

Then a trembling hand rose over the ledge at our feet and clutched at the rock shelf. Roy and I sprang back, but Ganarlaith and Alyra ran over to the clinging hand. "Loryk *Chodan!*" they shouted. They got a hold of his arm and hauled him up, and a moment later he was back on his feet and surrounded by elves babbling in relief.

For my part, I did not feel happy to see him. It dawned on me that without Tommy here, Roy and I were all but defenseless.

And then Roy said, "Alyra. . ." He sounded like he'd just been punched in the solar plexus.

Oh, no. I already knew what he was going to say.

So did she. She turned toward him with horror in her eyes. "No. No, Roy, please—"

"Alyra, he's one of them. He let them in."

29

We're so screwed, I thought fleetingly as I stepped toward Alyra. My instinct was to yank her away from Loryk before he could snatch out her larynx or whatever he planned to do. But she held up her hand and I stopped. Maybe she knew what she was doing?

"My lord," she said. "How did you come to fall into the Void? How did you manage to climb out?"

He smiled like a shark. There was nothing overtly horrifying about him—his eyes weren't glowing red or anything—but to my qi-sight, he was a bloated scarecrow stuffed with a hundred crucified children and looking for more. "You need not fear," he said. "I am still, aha ha, still the Loryk that you know. But now I carry within me the knowledge of the elder ones, the ones before the world. Theirs is the only, hee, only true light— *Alyra*. Now—ehhh, heh heh heh, now we can rule all worlds. All the worlds that there are."

She looked at Ganarlaith. "This is not our king."

Ganarlaith looked at the ground. "He is still my king."

The racist with the spear shifted away from Alyra, and I could see the energy coiling in his arms. "You speak treason, Princess. Have a care."

"Cave-dweller," she said fiercely, "you care not what sits on the throne as long as it keeps your tunnels safe from the fire-serpents. Would you sell your honor so quickly for these empty promises of lordship?"

Oh, good. Insult his tribe, that'll calm things down.

Ganarlaith raised his head and growled something in elvish and she responded in kind. My opinion of the Captain had changed a lot after his appeal to Tommy back in the Spire. Guy might be kind of a jerk, but he was a soldier and a patriot, and it was hard not to respect that. Too bad he was stuck serving a crappy king.

Now everyone was arguing, even Vala. I could feel my own aggressions rising rapidly, which is hardly unusual for me, but I had enough tactical sense to know that a fight would not go well for me and Faith right now. We glanced at each other, and her face was a mirror of my own anger and fear. I suspected the presence of the *raakkk* was stirring up everyone's bloodlust; even without that, the whole situation was a powder keg. 'Least if we died here, it'd be a short walk to the afterlife.

And then, like a cobra-strike, Loryk's hand shot out and caught Alyra by the throat. And instantly, without thinking, I sprang at him. And everything went bad.

Everyone was looking at the king and the princess; no one paid attention to the mortal. I took three running steps, bounded into the air, and made probably the greatest flying jump kick of my martial career. Caught Loryk right square in the face. He dropped Alyra and went stumbling back to the very brink of the Void, and I landed fair on my feet and came running up to knock him into the pit. Let's see if he can crawl out twice. But then Ganarlaith tackled me from the side. Just like me, he was reacting on instinct: a threat to the king he was sworn to protect, the meaning of his life. I did not anticipate this.

We hit the rocks hard, already scrambling for position, and I could instantly tell this guy was fifty times my equal on the ground. If I could last a minute, it would be a miracle and the hardest minute of my life, as well as the last. I turtled up so he'd at least break a sweat breaking all my limbs, but he started raining elbows on my head.

Through slitted eyes, I saw a flash and felt a scourge of heat, and Faith's fire engulfed the Captain's head. His first reaction was what you'd expect, leaping up and swatting madly, but a second later he shook his hair and shouted something in elvish, and a gallon of water came spraying out of his scalp and doused the blaze. I took the opportunity to put my boot in his crotch with every single ounce of power I could muster.

The racist soldier was charging at Faith, spear leveled. I couldn't get up, couldn't even hope to get there in time, but Vala launched a fireball at his back and blew his lungs all over my best friend's face.

The other two soldiers had been hesitating, but that tipped the scales. They attacked Vala with swords and daggers, and she back-pedaled desperately, trying to weave another spell. Alyra crow-hopped and drilled one of them in the kidney with a sidekick, and he went down for a moment, but I could see his qi gathering for a spring. I rolled to my feet and felt a hand close on my windpipe.

Loryk. From what Ganarlaith had said about Koshin, the demons gave unnatural strength to their host bodies. To make it worse, their qi threw off so much static that I couldn't predict their movements. The ex-king spat out a mouthful of teeth and grinned at me, and I could feel my feet coming off the ground as he slowly lifted. I jabbed a thumbnail into his eye-socket, buried my thumb to the last knuckle, felt a warm spurt of blood and salt splash over my wrist, and watched his grin get wider. What did they care what pain their body felt?

She saved me again, another slash of flame that melted his forearm, exposing the bones. I raised my hand and dropped a hammer-fist on his charred, smoking radius and ulna, snapping them like overcooked breadsticks. I fell at his feet, gasping for breath, with a severed hand still clutching at my neck. Loryk stepped past me and went stalking toward Faith, and I could see his other hand rising with a silver stylus clutched in his twisted claws. I tripped him as he went by, but he only stumbled for a moment.

Over to my right, the elf-girls were battling the elf-guards, and Faith and Loryk were about to have a magic-duel while I was lying in the dust, half-helpless. My God, if only someone would have handed me the powers of an angel. . .

I'd forgotten all about him in the scuffle, but the peripheries of my qi-vision registered an angry force gathering like a gale. The Captain of the Guard had fallen when I kicked him, but he was shaking it off now and getting back to his feet. This was my one chance to contribute to this fight, this otherworldly battle of immortals. I am Roy Galahad Belmont and no elves or devils will determine my destiny.

We rose to our feet, glowering, panting, both of us ready to kill and to die. At my back was the everlasting Void; at his, the everlasting Flame. The sounds of rage and pain were all around us, but none of that mattered now. It was time to settle this, warrior to warrior.

But not for myself—not this time. Not for my fighter's ego. Faith had no chance at all against Loryk, so I had to win this fight, *had to*, for her. This is who I am, and I will not let my friends die.

I bared my teeth. "Come on, you pointy-eared son of a bitch."

"When we meet beyond the Flame, Earth-man, it will be my honor to share a drink with you. Farewell."

He charged.

This trick worked on Tommy. Ganarlaith's energy was like a bulldozer, blasting forward to crush me where I stood, but I could read his momentum and direction as clearly as if he were calling out his moves in advance. I took a step forward to meet him, then fell straight back, grabbed him by the shirt, and put my foot in his chest. Everything happened slowly somehow, and I could see the murderous resolve in his face becoming realization and horror as he went sailing over my head. He didn't scream—didn't say a word. Just fell. Forever and ever.

I leapt to my feet. I'd never been so high on qi in my life. The slow-motion effect wasn't stopping. Off to the right I could see Vala falling to the ground, wounded, and the second soldier dropping with a cloven skull. The third one was already dead. Alyra was turning toward Vala, hands outstretched, glacial, half-frozen in time. To my left, Loryk had unleashed a howling torrent of flame at Faith from his wand, his Pen of the Varodrim. She had her arms crossed over her face and was being pushed down on one knee, shrieking out garbled words, trying and failing to hold back the fire. The nearest soldier had dropped a sword, and I scooped it up as I passed.

Loryk heard me coming, turned, and pointed his Pen. But I wasn't aiming for him, I knew I'd never make it in time. I put absolutely everything I had into one swing, aiming for his other hand, his Pen-hand, and I felt the sword bite into the flesh of his arm just as the rampaging flames swept over my body like a wave.

30

INSIDE THE FLAME, it was snowing. It hadn't burned me as I passed through, but it was uncomfortable, like a really hot day in summer when all you want to do is find a pool and jump in. But once I came out the far end, I found myself in a little garden full of cherry trees. The air was cool, and the skies were white with snow clouds, and big soft flakes were drifting slowly down. Ahead of me was a small brook running quietly over smooth-worn stones. Beyond the trees I could see a high stone wall encircling the garden, and the Flame was still burning at my back.

I looked down at the torch in my hand. It wasn't lit. I stuck it back in the Flame and waved it around, but nothing happened.

"Aw man, come on," I muttered.

Maybe there were some clues in the garden. I took a few steps further in, and then I stopped. There was someone on the other side of the brook.

It was a little girl, no more than four or five years old, with long hair and a green dress. She was a few yards off but coming in my direction. There was a basket in her hand, and she kept kneeling down to collect the pink cherry petals that strewed the banks of the water. She looked very serious about it.

I waited till she got closer and then said, "Hi."

She looked up, and she didn't smile, but she waved at me. She didn't seem at all surprised to find an uninvited guest loitering around in here. I waved back, and she stood watching me for a few moments without speaking, so I added, "I'm Tommy."

"I'm Grace," she said, and pointed to herself.

"That's a pretty name."

She still didn't quite smile, but she looked pleased. "I think so too."

"Grace, this might sound like a weird question—"

"Did you get that from the squirrel-man?" She pointed at my torch.

"Yes! Yes, I did. Or, well, no, actually, but it came from them. Do you know how it works?"

She made a big swooping "come here" gesture with her hand, so I stepped into the brook and started wading across. It only came up to my knees. Just before I got to the other bank, she held up her hand again, and I stopped. "You have to put it in there," she said, and pointed at the water.

"Are you sure? If I get it wet, won't it—"

Grace stomped her foot and pointed at the water again, looking very imperious in the way that only a five-year-old girl can do. So, I crossed my fingers and dipped the torch into the stream where it instantly flared into life. I held it up and a bright blue fire crackled from the tip without smoke or even heat. It didn't seem to be harming the torch, and I wondered how long it would burn for, but I figured that was Loryk's problem. If he ever showed up again.

"I guess you were right, Grace. Thank you very much."

She bounced up and down on the balls of her feet, swung her basket, and nodded.

"Hey—can you tell me how long ago the squirrel-men were here?"

"There was only one. It was a few days ago."

"Really? Just a few days, are you sure?"

"Mmm—it might have been longer."

"Did he say anything to you?"

She shook her head. "He didn't see me. I was climbing trees. He took some rocks, and he took some sticks, and he took some cherry blossoms."

"Are you not supposed to do that?"

She shrugged.

"Is it okay if I take this torch out of here?"

She shrugged.

"Well—I hope it's okay. I kind of have to."

"Are you taking it back to the squirrel-man?"

"No. I need it to help my friends. Say, how did you know how to light it, anyway?"

"I just know."

I was starting to get worried about Faith and Roy, but I was also a bit worried about leaving Grace all by herself.

"Are there any grown-ups around? Does someone take care of you?"

"Grown-ups can't stay here. Only to visit."

". . .Grace?"

"Mm-hmm?"

"Who are you?"

She finally smiled. Then she reached up and poked me, very lightly, on the tip of the nose and said, "Boop." And then she skipped away into the trees.

31

The whole fight took less than a minute. Roy kicked Loryk, I burned Ganarlaith, Vala splattered the guard with the spear, and I burned Loryk's arm in half. It all happened really fast. And a moment later, a blazing torrent of elf-magic was coming straight at my face. I don't know how long I held it off—it couldn't have been more than a few seconds. If it had lasted a few seconds longer, I would have gone home in an ashtray.

Then it stopped. I was on my knees in the dust, retching for air, blinded by a fog of smoke. I heard Roy screaming in agony—*screaming*, my God, I'd never heard him scream like that. A spike of ice and venom went from the back of my throat to the pit of my stomach. This can't be happening. Not to Roy.

It took everything I had to get back up. As the smoke cleared away, I saw Loryk standing there with an almost comical look of frustration and both arms missing below the elbow. Alyra came sprinting toward him with a broken spear-shaft and swung at his head like Babe Ruth knocking one of the stadium. There was a great sodden crack and a spectacular gush of blood, and the king of the elves went down in a heap at our feet.

Right next to Roy. He was writhing on the ground, his flesh scorched and blistered, with black steam pouring from his body. I stood there staring, and I heard myself saying, "No, no, no". I couldn't stop myself. I'd never felt so helpless in my life. After everything I said to him back in the Spire, he still saved me, and he burned for it. He'd never be handsome again.

Alyra was kneeling by his side. There was something in her hand, a crumpled napkin, and she unwrapped it to reveal a bright golden fruit the size of a grape.

"Roy," she said urgently. "Roy, eat this. Quickly. Roy, trust me." His mouth opened, and she popped the fruit inside.

He was still writhing and groaning, but a few moments later he grew quieter. Then he lay still, and I heard him sigh. Even as I watched, the blisters began to close, and his skin began to knit itself back together again.

My knees gave out. I sat down with a thump, and let the relief and gratitude pour out of me like a cup filled past the brim. If I'd ever doubted there were miracles, this was the moment that cured those doubts forever.

Slowly, still wincing, he sat up. He took Alyra's hand and said, "Hey there."

She made what I knew was his favorite expression—the trying-not-to-smile smile—and said, "Hey yourself." Then she leaned close and kissed him on the lips.

Roy, you sly dog!

Vala came limping over to us. She was clutching her ribs with a grimace, but she seemed to be in one piece. "Faith, are you hurt?"

I shook my head. "I'm fine. Thanks to Belmont here."

He made a huge show of waving it off. "Awww shucks, 'tweren't nothin'. Anybody'd done likewise. 'Long as they were a red-blooded American, that is."

"Okay, we get it, you're awesome. Can I have your autograph?"

"Hey, guys," said another voice from behind me. "What'd I miss?"

"*Tommy!*" All my strength came back in a burst, and I spent it leaping up and hugging him as fiercely as I could. He held me close with one arm, and I gradually realized the other was busy with a burning torch.

Roy and Alyra were back on their feet, and the five of us surveyed the carnage on this narrow, dusty ledge between Heaven and Hell. A stone's throw away, the marching dead continued to pass from the Bridge to the Flame, showing no interest in our affairs.

Tommy nodded toward the fallen monarch.

"So he let 'em in, huh?"

"Yup," said Roy. "Guess that means the torch is yours now champ."

"I don't want it," Tommy said, and drew back his arm to cast it into the Void.

But as I gazed down at Loryk, my eyes happened to fall on two things: The pen still grasped in his nearby hand and the keys of the lyrilim on his belt. And I remembered a dream, and a man in blue.

"Tommy, wait. Can I see it for a second?"

"Sure."

"Roy—this is gonna sound gross, but—do you mind getting me the Pen?"

"Uh. . . sure?"

As he was prying it loose, I leaned down and lifted the keys from Loryk. And the instant Roy put the third item in my hand, the man in blue materialized out of thin air, not five feet away from us.

The others leaped back, shouting in alarm, but I simply smiled.

"Hi there. Do I get to know your name this time?"

"Perhaps I will have told you the time before. For now, it would seem you and your friends had done well here."

"Faith, who is this guy?" Roy demanded. "How did he get to the Firmament?"

"I have no idea. But I told you about him once before."

"The guy from your dream?" Tommy asked.

"The same."

The man in blue bowed very slightly in our direction.

"It would always be a pleasure to have seen you all again. Now that Ms. Avalon chooses to retain the three items, new branches of possibilities had been opened in the universe. That is how I would have come here."

Roy made a face. "Wow, that's—that's really informative, thanks."

Alyra took a step forward.

"I am Princess Alyra of Ardmore. Are you man or angel?"

"Oh, I shall not be more than a man. And for me this was not our first meeting, Princess. You would always have my condolences for the fall of your king."

". . .Thank you." I could see her opening her mouth to ask how he knew, but she already seemed to get that he didn't do straight answers. She hesitated and said nothing.

"So," I said. "Come here often?"

"Now and again. I had come once because of the widening branch of possibility, of which I will have spoken. One now-possible outcome is that your mother might be found."

My smile vanished. "What did you—what did you say?"

"It's to be revealed that she had been taken by one known only as the Dark Xaxon. Were she to be found, it may be upon their home world."

"But there's no doors there. How can we—"

He shook his head sharply. "Nothing more might be known to me at this time. I'd wish it could have been."

"But—"

"There could be nothing more." His face was impassive, but I thought I glimpsed genuine sorrow in the corners of his mouth. "However—there shall have been one small gift that I took it upon myself to give you."

"What gift?"

"To tread the Bridge is a long endeavor. I would offer a shortcut."

"What of King—what of Loryk?" Vala said.

"He'll return with us," Alyra decided. "All his people will see the *raakkk* within him and know what he's done."

"Hold on," Roy said. "What about Captain Ganarlaith? He fell into the Void, but he was a good man. Er, you know, elf. He doesn't deserve what happened to Loryk."

"Possession could never occur save by the consent of the host," the man in blue said gravely.

"For those who had fallen into the Void, many different outcomes might have occurred. Some shall die, some shall give in to the demons, and some shall emerge in distant times and places. The Captain's fate could not yet be seen."

"Did you say distant *times?*"

"I may have. I can no longer be sure."

"Dude, there's something seriously wrong with you."

"Roy!" I said. "Don't you see he's doing everything he can for us?"

"By being cryptic to the point of incoherence? How do you know we can trust this guy?"

"I don't know how I know, I just know. Okay?"

He sighed. "See that look on her face?" he said to Tommy. "You're gonna be seeing it a lot. She looks like that, don't even bother trying to reason with her."

"We should go," Alyra said, and gestured at Loryk. "Elves rarely bleed to death, but it's not impossible."

"Will his hands grow back?" Tommy asked curiously.

"They will if we decide to grant him one of the Ultra Luna-fruits. They take decades to prepare, but there's nothing they can't heal. The one Ratoska gave me was meant for Loryk, in case he should be injured in the quest."

"But you gave it to Roy," I said. She nodded, and I went over and hugged her.

She hugged me back. "Thank you, Faith. Does this mean I'm forgiven?"

"You are so, *so* forgiven, Alyra. But you know, I don't think you did anything wrong. Loryk fooled us all."

"I let myself be fooled." She glanced at Roy. "You were right. The flowing years can bring complacency as well as wisdom."

"It's always alarming when people tell me I'm right."

"Come," said the man in blue. "My allotment has been at its end. Join hands."

We did as he said, and Alyra reached down and took hold of one of Loryk's oozing stumps. I reached over and took the hand of our strange visitor, and once again his brow unfurrowed at me just a tiny bit.

"Close your eyes," he told us.

I did, and he immediately let go of my hand. I opened my eyes again, puzzled, and then caught my breath in astonishment. We were back in Ardmore.

"Whoa!" Roy exclaimed. "Now that's a nice trick."

I could tell where we were because the man in blue had deposited us right in front of the Spire of Vissarion, and there was absolutely no mistaking that place. But the rest of the city was covered in a deep, thick fog. The air was frigid, and I found myself shivering. Roy bent down, ripped off Loryk's cape, and draped it around my shoulders.

"How long have we been gone?" I asked, involuntarily dropping into a whisper.

Alyra sniffed the air. "One full day, by my reckoning. Long enough that anything might have happened."

That made it Saturday. Named for Saturn, known to the Greeks as Chronos—god of time.

"So, what now?"

She and Vala glanced at each other.

"There are no sounds of battle from within the Spire," Vala said.

"Or anywhere else," Tommy added. "It's like the whole city's in hiding."

"The gates are open," Roy observed. "Should we. . ."

We all looked at each other.

"Well," Alyra said. "We can't stand out here forever. Tommy, would you be so kind?" She pointed at Loryk. Tommy scooped him up and slung him unceremoniously over one shoulder.

I had put the keys and Pen in my pockets and tucked the torch into my armpit when we all joined hands. Now I held it aloft, but it cast a scanty light in the fog. We slowly advanced on the Spire, straining to hear any sound, and passed through the wide-open gates. The air was clearer inside, but the courtyard was still shrouded in a pale grey mist. Nothing stirred.

Vala's hands were half-cupped, as if she were holding an invisible ball, and I knew she was ready to start throwing fire at any second.

"Let us head for the great hall," she whispered. "Perhaps—"

She stopped. Shapes were coming out of the mist. Great prowling, slinking shapes, long and sinuous, with glinting eyes and fangs and looming wings. We were surrounded by dragons.

32

I felt great after eating that fruit. We'd been up since Thursday afternoon, running and fighting and taking emotional beatings, and the strain was catching up to me even before I got burned alive. The rejuvenation process was like getting the best night's sleep you ever had, rolled up into about fifteen seconds. When we arrived back in Ardmore, I had a few blissful moments of thinking we were almost home free. And then the dragons came.

There weren't all that many of them—a few dozen, maybe—but that was way more than plenty. We were in the middle of an open space, surrounded by creatures that could literally kill us by breathing, and we had no weapons, no cover, and no reinforcements coming. After everything we'd been through—just like that, we were toast.

Welcome home, wayfarers.

"Hi, Ka," Tommy said. His voice was level, but I could see him sagging. Even for him, this was hopeless. "We really don't want any trouble, okay?"

Why, nor do we. We want only one thing.

"What's that?"

To relieve thee of thy burden.

"What bur—oh." He jiggled the unconscious politician on his shoulder. "You mean this guy?"

None other. In search of him we took this citadel, only to find it empty. But now the will of fate hath brought him to our very feet.

"Well, you know what? I did promise him that I'd hand him over to you if he threatened my friends again."

And did he?

"Sure did."

Alyra looked shocked. "Tommy! You can't be serious."

"I don't know if I'm serious. I don't want him dead. But I can't stand here and watch you all die."

"They'll get him either way," I muttered.

"That's not the point," she snapped at me. "Vala and I have a duty to perish defending our king, if necessary."

"Alyra, he's not your king. You said those exact words yourself."

"I..." She shook her head. "It doesn't matter. I cannot stand by and let him be eaten alive by these accursed reptiles."

Not thy king? The frost dragon sounded intrigued. *Why so?*

"That is elven business, worm, and no concern of yours!"

Faith stared at her. "For Pete's sake, are you *trying* to get us killed?"

The insults of a fool are as the wind in a hollow tree. But thou wilt answer my question or die here and now.

"He's possessed," Tommy interjected. "He let the demons take him, so he'd be strong enough to hurt us."

There was a rustling sound, and the dragons drew slightly back from us.

And thou hast brought him here? We did not cloak thee from the demon-sight only to have thee infest our sacred mountain with their blasphemy and filth.

"No, no, it's okay. Alyra wanted all the elves to know what he'd done so he could be punished. See, you guys are kind of on the same side here."

She and Alyra both snorted at the same moment. It was oddly endearing.

"Dragon," Vala said quietly. "What would you do with him, if we gave him to you?"

Nothing, now. Thy companion was correct, we craved his flesh in answer to the wrongs he wrought against us long ago. But if he harbors such evil as thou sayest, then no dragon will taste of him. Tell us then, in turn: if thy people render justice against him for embracing unclean spirits, what will become of him under elven law?

There was a pause, and Vala lowered her head. She clearly knew the answer but deferred to

Alyra. I watched my fairy princess struggling with her pride and put forth a supreme effort of will to keep my mouth shut. She needed to work through this on her own.

"The penalty is exile," she said at last. "He will be bound by the Circle of Nine and stripped of his sorcery. Then he will be taken to the borders of the Wasteland of Dagaroth and left to wander in despair until the carrion-birds have feasted on his entrails."

There was another pause. The sleek, fanged heads all around us swiveled back and forth in silence; apparently they were conferring amongst themselves. Finally, Ka turned back to us.

This we accept, she said. *Our quarrel with thy folk is not ended, elf-maid. But we will pursue it another day.*

"May the day be not too long delayed," Alyra said coldly.

Tommy—thou art a credit to thy long-dead race. I hope to see thee again.

"Uh, yeah. You too, Ka."

And they rose into the air, flapping and croaking like a murder of horrendous crows. They circled above the parapets and then went soaring away. From outside the Spire, we heard the sound of shouts and tramping feet, and a few moments later a platoon of elves hustled into the courtyard, bristling with swords and guns.

"Vauksness *afestha!*" the leader called out. "*Zurula fels tathana?*"

She gestured wearily at the sky. "They're gone, Lieutenant. You can stand down."

The soldiers lowered their weapons.

"Are you all right, Princess? They took the Spire in the early hours, and then this cursed fog enveloped the city. We thought everyone had evacuated, so we decided to wait till the fog lifted to re-take the castle."

"We've just returned from the Firmament. The king is hurt. Please take him to his chambers at once."

When they recognized the figure Tommy was carrying, they cried out in dismay. Three of them ran forward, lifted the ex-king, and brought him inside. The lieutenant was about to follow, but Alyra called after him.

"Lieutenant! What became of the Xaxons?"

"Nearly all of them have been slain, Lady. The survivors flew west from the cliffs into the wilderlands beyond. We will organize a pursuit as soon as we secure the Spire."

"Very well, carry on." He bowed and followed the others into the castle.

"All right," she said, sounding even more weary. "Let's go inside and get cleaned up."

"Actually," I said, and stopped. The others looked at me, and Faith started to nod. "I was thinking—maybe it's time we were heading home. It sounds like you've got a lot of house-cleaning to do and we'd only be in the way. Besides, our parents must be worried sick about us by now."

She looked surprised, and a little sad (which I admit made me more than a little happy), but she nodded as well. "Perhaps you're right. You've freed us from a great many lies, my friends. Thank you."

"We also started a couple of wars."

"Those are ancient feuds, for which you are not answerable. You've acted with nothing but honor."

"Is Loryk really going to die?" Faith asked.

Alyra sighed. "Most likely. If he's still alive after one hundred and one years, he'll be given an exorcism and a second chance—a parole, of sorts. I will beseech the Council to give him the Ultra Luna-fruit before they send him into the desert, so he'll have at least some hope of survival out there, however meager. King or no, he's still my uncle."

"Are you gonna be king now?" Tommy asked. "Or queen, or whatever?"

"No, Prince Gaelric will be called back from the Sea-elves' domain to assume the throne. He's young, but—that does not mean unwise."

Faith stepped forward and offered her the burning torch. "Here. You might need this."

But Alyra shook her head. "I understand very little of what's happened today, but I can see that those items are meant for the three of you. Roy, why don't you take the keys?"

"Well—if you say so," I replied, dubiously. Faith dug them out of her pocket and handed them to me. "How do they work?"

She pointed to a large shimmering key. "That one leads to the Vale. It fits any lock, and since it's Loryk's, it will work here in Faerie despite his enchantment on the doors. Insert the key and picture a specific door in your mind, and that's where you'll emerge."

"How about all the other keys, where do they go?"

"You're a scientist, Roy. Experiment." She turned to Faith. "As for the Pen of the Varodrim. I've never used it, but I know how it works. Simply compose a spell in your mind and write it down with the Pen. The power will be stored away, and then you can invoke it at will."

"Thanks, Alyra."

"How about the torch?" Tommy asked.

"I'm afraid I can't help you with that. I have no idea how to call forth its power, or even what it's meant to do. But I doubt it would have come to you if you weren't equal to the task of finding out."

"I hope so." He accepted the torch from Faith and scratched his head. "I kinda don't know what to say now."

"Oh, we'll meet again, Thomas Gabriel Connor. No farewells."

She bowed to us, and we bowed back. Then Faith embraced her Wood-elf sister, and Alyra took me by the hands.

"Watch over these two," she said. "They obviously need you."

I couldn't think of anything wise to say. I pressed my forehead to hers, and I heard myself murmuring, "My lady."

She drew back, and a glimmer of the old twinkle came into her eyes. "Let's not get ahead of ourselves, Earth-man. I'm not your lady yet." And she kissed my cheek and stepped away.

I pulled myself together and got businesslike. "All right, guys. Are we ready?"

They nodded.

We went to the nearest door—the one leading to the ice-fox stables, if memory served— and I put the key in the lock. We turned and waved to our elvish friends, and they waved back, and a golden shaft of daylight pierced the mist and lit the diamond courtyard all around us. We gazed upwards, and as the last few wisps of fog cleared away, the first snowfall of the season began.

Tommy whispered something. I could barely make it out, but it sounded like, "Hi, Grace."

Then I turned the key and opened the door, and we were once again adrift on the Shoreless Sea.

33

The next day was sunny and clear. Ma Belmont made us pancakes, and then she dragged Roy and the little ones away to morning Mass. Tommy and I were left standing alone in the living room, holding hands. Roy winked at me as he left and said, "You'll be safe with feathers here."

Once everyone was gone, Tommy gave a slight sigh and said, "He's not gonna start calling me 'feathers' all the time, is he?"

"Um. . . yeah, he probably is. Just try and remember it's a sign of affection."

"I mean yeah, I get that, it's just that I don't actually have wings or anything, so it's kind of—"

I put a finger on his lips, and he shut up. Then I kissed him, and his hands closed on my waist and pulled me near. My arms encircled his neck, and for a few brief moments the universe was perfect.

Suddenly, there was a knock at the front door and Hope came running in and threw her arms around the both of us. "Hey, guys! How'dja sleep? Did I miss Roy?"

I hugged her back. "Slept good, honey. Everyone's gone to church. They'll be back soon. Where's Mom and Dad?"

"They're letting me handle Faith retrieval duty. I promised not to come home without you."

"Fair enough."

"Hi, Hope," Tommy said.

"Hi, Tommy!" she said, and blushed, and buried her face in my shoulder. I rolled my eyes a little and kissed her hair.

"By all means, let's make this as awkward as possible."

She'd been the first person I called yesterday when we emerged from the kairos field and found ourselves back in Roy's bedroom. But not right away. First, we held a whispered council to determine exactly what we were supposed to tell our parents about where in God's name we'd been.

"Can't we just tell them the truth?" Tommy asked.

Roy and I exchanged skeptical glances. The habit of not telling the truth to grown-ups dies hard, especially when the truth involves actual dragons.

"Why don't we tell them the truth, but leave out some of the place-names," Roy suggested. "We can say we had to leave town and help some people who are also fighting against Wingrove and The Eye. We can be fuzzy on a few details."

"They'll want to know where we went," I pointed out.

"So, we say we don't really know. It's not like *that's* a lie."

"And when they ask why The Eye was after us in the first place?"

"We, um. . . okay, lessee. . ."

"We say Wingrove is after me because of my father," Tommy said. His voice was unusually flat. "That's not a lie either. And maybe it'll give me a reason to push Uncle Syme for more answers about my mom. I've never thought about it much before."

"Me neither," I said. "I need to start looking for my birth father too."

Roy nodded. "And from what that guy in blue was saying, we'll have to start thinking about how to get to planet Xaxos and rescue your elf mom."

"One thing at a time." I put my head in my hands. "There's so *much*."

"It's cool," Roy said, and put a hand on my shoulder. "Now that we'll have at least a week or two with no one trying to set fire to us, we can sit down and figure everything out at our own pace. For now, let's get all the crying and interrogating over with."

There was a lot of both. Our families were overjoyed to see us and we were pretty happy to see them as well. Everyone gathered at chez Belmont once more, and Tommy and I ended up sleeping over as we were supposed to do on Wednesday night—which, even though we'd magically skipped over a day in kairos, seemed like an awfully long time ago. This time we slept in the living room, a cluster of blankets around the crackling fire, with Joseph and Amarantha keeping watch to make sure we didn't disappear again.

We also checked in with Officer Tooley, who seemed dubious about our story (or lack thereof) but mostly glad to see us all in one piece. There was still a police car parked outside the house, and apparently there were a couple of FBI agents who wanted to talk with us. And although they weren't pushing the matter quite yet, our parents clearly weren't buying our "I have no recollection, Senator" routine. Once everything settled down, we were going to have some serious explaining to do.

But for now, it was time to go home and check on my cats. I collected my purse and phone and history book (all of which Officer Tooley had found in the stolen van used by The Eye), kissed my Tommy again, and followed Hope to the Avalon family station wagon.

Dad greeted me at the door as we came in. "There's my darling girl," he said, and tossed a mock punch at my head. Without thinking, I used one of the haradir arm-traps I'd learned from Vala, and something like awe came into Dad's face. "Nice technique! That's not one of mine."

I waved modestly. "Roy and I have been doing some extra training."

"My opinion of the lad continues to rise."

"Mine too. He's fighting for much bigger things now, Dad."

He nodded seriously. He was an imposing man, with iron grey hair and a presence so solid that you didn't need a qi-sense to feel it; when he was grave about something, the gravity was like a palpable weight. "I can tell. He's grown in the few days since I saw him last."

"Faith," Mom called, "do you want some coffee, love?"

"Hi, Mom. Yes please, thanks."

I headed into the kitchen, where she was already topping off a mug for me. Obviously she had anticipated my reply. Pendleton zipped over and nuzzled my leg. I picked him up, and he let me pet him for a few seconds longer than normal before going into a frenzy and exiting the room at top speed.

"So, Roy's doing well," Mom said, handing me my coffee.

"Subtle. I see where you're going."

"I was just wondering about the other young man in your life."

It drove me crazy that I couldn't physically stop myself from smiling at the mention of him.

"He's not a young man in my life, Mother. He's just—Tommy."

She nodded as well, but her solemnity was always straining to contain a sparkle. Apart from some lines around her eyes and a sprinkle of silver in her hair, she and Hope could have been twins.

"Well, I trust we'll be seeing more of him. He seems very nice."

"He does rather, doesn't he?"

Then Sarah burst into the house. "Faith! Hey!"

I barely had time to say, "Hey yourself," before she wrapped me up in the fiercest hug she'd ever given me.

"Hey, sweetie," I murmured. "I'm fine. We're all fine. I'm sorry we worried you."

"You're really okay? You're sure?"

"I'm sure."

"Well." She pulled back and was instantly all business. "Good. That's settled, then. Hey Hopestress, you ready for I don't have to run day?"

Hope beamed. "Absolutely! Let's do this thing."

"I don't have to run day" meant that we camped in the living room and watched zombie movies while earnestly endeavoring to eat all of the popcorn on Earth. Queensbury slowly lowered her palpitating bulk into my lap, and for a few hours I was able to forget my troubles and be a rapturously ordinary American girl. It was a good day.

In the evening, Roy came by to visit. After he said his hellos to Hope and Sarah and my folks, he offered me his hand and said, "Got a minute?"

"'Course." I took his hand and we strolled outside to look up at the first few stars. The air was bitter, and the moon was new. The night seemed darker than usual, somehow. "Lotta space up there."

He squeezed my hand. "We'll find her, Faith."

I nodded.

"Heck of a week, huh?"

"Say that again."

He blew air through his cheeks. "It freaks me out, the sheer amount of luck that happened back there. I mean, do you realize how insanely lucky we got? We should've been dead about a dozen times over. Even Tommy."

"Maybe somebody's looking out for us."

"Maybe. But we can't count on that. Next time we've gotta be ready."

"We will be. We know what's out there now."

"We know *some* of what's out there. Enough to know how little we really know."

"It's a start. And we've got each other."

"Yeah." Uncharacteristically gently, he raised my hand to his lips. "We do."

"Why, sir! Whatever would Ms. Vauksness say?"

"Something in elvish, I expect. You know how elves are." He let me go and headed back to his car. "Anyway—just wanted to say good night. See you in school tomorrow."

"I'll be there."

After he drove off, I stood outside awhile and watched the distant lights come into the sky. I'm no physicist, but I do have some idea of how far away they are. And how old, how alien. Loryk said the light of today's dawn would not reach Xaxos for a billion years. And somewhere in that hostile place was a lady I'd never seen—the lady who gave me green eyes.

Roy was right, we were nowhere near ready for this. But right now I wasn't thinking of what Roy had said. I was thinking of what Vala told me the day we met:

"We did not choose the fire. The fire chose us."